M000282428

CRIME

DELAYED

A BUCK TAYLOR NOVEL

BY

CHUCK MORGAN

COPYRIGHT© 2018 BY CHUCK MORGAN

Printed in the United States of America

First printing 2018

ISBN 978-0-9988730-3-9

LIBRARY OF CONGRESS CONTROL NUMBER

2018933911

DEDICATION

This book is dedicated to the men and women who wear the uniform and work as Rangers. Whether local, state or national, these men and women have dedicated their lives to protect the natural beauty all around us. For all their service and sacrifice we are truly grateful.

Chapter One

How could they be so dumb? All they had to do was stash the carcass and come back for it later. Why did that lady ranger and her dog have to show up? Up to that point, everything was perfect. The bull elk was huge with a monster rack. He was the biggest elk they had seen in the last month at least.

Sure, they were a little out of season and they didn't have a permit for a bull elk, but they weren't hurting anyone. The elk was just standing there waiting to be shot. What did it hurt? God must have intended for them to shoot it or he wouldn't have put it there, right?

They were going to stash the elk in their hunting camp. Well, not much of a hunting camp. It was basically a lean-to made of sticks and pine boughs but it was a great place to hide out when they weren't hunting. They had all the comforts of home. They had a gas lantern for light, they had a small cooler for drinks and they had a couple sleeping bags for when they stayed out at night. They really didn't need the sleeping bags because the nights were still warm even at this altitude.

Tonight, they would have come back and butchered the elk. The sled they use to haul out the meat was hidden in the ravine next to the lean-to. All they had to do was load it up and drag it back to the cabin. It was only a couple miles and they had done it a lot lately. They always took a different track back so that the undergrowth wouldn't get worn down and show the way back to the cabin.

They were the hunters, and everyone depended on them for food. They were the best shots in the group and they knew how to skin and gut what they shot. The elk would have lasted them a week or two. But now this. The Teacher is not going to be pleased.

The lady ranger came out of nowhere. One minute they were dragging the elk back to camp and the next minute there she was standing on the little ridge with her stupid dog. All she had to do was walk away. Her and that stupid dog. But she didn't.

They had hidden in the bushes. She should have walked right by them and not seen them, but no. The dog had to sniff them out. He had to start barking. She could have kept walking but she must have sensed them because she pulled the gun out of her holster. They couldn't let her find them or the cabin.

The first rifle shot hit her in the thigh. There was no ballistic armor around her thigh. She went down hard and rolled down the ridge into the ravine. The dog tried to go after her but the second bullet hit the dog right in the chest. The dog went down hard too. There was a lot of blood. They broke cover and rushed over to the edge of the ravine. The lady ranger was trying to reach her pistol with one hand and she was trying to key the mic on her shoulder with the other.

When she saw them, she just froze. Blood was pumping out of her leg. A crimson fountain exploding with each heartbeat. She looked at them and began to plead with them to help her. She had tears in her eyes. They just looked at her. The lady ranger started to shake. Her breathing got shallow. She looked so helpless just lying there in the ravine. The Teacher had taught them not to let anything they hunted suffer. They understood the kill shot. He raised up his rifle and without any hesitation or doubt shot her in the forehead.

Where was the dog? They had seen the crimson stain explode from the dog's chest. He went over the ridge, so he must just be on the other side, but he wasn't. Where could he have gone? They wanted to make sure he didn't suffer like the lady ranger, but he wasn't on the other side of the ridge. They looked around trying to spot the blood trail, but there was none.

Maybe he was some kind of mystical forest creature. Just like in the stories the Teacher use to tell them around the campfire. It would be a grand prize to take back to the Teacher. He might award them with a knife or a hatchet. But, where is he? He couldn't have gone far, but after an hour searching, there was no sign.

They went back to the lean-to and found a camp shovel and headed back to the lady ranger. The Teacher had told them that all life was sacred, so they knew that he would not be happy if they didn't give the lady ranger a proper burial and that's just what they did. The covered her body with dirt and rocks, cut some pine boughs and further covered the grave in the ravine. Then they said the Lord's Prayer just like the Teacher had taught them. Finished, they headed back to the elk carcass.

Instead of waiting til tonight to butcher it they decided to do it now. Someone might have heard the extra shots and they also figured that sooner or later someone would come looking for the lady ranger and her dog. They finished dragging the carcass to the lean-to hunting camp. They spent the next two hours butchering the huge elk, loaded up the sled and hauled it back through the woods to their cabin. They would have a big feast tonight.

They would tell the Teacher about the lady ranger. He would be happy that they had protected the others. They were not sure if they should tell him about the missing dog. The Teacher might not be pleased that they had missed the shot and not killed the dog. He might give one of the others the rifle and let them go on the next hunt. The more they thought about it, the more they convinced themselves that they would not mention the dog.

Chapter Two

Buck Taylor, Colorado Bureau of Investigation Agent and his son David had volunteered to work the burger and hot dog tent at the annual Gunnison Labor Day community picnic and were doing a brisk business. Buck tried to make the burgers the same way his friend Jimmy Palumbo did at the La Bon Café in Durango. Jimmy's burgers were huge and legendary and the only food item besides french fries that Jimmy sold in his café/bar but Buck just couldn't get them to taste the same. Someday he would find out Jimmy's secret.

Gunnison, Colorado, population of roughly 6,200 people, sits at an elevation of 7,700 feet and is the largest city in Gunnison County. Situated along the Gunnison River, the city was incorporated in 1880. The area is a mecca for hunters, fishermen and anyone who enjoys the outdoors. It is home to Western State Colorado University which was founded as The Colorado State Normal School for Children in 1901.

One interesting historical fact is that during a two-month period at the end of 1918 the residents of Gunnison isolated themselves from the rest of the area to prevent the introduction of Spanish Influenza. All roads were blocked at the county borders and people traveling through the area by train were not allowed to leave the train. Because of the isolation, no one in Gunnison died of the flu.

North of Gunnison lies Crested Butte, a ski resort community which helps contribute to the winter tourist trade since you must pass through Gunnison to get to the Crested Butte ski area. Gunnison is a picturesque little community in the heart of the Rocky Mountains and appears to be a perfect place to raise a family.

Buck Taylor stands six-foot-tall and weighs in at 185 lbs. Very little of it flab for a 58-year-old man. Buck's hair is salt and pepper with what seemed like a lot more salt than pepper and he wore it slightly longer than was typically the fashion of the day. Buck lived in Gunnison all his life. He spent seventeen years with the Gunnison County Sheriff's Department before accepting a position with the Colorado Bureau of Investigation. He met and married his high school sweetheart Lucinda Torres and they raised three children, David, Cassie and Jason. Life was good until Lucy was diagnosed with breast cancer and for five years she and Buck fought the battle of her life. A little over a year ago Lucy lost the battle.

They were just finishing up the latest rush of people when his son's cell phone signaled an incoming call. David looked at the call and answered.

"Taylor," he said. He listened intently to the call then hung up. David was a police officer with the Gunnison Police Department. He looked a lot like his dad when his dad was his age. Slightly taller than his dad and slightly heavier than his dad but the resemblance was striking. Unlike his father, David still moved with the ease of a young man.

David had recently been promoted to sergeant and was now the night shift supervisor. He liked working the night shift and had been a patrolman on that shift for many years. He enjoyed the calmness and quiet of a small mountain town in the early morning hours. He also enjoyed those rare occasions when he was able to spend time with Buck. They had a lot in common and he enjoyed hearing about Buck's latest investigations.

The pair didn't have a lot of time to talk today. The picnic was in full swing and the park was packed with locals and tourists alike. This weekend was the unofficial end of the summer tourist season and most of the tourists should have already gone home but the weather was perfect and the town was still living the good life.

Tourism was essential for the survival of the town. In the fall, the hunters would descend on the town to get themselves outfitted for the annual trek into the mountains in search of elk and deer and an occasional moose. As soon as the hunters were gone the skiers would start showing up.

Fishermen would show up all year round and it was not unusual to see a fly fisherman standing in the middle of the Gunnison River stalking a beautiful Brown or Rainbow trout while the snow came down around him. If there was open water on the river, there would be a fisherman standing in it no matter the weather. Buck Taylor was typically one of those fishermen. Buck's passion for fly fishing was only exceeded by his love of his job as a criminal investigator.

Fly fishing was also his escape from having to deal with the death of his wife of 35 years. Lucy Taylor had spent five years battling metastatic breast cancer. She lost the battle when the cancer metastasized into her brain. She held out as long as she could but eventually, the chemotherapy and the radiation were no longer effective. She died peacefully in her sleep wrapped in Buck's arms. Buck was devastated by the loss and now more than a year later he still missed her. She was his rock and his soul mate.

Buck and the family had gathered one Sunday morning to scattered Lucy's ashes in the Gunnison River, not far from where Buck and his son were now cooking burgers. It was supposed to be a private family affair but somehow word had spread around town and a huge group of people showed up. The private affair turned into a huge picnic and celebration of Lucy's life. Lucy would have loved it.

Buck looked at his son as he hung up the phone.

"Something up?" Buck asked.

"Yeah. I need to go into the office. We got a call from the Pitkin County Sheriff's office. They are searching for a missing Division of Parks and Wildlife ranger and they have asked for us to start on our side of the mountain and work towards them. She's been missing almost twenty-four hours. The Sheriff has activated the Gunnison Search and Rescue team and we have been asked to assist."

"Do you need some help?" Buck asked.

"Who's gonna cook the burgers and dogs for this crowd if you leave. I will let you know later if we are looking for volunteers. Can you make sure Judy gets her tent closed up and gets the kids home?"

David's wife Judy was in charge of the dessert tent. She also ran the little deli/ice cream shop that Lucy owned and ran for a significant part of her life. When Lucy passed away, Buck had been thinking about selling the little place but Judy offered to take it over and eventually buy the shop from him. Buck was pleased that Lucy's legacy would continue and besides the people in town loved her little place.

But today Judy's assistant was working the shop while Judy and her and David's three kids, Amy, age 16, David Jr also nicknamed Buck, age 14 and Rosalie, age 10, named after Lucy's mom, ran the tent in the park. Buck told David he would take care of everything and not to worry. He also told him to be safe.

David shed his apron and headed towards the dessert tent to let Judy know where he was heading and dashed for his car. Buck threw some more burgers on the open grill and prepared for the next group of hungry tourists. The Mayor of Gunnison, Pamela Sanders, saw Buck working alone and jumped in to help. Buck's mother in law Rosalie, who had been sitting in the shade, also walked over and put on an apron.

Rosalie Torres was one of the elders of the community. Pushing seventy-five and five feet two, she was a force to be reckoned with. What she lacked in stature, this still active Latina more than made up for with drive. She was still on the organizing committee for the

Labor Day picnic and she served on almost every volunteer committee that functioned within the county. Nothing went on in Gunnison that Rosalie was not a part of.

Fernando Torres, Rosalie's husband and Lucy's father, had run a small horse ranch just outside the city border. He had also been an outfitter and hunting guide. His love of the outdoors was something he was proud to have passed on to his two daughters, Lucinda and Rachel and his son Michael. Life was not always easy for Fernando and Rosalie, but they did the best they could and made sure that their children never wanted for anything.

It was a sad day five years ago when Fernando suffered a heart attack while guiding a couple of hunters up near Monarch Pass. Although the hunters had made a valiant effort to revive him and had succeeded several times, by the time search and rescue had reached them Fernando was gone. The family still missed Fernando every day, but it was ok. His daughter Lucy was with him.

By the end of the day every one of the fifty or so volunteers were dog tired, but they all had a wonderful time. Buck had also volunteered to be on the teardown team so after clearing out the burger tent and making sure Judy and the kids had torn down the dessert tent he spent the next couple hours helping clear the rest of the tents and clean the park. Just before he left the park he walked over to the little handicapped fishing dock where the family had scattered Lucy's ashes and spent a minute in quiet reflection. He said goodnight to Lucy and headed for home.

Buck was due in the office in Grand Junction the following afternoon for the monthly staff meeting and he had a bunch of paperwork that needed to get turned in for the cases he had recently closed.

Chapter Three

Buck is assigned to the Grand Junction office of the Colorado Bureau of Investigation but he typically works from home and handles cases in the central and southwestern parts of the state. He is highly regarded as an investigator by those who know him and he is often called upon by Governor Richard Kennedy to handle special cases of a sensitive nature.

The phone call he received just as he was getting ready to leave the house for Grand Junction was regarding one of those sensitive cases that required special handling.

Buck recognized the number on his phone as one of the main numbers for the CBI office in Grand Junction. He wasn't sure who was calling but he hit the answer button.

"Buck Taylor."

"Hey Buck, this is Paul Webber. Did I catch you at a good time?"

Paul Webber had just recently joined the Colorado Bureau of Investigation as a field agent and had been assigned to the Grand Junction Office. He came to

CBI from the Dallas, Texas Police Department and was very highly regarded as an investigator. Paul was a big guy. He stood six feet four and weighed in at two hundred forty-five pounds. A former college football standout at the University of Texas, Paul had spent four years in the Marines before joining the Dallas, Texas Police Department where he spent six years and was most recently assigned as a homicide detective.

Paul Webber had been assigned to work with Buck on a corruption case out of the city of Montrose, Colorado. The governor had been approached by the Montrose Chief of Police and asked to have CBI start an investigation of the five city council members. A complaint had been filed by a local real estate broker indicating that something shady had gone on during the annexation negotiations for a new subdivision. The Chief of Police was concerned that handling the investigation out of his department might ruffle some feathers. Montrose was a small western slope town and everyone knew everyone. He wanted the investigation to be impartial.

Buck had liked Paul Webber from the first time he met him. Paul was smart and he had a tremendous amount of drive. Like Buck, he was also very passionate about investigating crimes.

Buck and Paul had been investigating the entire annexation process for the past couple weeks and had finally gotten a warrant to look at the finances of each person involved. They were expecting a call from the forensic accountant any time now.

"Hey, Paul. I was just getting ready to leave the house and head to the office. What's up?"

"The forensic accountant just called. We were right. Councilman Meyers definitely tried to hide fifty thousand dollars. The accountant was also able to backtrack the money to the developer's daughter's personal bank account. He is emailing us the findings. We should have enough to make an arrest."

"Great news, Paul. Go ahead and type up the arrest warrant for the developer, his daughter and the councilman. Fax that to the city attorney in Montrose and have her call the judge to get the warrants. I am leaving the house now and will meet you at police headquarters in about an hour. See if you can pull Richards and Baxter away from their desks. We could use them to arrest the developer."

"Will do Buck. See you in a bit."

Paul hung up and Buck smiled. He hated when elected officials disregarded their oaths and violated the trust of their constituents. Besides Councilman Meyers was an arrogant prick. He pushed the speed dial button on his phone and heard the Director's phone ringing.

Colorado Bureau of Investigations Director Kevin Jackson answered the call.

"Hey, Buck. What's going on?"

Kevin Jackson was the youngest person ever appointed to run the Colorado Bureau of Investigation. He had spent years working his way up the administrative side of the Colorado Springs Police Department and had made significant changes along the way. But he wasn't just an administrator; he was also a cop and a very good one. Buck had become very familiar with the Director, and sometimes it seemed as though he worked for the Director instead of for the agent in charge of the Grand Junction field office.

Buck filled the Director in on the events getting ready to unfold in Montrose. He explained what the forensic accountant had discovered and that he had Paul Webber preparing the arrest warrant. He also asked him if it was ok to borrow Agents Richards and Baxter to help with the arrests? He would use the Montrose police as back up. The Director told him that he would call the governor and fill him in. He had no issues with anything Buck had told him and told Buck to let him know when the arrests were finished. He told Buck to stay safe. Buck hung up

Richards was Agent James Richards, a ten-year veteran with the Colorado Bureau of Investigation. Richards had spent several years with the Ann Arbor, Michigan Police Department before deciding to relocate his family to Colorado. He had a slight build and a very bookish look about him. Buck thought he was an accountant the first time he met him.

Baxter was Agent Ashley Baxter. Ashley was five feet four with long blond hair that she usually wore in a ponytail. She joined CBI five years before, right out of the University of Wisconsin. A Denver native, she had no issues moving to Grand Junction and had thrived in her new environment. She typically worked with Richards and their focus lately was mostly on property crimes like burglary. They had just wrapped up a successful investigation into a series of home invasions and were waiting for their next assignment.

Chapter Four

Jimmy Corey was concerned when he woke up Labor Day morning and his mom still wasn't home. She had promised to be home last night. They had planned to spend Labor Day together and then they had an important meeting at his school on Tuesday.

Susan Corey had worked as a ranger for the Division of Parks and Wildlife since graduating from Colorado State University in Fort Collins, Colorado seven years earlier. She had earned a bachelor's degree in animal biology and had jumped at the chance to work for the CPW. At five feet seven and one hundred forty pounds she was in excellent condition to hike the backwoods of the Colorado mountains to enforce hunting and fishing laws and protect the animals in her charge. It was not unusual for her to spend several days in the field searching for poachers or anyone else breaking the law. She didn't mind working alone since she always traveled with Duke, her five-year-old golden retriever.

Jimmy took out his cell phone and pressed the number one key. His mom had always told him that if anything ever happened to her that he should call the first preprogrammed number in his phone.

Miguel Vargas answered on the second ring. "Vargas."

"Hi Mr. Vargas, this is Jimmy Corey, have you heard from my mom?"

Miguel Vargas was the Chief Ranger at the Colorado Parks and Wildlife office in Glenwood Springs. Vargas was fifty years old, five feet ten and weighed one hundred seventy pounds. He was in excellent health from spending almost thirty years as a CPW ranger. A job he loved.

"Hi, Jimmy. Last I heard she was due back home yesterday. Did she not get home?"

"No sir," responded Jimmy. "I have been trying her cell phone since last night and it just goes to voicemail."

Vargas was now concerned. It wasn't like Susan Corey to stay out of touch.

"Jimmy let me see if I can find her. Keep trying her phone and if she comes home have her call me. I will be back in touch as soon as I hear anything."

Vargas hung up and dialed the CPW dispatcher. Because of the holiday and the perfect weather, most of the eleven rangers that worked out of Glenwood Springs were on duty. There were still a lot of campers in the woods and encounters with wild animals were always a concern. He asked the dispatcher to call the troops and have them start looking for Susan Corey's car.

Vargas knew Susan Corey was working a poaching case somewhere south of Aspen but he didn't have an exact location which was going to make this tough. He was going to need some help. Susan Corey could be anywhere.

Vargas's next call was to the Pitkin County Sheriff. Vargas and Sheriff Earl Winters had been friends for years. The Sheriff recognized the number on the screen and answered his cell phone immediately.

"Hey, Miguel. What's up?"

"Mornin Earl. Hate to bother you on the holiday but I have a missing ranger and could use your help."

Vargas went on to explain the situation and that she could be anywhere in the area. Vargas knew Susan Corey was heading into the mountains south of Aspen looking for elk poachers but she could have been heading home and encountered another issue. The last time the dispatcher had talked to her was three days earlier and she told them she would be hiking into the area around Hunter Peak. The problem is, Hunter Peak is not easy to get to and there are several old Forest Service roads that you can use to get into the area. After that, it is still good couple hours to hike in.

The Sheriff listened intently, asked a couple of questions and told Vargas that he would have his deputies start looking for her truck. He would also activate the Pitkin County Search and Rescue team and call Gunnison County to see if they could start looking from their side of the mountain. There were several old access roads she could have used from Gunnison County as well. The more folks they could get out on the roads looking for her the faster they could find her truck and narrow down the search area. The Sheriff hung up.

The Sheriff was good to his word and his first call was to Gunnison County Sheriff James McCauley who listened to him and then promised to have his deputies start looking along the back roads and to also have his search and rescue team start covering what the deputies couldn't.

His next call was to his dispatcher to call in all his deputies and his search and rescue team and have them meet at the Sheriff's office. His plan was to spread as many cars around the county as possible to try to find Corey's truck.

Meanwhile, Miguel Vargas was doing the same thing with his rangers and after assigning search areas, he jumped in his truck and headed for Aspen. As more time passed the more his concern grew. He knew Susan Corey could take care of herself but anything could have happened. She could have fallen or somehow gotten injured, she could be lost, although that was unlikely, or, god forbid, she could have encountered the elk poachers and things could have turned ugly fast. He hoped it wasn't the last scenario.

Vargas called Jimmy Corey back on his cell phone. When Jimmy answered, he explained what was going on and that a lot of people were going to be looking for his mom. He also asked him to look around her small office and see if she left any notes about where she planned to go when she left the house. Jimmy promised he would.

Finally, as he was getting ready to head to Aspen Vargas asked his wife to head over to Susan Corey's house and sit with Jimmy. His wife could read the concern in his eyes and told him not to worry. She would take care of

Jimmy and she would also call his grandparents in Pueblo and let them know what was going on.

Chapter Five

The Sheriff arrived at his office and waited for his search teams to assemble. While he waited, he pulled up Susan Corey's truck registration through the Division of Motor Vehicles website. The ranger drove a state-issued 2014 Chevy Tahoe, white, with the Division of Parks and Wildlife logo on the front doors. Just to be on the safe side, he asked dispatch to put out a BOLO, Be On The Lookout, for her truck, just in case she was stranded someplace. He also put in a request through her cell phone provider for the last location her cell phone had been used. This might help narrow down the search area.

Once his search teams and deputies arrived at the office, he provided them with Susan Corey's picture, her vehicle registration and assigned each searcher with an area to search. The search teams headed out. The day did not go well and by nine PM that night the Sheriff called the searchers in and asked them to meet again the next morning to start searching again. Susan Corey had fallen off the face of the earth and the Sheriff hated to call off the search but with darkness setting in it would make looking down old access roads even harder. Best to wait for morning.

Tuesday morning dawned clear, bright and warm. Strangely warm for a September morning in the mountains. The searchers started to arrive at seven AM and were just getting their assignments when the Chief Deputy walked into the room and asked everyone to just sit tight for a little bit. The Sheriff was out on a call which might prove helpful to the search.

The Sheriff and another deputy were on their way to talk with a couple of hikers who found a dog that appeared to have been shot and was lying under a Colorado Parks and Wildlife Chevy Tahoe.

Pitkin County Sheriff Earl Winters was the epitome of a western Sheriff. Tall and broad at the shoulders, Earl wore jeans, a button-down shirt and a broad-rimmed Stetson. He had a bit of a gut hanging over his belt but was still an impressive man. The large handlebar mustache only added to the old western look. Earl had been Sheriff for over twenty years and had no intentions of retiring anytime soon. He loved his job and he loved his county.

The Sheriff was first to arrive at the location of the call. County Route 13 led south from the Aspen Highlands ski resort and the road ran out at the Maroon Snowmass trailhead. This was a very popular trail that led to Maroon peaks and the parking lot was still crowded even though it was late in the season. The Sheriff didn't have to look hard to find the hikers who had called in the report. There was a crowd of hikers standing around the white Tahoe that was parked down a small side road that led to the parking lot restroom.

The group separated as the Sheriff walked up. The reporting party, Henry and Lidia Franklin, were kneeling next to a full-size golden retriever. On the other side of the dog another hiker was cleaning the wound and talking softly to the dog while working out of a first aid kit. The dog was shaking. The Franklins introduced themselves to the Sheriff.

The Franklins had started on a day hike just after dawn and had not noticed the dog at first. As they were walking to the restrooms they heard what sounded like someone whimpering. That someone turned out to be the golden retriever. He was lying under the truck crying and when Lidia crouched down to see if he was ok, she noticed the blood on his chest. She was able to pull him out from under the truck and that's when she had her husband call 911.

The other hiker who was working on the dog identified himself as Steven Blair. Blair was a registered nurse who had started for the trailhead a few minutes after the Franklins and immediately pulled out his first aid kit and started working on the wound. He reported that the blood around the wound had mostly congealed but he couldn't be sure if there was any internal bleeding. He felt the wound might be a day or two old. The dog was too weak to stand and did not look good but he still managed to lick Blair's hand while he spoke to the Sheriff.

The Sheriff knelt next to the dog and stroked his fur. He slid the dog's collar around and found a name tag. "Duke." The name on the back of the tag was Susan Corey with a phone number.

While the Sheriff was checking the name tag, the deputy arrived and knelt next to him. The Sheriff showed him the name tag and the deputy nodded. The Sheriff told the deputy to get an emergency blanket out of the back of his patrol car, a Ford Explorer and he then asked Blair to help him carry the dog to the back of the car. They gently placed the dog in the back of the Explorer and the Sheriff told the deputy to head for the Pitkin County Emergency Vet clinic.

The Sheriff called dispatch and told the dispatcher to call the emergency clinic and let them know that the deputy was on his way and that the dog looked critical. He then thanked the Franklins and Steven Blair and took down their contact info in case he needs to contact them later on.

The Sheriff went back to his truck and pulled a Slim Jim out of his toolbox and made quick work of getting into the ranger's truck. Once inside, he found the registration and confirmed that it was indeed Susan Corey's truck. Other than some papers sitting on the passenger seat he couldn't find anything that might indicate where she had gone. The Sheriff was very concerned and it was now time to call in the cavalry. He locked up the ranger's Tahoe and headed back to his truck.

"Dispatch, come in."

"Go ahead, Sheriff."

"Dispatch, activate search and rescue and have them report to me at the Maroon Snowmass trailhead. Call in all off-duty deputies and reserve deputies and have them assemble here as well. Contact Gunnison County and ask if they could activate their search and rescue and coordinate with me when they are ready. I will try to give them a search perimeter as soon as I can. Then put out a statewide broadcast that we have a missing and possibly injured law enforcement officer and we are requesting assistance to search a massive area. Foul play is assumed at this point. Got it?"

"Yes, sir. Do you want a call for volunteers for the search?"

"Not until we know what we are dealing with."

The Sheriff then called Miguel Vargas and filled him in on what they had just discovered. Since all of Vargas's rangers were also armed law enforcement officers, he would mobilize the entire team and have them head to Aspen to assist with the search. The Sheriff asked all the hikers who were still in the area to remove their cars from the parking lot and evacuate the area. This was about to become a crime scene. He used a couple of old buckets and a chain to close off access to the parking lot. It was going to be tight trying to get a lot of vehicles in here but they would figure it out. Now he just needed to wait for the troops

The Sheriff stood at the trailhead and looked deep into the woods.

"Where are you, Susan Corey?"

It was time to get organized.

Chapter Six

Buck Taylor turned left off Main Street onto S Park Avenue, turned right onto S 1st Street and pulled into the Montrose Police Department parking lot. He parked his state-issued Jeep Cherokee in one of the visitor's spaces and headed for the building. Once inside he identified himself to the duty officer at the desk and was buzzed into the back and headed for the Police Chief's office.

The Police Chief, Paul Sawyer, was seated at a small conference table across the hall from his office. Also in the room was the City Attorney, Beverly Jensen, Paul Webber, James Richards and Ashley Baxter from the Colorado Bureau of Investigation. Two Montrose police officers Nunez and Harding were also in attendance. Buck was pleased. He had worked with Nunez and Harding before and knew they were top notch cops. Buck shook hands all around.

"Ok," he said. "Do we have the warrants?"

Beverly Jensen nodded. Beverly was a twenty-eight-year-old, medium height black woman who had landed in Montrose after completing her law degree at THE Ohio State. She was looking for a place to start over after a failed marriage and had fallen in love with the area during a trip early in her college years. From the few encounters Buck had with her in the past, he knew she was smart and dedicated.

"You bet. We have arrest warrants for City Councilman Benjamin Meyers, Reginald Carstairs and his daughter Regina Carstairs. We are good to go."

"Great," said Buck. "I will take Meyers with Officer Nunez. Paul, you and Harding will take Regina Carstairs and Richards and Baxter will take Reginald Carstairs. You all have the addresses. This should be simple but keep on your toes. You never know how people are going to react. Chief you will be our back up if the shit hits the fan. We all good?"

Everyone nodded and they headed out the door to their cars. The Chief stopped Buck before he left the building.

"Hey Buck, I really do appreciate the work you guys did. This was going to get hairy if we had to deal with one of the city fathers and you are really saving our bacon. Thanks."

"No problem, Paul. As far as we are concerned the information we received came from a source outside the city and the first you guys found out about the investigation was when we showed up just now with arrest warrants. That should give you plenty of cover."

Paul Sawyer smiled and they headed to their cars. Buck, followed by Officer Nunez in his patrol car, pulled out of the lot and headed back down South 1st Street, turned right onto South Park Avenue and turned left onto

Main Street. Benjamin Meyers and Associates Real Estate office was just four blocks down on Main street so just before they got to Junction Avenue the two cars pulled over to the side and double parked. Buck put his red and blue flashers on, grabbed the warrant and exited the car.

Walking briskly, he pushed open the front door to the real estate office and walked right past the receptionist who started to say something but Buck wasn't listening. He turned the handle of the door marked Benjamin Meyers and pushed open the door. Meyers was seated behind his desk talking to two clients one male and one female and he looked startled when the door burst open and in walked Buck followed by Officer Nunez.

"Benjamin Meyers. We have a warrant for your arrest on public corruption charges. Please stand up, step around the desk and keep your hands where I can see them."

Meyers looked at his two clients who started to get up and were immediately told to remain seated by Officer Nunez. Nunez then looked at Buck.

"Agent Taylor, this is Reginald Carstairs and his daughter Regina."

"Well well," said Buck. "You two are under arrest as well. Please do not move. Nunez, call it in."

Regina Carstairs started to give Buck a lot of lip and reached into her purse, which was in her lap. Nunez who had the better angle saw the handle of the gun before Buck did and immediately drew his service weapon and placed it at the back of Regina's head. Buck grabbed

Meyers who had just started to stand up and pushed him flat down on his desk and drew his own weapon and pointed it at Reginald Carstairs.

Carstairs looked bewildered until Nunez pulled the gun all the way out of his daughter's purse and then he looked scared. Regina just looked hostile and continued to yell profanities at Buck. She finally ran out of steam and sat back in her chair. Nunez called dispatch and told them to send everyone to the real estate office and proceeded to search each person, one at a time and put flexicuffs on their wrists while Buck held Meyers down and held his gun on the Carstairs.

The Police Chief was the first to arrive, followed immediately by the rest of the crew from his office. They were each read their Miranda rights and were then walked through the real estate office and out past the crowd that had gathered on the street. Each suspect was placed in a different patrol car and driven back to police headquarters to be booked, fingerprinted and formally charged.

Paul Webber watched the booking process and said to Buck.

"What are the odds that they would all be together at just the right time?"

"You got me Paul but boy that Regina sure wanted to go down swinging. I can't believe she went for a gun. What an idiot."

"You got that right," Paul replied. "I will stick around and make sure all the paperwork is covered if you want to head to the office."

Buck nodded told Richards and Baxter that they could clear out as well and stopped and shook hands with the Chief and officers Nunez and Harding and asked Beverly Jensen if she needed anything else from him.

Beverly told him she was good and she would call him if anything came up. Buck wished everyone well and headed for his car. Once in the parking lot he called the Director and filled him in on the arrests.

The Director said, "she actually went for a gun in her purse. What the hell did she think she was going to do? Shoot her way out of the office."

"You got me, Director. I was as surprised as anyone. This could have gone from simple to messy in a heartbeat. I'm heading up to the office. Call if you need me."

Buck disconnected the call, slid into his car, turned onto Highway 550 and headed for Grand Junction. Buck had just gotten to Delta, Colorado when he pulled over to the side of the highway and turned up the police radio. Buck hardly ever used the police radio in the car. It was mostly there just for emergencies. He preferred to do most of his calling on his cell phone. It was a little more private.

Buck listened to the state-wide officer assistance call. This must be the same ranger his son David had mentioned. It sounded to Buck like the situation had gone from a missing ranger to something else entirely especially when the bulletin mentioned that her dog had been shot. Buck never ignored an officer assistance call. He always figured that someday it could be him on the other end and he would want everyone to respond. He pulled out his phone and called the duty officer at the Colorado Bureau of Investigation office in Grand Junction. He told the woman who answered that he was responding to the officer assistance call from Pitkin County and would be in touch.

There was no easy way to get to Aspen from where he was in Delta, so he turned onto Route 92. At Hotchkiss, he turned onto Route 133 which would eventually take him to Carbondale where he would turn south on Route 82 and head for Aspen. All told the drive would take him almost three hours and he would arrive late in the afternoon. He had no choice. A law enforcement officer was in trouble. Buck flipped on the emergency flashers in his engine grill and hit the gas. He needed to shave some time off the three-hour drive.

Chapter Seven

The Sheriff was standing next to the Pitkin County Search and Rescue mobile command center when Buck walked up. Buck had to park almost a mile down the road leading to the trailhead. Between tourist cars and all the emergency vehicles, there was barely room for all the people.

"Sheriff," said Buck. "Heard you could use a hand."

The Sheriff turned and shook Buck's hand. "Buck Taylor. How the hell are you? Been a while."

It had been a few years since Buck had worked with Sheriff Winters and he was amazed to see that the Sheriff looked exactly the same as the last time he saw him.

"Doin good. Want to fill me in on what you got goin?"

"You betcha," said the Sheriff. "Hey, by the way, was really sorry to hear about your wife passin. Always liked that lady. And hey, nice job in Durango last month. Knocked the shit out of the cartel boys." Bucked nodded.

The Sheriff filled Buck in on the search so far. Since Susan Corey hadn't left any information in her car, so the Sheriff had no choice but to use it as a starting point for the search and send his teams out in several different directions. Because the dog had been shot, the Sheriff had assigned a deputy or an armed ranger to work with each two-man search team. He wanted someone armed with each group just in case. He was happy to report that the dog was out of surgery and the emergency room vet felt good about his chances.

The Sheriff walked Buck through the search grids on the topographic map he had laid out on a table inside the command center. Right now, he had fifteen search teams working from several directions and all heading generally toward Hunter Peak. The Gunnison County search and rescue teams were working their way toward Hunter Peak from the south. From this point on it was just a matter of waiting. And it would be getting dark soon and he wanted everyone back before dark.

Buck looked at the grids. "Lot of area to cover. Any tracks from the dog?"

"No," responded the Sheriff. "None that anyone could find."

"You got PIS out there? Anyone could find tracks it would be him."

"Can't find him. Truth is I think he is pissed at me."

Buck waited for an explanation. The Sheriff went on to explain that one of his newer deputies had gotten curious about PIS and had pulled his prints off a soda can and ran them through AFIS, the Automated Fingerprint Identification System. As in the past, the prints came back as unknown and as in the past, PIS found out that they had run them and he stormed off to god knows where.

Buck let out a low whistle. "You guys violated his trust. No wonder you can't find him. Geez. We promised we wouldn't do that anymore. Try to find out his identity."

"I Know. Jumped all over the deputy. But nothing I can do now."

"Ok," said Buck. "Since your search teams will be heading back in a little bit, I am going to check into the hotel and I will try to find PIS and see if I can get him to help."

Buck shook the Sheriff's hand and started the long walk back to his car. Good thing he was in good shape. Buck reached his car, managed to turn around on the narrow road and headed for Aspen.

Aspen, Colorado, playground of the rich and famous, is the county seat of Pitkin County, Colorado. Aspen had a population of around 7,000 people and sat at an elevation just shy of 8,000 feet. It was originally built as a mining town in the 1880's and was almost abandoned after the collapse of the silver mines in the early 1900's. In the 1930's skiing started to take the place of mining and Aspen started looking towards the future but all that got put on hold during World War II. In 1946, skiing took off for real and Aspen hasn't looked back since. Once the county seat of the counterculture movement in the United States, Aspen is now home to movie stars and corporate CEO's and boast the most expensive real estate in the country. A lot had changed over the years and Buck was never sure if it was a good thing or a bad thing. Mostly it just was and Buck accepted that.

One thing Buck loved most about Aspen was that it still had its share of quirky characters and in spite of efforts to "clean up the city," the city still had a fairly good size homeless and counterculture population. Buck was on a mission to find one of those quirky characters as he pulled his car into a parking space along South Monarch Street next to Wagner Park.

Buck had first encountered PIS about ten years back. PIS, as he was affectionately known, had arrived in Aspen about twenty years ago and had immediately stood out. At that time the counterculture movement was in full swing and drugs were everywhere. Everyone in Aspen had either heard of or knew PIS except that no one really knew much about him. PIS was tall, about six feet two and gangly as folks used to say. He probably weighed one hundred fifty pounds soaking wet. He had long grey hair pulled back in a ponytail and a three-day growth of stubble on his face. The odd thing is that no matter what day or time of day you encounter PIS his stubble was always the same. It never seemed to grow out or look untidy.

Unlike most of the homeless characters at the time, PIS never smelled like a homeless person. He wore the same clothes every day but never looked dirty or unkempt. His outfit hadn't changed since Buck first met him. He wore calf height, brown leather lace-up moccasin style boots, light grey tuxedo pants with a dark grey stripe down the legs and a worn white dress shirt now frayed and yellow with age. Around his waist he wore a bright red cummerbund and around his neck he wore a bright red ascot.

No matter what time of year or what the temperature was PIS always wore the same tattered brown linen coat and a black beret. He looked rather elegant for a homeless person. His only other possession was a well-worn leather backpack that looked like it had traveled the world. The initials, P-I-S, were engraved on the flap and since no one knew his name, everyone just called him PIS, which he never seemed to mind. His demeanor was always jovial and friendly and no one ever complained about feeling threatened by his presence. Most striking was his British accent. Not the harsh Cockney accent you associate with street people but a very elegant silky-smooth accent that just exuded sophistication.

No one ever saw him panhandling for money, yet he always seemed to have enough to visit one of the local pubs for his nightly glass of cognac. As it turned out, PIS also had an incredible talent which helped him generate some income on a fairly regular basis. PIS was an amazing tracker. There wasn't anything he couldn't find whether it be an animal or a missing child and his abilities had come to the attention of many of the local hunting guides who paid him a daily fee to help them find game for their out-of-town clients. PIS's tracking skills had also come to the attention of the local police and Sheriff and over the years he had been involved in finding many lost hikers or missing persons in the rugged mountains surrounding Aspen.

Early on, when he first arrived in Aspen, many people tried to engage him in conversation to try to determine his real name or his background. It was rumored that several times people had tried to follow him as he left the downtown area and headed for the forest at the end of the day. No one was ever successful. Within minutes of entering the forest PIS would completely disappear leaving his followers bewildered. No one had any idea where he went at night or where he slept but every morning he was right back downtown walking the alleys between East Hopkins Avenue and East Hyman Avenue rummaging through trash dumpsters. If you asked people to guess PIS's age you would get answers from forty to eighty. He truly was a mystery.

The Sheriff had run his fingerprints once when an overzealous deputy had tried to arrest PIS for vagrancy and his prints came back as unknown. PIS had become furious at the intrusion into his privacy and ever since there was a truce between local law enforcement and PIS. He would provide his tracking services for free to any agency that had a need for such services, in exchange local law enforcement would no longer try to determine his true identity. That truce had lasted almost twenty years, til now.

Buck had first met PIS during a missing person's case Buck had been working in the Aspen area. The case involved a missing heiress, a thirteen-year-old girl, who had disappeared from her home in the Woody Creek area. It was never clear if she had walked away from her home or if she had been taken. Security had been tight around the family home and there were no signs of a break-in. No ransom had ever been demanded and no body was ever discovered, even though Buck and PIS with the help of the Sheriff's department had worked tirelessly for two weeks and had scoured every inch of the forests around Aspen. It was Buck's only case that remained unsolved and the case file sat in a prominent place on Buck's desk as a reminder of the one he couldn't solve.

Buck had gotten to know PIS pretty well during those two weeks. More so than anyone else had ever been able to and had developed a fondness for this unusual character. During those two weeks of hiking around in the woods, Buck had learned two things about PIS that he had kept a secret to this day. He found out that PIS's real name was Pheasant Iverson-Smythe. PIS had refused to say anything more about why his first name was Pheasant and Buck let it go. The other thing he learned, while they sat around a small campfire one afternoon, was even more of a mystery. PIS had pulled an old tin cookie box out of his backpack. Inside the cookie tin wrapped in fine silk was a beautiful china cup and saucer, a silver spoon, a small tea ball for brewing tea and a tiny silver teapot. PIS had also removed a smaller tin containing loose leaf Earl Gray tea which he proceeded to brew up for himself. The whole image seemed completely out of place. Buck had spotted a worn black and white picture of a very beautiful young woman sitting in the bottom of the cookie tin but when he asked PIS about the picture, PIS almost reverently closed the tin and softly explained that some things were best left unsaid. Buck could have sworn he saw a tear develop in PIS's eye.

Those two weeks had created a strange bond between these two men. Buck couldn't really explain it and he never tried. He had worked with PIS several more times over the years and it became clearer and clearer to Buck, that as he got older PIS never seemed to age. PIS also seemed to understand how much it troubled Buck that the case of the missing heiress remained unsolved.

Chapter Eight

Buck had spent the next couple hours until well after dark walking the streets and alleys of downtown Aspen searching for PIS. His inquiries with local shopkeepers, hoteliers, bartenders and the homeless he encountered had netted the same response. No one had seen PIS for a couple of days. Most couldn't remember the last time they saw him, but they would be happy to let Buck know if he showed up.

Buck checked into his hotel and crashed for the night. Tomorrow was going to be a very long day. Before he nodded off to sleep, he asked the spirits of the woods to keep an eye on PIS and Ranger Susan Corey and keep them safe. Buck wasn't religious in the typical sense of religion. He had been raised Catholic and he and Lucy had tried to raise their children Catholic but only Jason, their youngest son, had kept organized religion in his life. Buck was more spiritual than religious. He had very little use for organized religion but he always believed that there were spirits out there keeping an eye on things. He always thanked the spirits for allowing him to catch fish or for allowing him to witness a beautiful sunrise or sunset. Lucy never questioned his beliefs and she never minded when he discussed his attitudes with his kids or grandkids.

Buck's internal alarm clock went off at five AM and he showered and dressed, clipped his badge and holster to his belt and headed out to get something for breakfast before heading down to the trailhead. Stopping at a small gas station and convenience store just before the turnoff for Route 13, Buck grabbed a couple bottles of Coke and water and a few snacks to take with him. He was sitting in his car eating a microwaved burrito and drinking his Coke when there was a knock on the passenger side window. Buck glanced over and there, standing beside the car was PIS. Buck hit the button to unlock the door and PIS climbed into the passenger seat.

"Good morning Agent Taylor. How very nice to see you again. What a pleasant day it is going to be."

Buck loved listening to PIS's accent and for a second he just stared. He had no idea how PIS had found him, especially this far from downtown. He swallowed the piece of burrito he was chewing on and smiled.

"Where have you been?" Buck asked. "People haven't seen you in a couple days."

"I've been around. I heard you were looking for me. Will we be embarking on another grand adventure?"

Buck nodded. "We have a missing person we need to find. I am heading to the trailhead now and could use your help."

PIS looked serious for a moment. "I told the Sheriff that I would not be available to work with him for a while. Did he send you to find me?"

"No. The Sheriff was very clear that you were pissed. I told him I would find you. This one is important PIS. A female ranger is missing and her dog was found shot. We need your help."

PIS stared at Buck for a minute without saying anything. His trust had been violated once again and Buck understood how important that was to him but he also had no doubt that PIS would do the right thing.

"I didn't realize it was a ranger who was missing. Had I known, I would have found the Sheriff and offered my assistance."

Buck simply nodded, started the car and pulled out of the convenience store parking lot. The sun was just starting to come over the mountains and Buck knew from past experience that the earlier PIS got on the trail, the better and morning light was the best for finding obscure footprints or trail signs.

Buck was able to pull into the Maroon-Snowmass trailhead parking lot and parked next to the rescue command center. The Sheriff, coffee in hand, was standing over the table looking at the search map with the head of the Pitkin County Search and Rescue team. They both looked up at Buck and PIS approached.

"Buck, PIS. Nice to see you," said the Sheriff.

Buck nodded but PIS reached out his hand, first shaking the hand of the head of the rescue team and then shaking the Sheriff's hand.

"I must apologize Sheriff. My behavior of late has been in very poor taste and if you will allow me, I would like to offer my services in the search for the ranger."

Buck had never seen PIS seem this contrite. He had filled PIS in on the events thus far and PIS seemed to be extremely concerned about the fate of the ranger's dog. Buck wondered if the wounded dog had somehow struck a nerve with PIS. Something from his past that triggered a serious response.

The Sheriff accepted his offer of help and Buck and PIS joined the Sheriff around the map. The Sheriff explained that the rest of the teams would be arriving soon and then he reviewed where they had searched yesterday and what the game plan was for today. PIS studied the map very carefully as if he was memorizing every trail and landmark, although Buck believed deep inside, that PIS knew these forests like Buck knew his own house.

PIS looked up from the map. "Is it possible to see where the dog was found?"

The Sheriff explained that the ranger's truck was still at the scene and he led Buck and PIS over to where it was parked. PIS got down on his knees and looked under the car. He had spotted a small splash of blood on the rocks under the truck and he reached in and touched it with his hand. He then crawled under the truck as far as he could go and started scanning the area around the truck. He basically had a dog's eye view of the forest around the truck.

The sun was just starting to cast long shadows across the parking lot as PIS slid out from under the car.

PIS was focused on something in the distance and both Buck and the Sheriff knew better than to interrupt PIS when he was this focused.

Chapter Nine

The Teacher was not pleased. Not pleased at all. They had never seen the Teacher this mad. They brought home all that nice elk meat and had the others cook up some for dinner. Some of the others had found some canned vegetables at one of the houses they raided and also some soup. It was a good meal.

The Teacher then asked them to tell the others how they had shot the elk and that is when the trouble began. Being the oldest, the hunter told the story the way the Teacher had taught him too. He used words and visualization to bring the others along on the trail as they stalked the huge animal. The others sat and listened, enthralled with the story. Even the youngest sat still during the telling.

They described seeing the animal in the distance, how they crawled and crouch stepped to within a couple hundred yards and how they had drawn a bead on the elk, sighted in on his massive chest, took a deep breath, just like they had been taught, held the next breath and fired. The shot was perfect and the elk had only been able to run a couple yards before it fell down in some grass. They chased after it and when they found it it was still breathing so, they slit its throat to stop the pain. Just like the Teacher had told them to do. The Teacher looked pleased.

They told the group about dragging the elk back to the hunting camp in the woods and how they were going to hide it and come back to butcher it later but that the lady ranger and her dog had spotted the camp. The Teacher froze. He asked them to repeat the part about the lady ranger which they did. A little more nervously this time.

They described how the dog had sniffed out their hiding spot and how they had no choice but to shoot the lady ranger in the thigh since she was wearing a ballistic vest. They described how they had found her lying in the ravine and how the blood was pumping out of her leg and she had pleaded with them to stop the pain and they told everyone that they shot her in the head, so she would no longer suffer, just like the Teacher had taught them.

The Teacher's face grew red with anger. He demanded to know what had happened to the dog. They were now too afraid not to tell the whole truth so they told everyone that they had shot the dog and had seen it fall but that after searching for a long time they were unable to find the dog. They explained that they had gone back to where the lady ranger was lying in the ravine and had covered her body with dirt and sticks so no one would be able to find her.

The Teacher could no longer contain his anger. He yelled at them for taking a human life, something he had always told them never to do. He understood that they were trying to protect the others but taking a human life was forbidden. He told them that they would be punished for taking the human life and he told them he was very unhappy that they could not find the dog. If the dog made it back to where it had come from there would be hell to pay and that they had put the others in peril.

The Teacher was certain that the outsiders would come looking for the lady ranger and her dog and he now feared that after all this time they would have to move their camp. He told them that it was all their fault for being so stupid and to get caught by the lady ranger. He called them dumb and stupid and a bunch of other words they did not understand and they knew the Teacher was mad, very mad. He said that if the outsiders found the cabin that they would take the others away to a bad place where they would no longer be able to see each other and that the hunter and the younger one would have to go to jail because of killing the lady ranger. They had no idea what jail was but the Teacher made it sound like a terrible place and the younger one started crying which just made the Teacher madder. He took the rifle that was in the corner and put it under his bed. He told them not to touch it again until he had come up with a suitable punishment.

The Teacher told the girls to clean up the table from dinner and then to start moving everything out of the cabin and deep into the mine. They needed to be prepared for when the outsiders came. He told the hunter and the younger one to go out into the woods and make sure the traps were all set. He did not want to be surprised by the outsiders.

The others had never lived anywhere else but the cabin. They were scared and nervous about having to leave. All their stuff, the Teachers books, and the awards he had given them for doing good things were here in the cabin. Momma was buried not far away and they were worried that they would never be near her again. Some of the others started to cry.

The Teacher, sensing their worry and concern, started to calm down. He told them all to come back to the table for a minute. He had them all hold hands and then he read his favorite passage from the bible. "Yea, though I walk through the valley of the shadow of death..." The other listened carefully to the words. They always felt better upon hearing the words.

The Teacher finished reading and told them that he loved them all, even the hunter and the younger one, and that he was sorry he had gotten so mad. He told them that human life was precious and that it was wrong to take a life but that they might now have to take more lives to protect their home. This would make him sad. He hoped that they could get deep enough into the mine so no one would find them and that someday they might be able to come back to the cabin.

The Teacher asked them all to gather up their things as quickly and quietly as possible and start moving things into the mine. They all followed his orders and the hunter and the younger one left to check on the traps.

Chapter Ten

While the Sheriff headed back to the rescue command center to help organize the searchers and give them their assignments, Buck stood next to Susan Corey's truck and watched PIS work. PIS was methodical in his approach to tracking and it would take all his skills for this one. The dog had left almost no trail to follow, so PIS gradually started to expand his circle around the truck. Moving out five yards each time he completed a circle around the vehicle. Several times he had gotten down on his knees or his belly to get a better view of the area.

Buck waited patiently. The rest of the search was going to be organized but not too precise since they had no idea in which direction Susan Corey had traveled. They knew from the Chief Ranger that she was supposed to be searching for the illegal elk camp in the area near Hunter Peak and that several of the search teams had been in that area but had found nothing. Once she arrived in the parking lot something could have changed her mind and she could have gone off in any direction. This was needle in the haystack time.

Buck's thoughts were interrupted by a call from PIS.

"Agent Taylor. Over here please."

Buck had tried for years to get PIS to call him Buck but to no avail. Even if no one was around, he still called him Agent Taylor. Buck walked over to where PIS was kneeling on the ground looking at something in the dirt. Buck knelt down next to him and looked at the spot PIS was pointing at. Buck got closer and finally pulled his reading glasses out of his back pocket. He looked at the ground next to PIS's finger and could barely make out a single, very light pad impression and contained in that impression was a tiny spot of something reddish brown. Blood.

Knowing where the first trail mark was, gave them a direction of travel from the ranger's truck and with that PIS started moving in that direction. Buck could hardly see the trail but there was enough indentation in the undergrowth to give PIS something to follow. Buck ran back to the rescue command center to let the Sheriff know that PIS had a trail and to pick up one of the search team radios. The Sheriff was still going to send out his search teams per the plan they had come up with earlier, just in case the trail PIS was following didn't pan out.

Buck headed back to his Jeep, put on his ballistic vest, grabbed his backpack, a topographic map, handheld GPS unit and his back up semi-automatic pistol and headed back to the ranger's truck. PIS was already fifty yards up the trail looking for the next sign which he found just as Buck was walking up behind him. A spot of blood on a leaf eighteen inches off the ground. Buck could barely see it but he trusted PIS so off they went.

The trail they followed was hardly more than a slight impression in the undergrowth but it made sense to Buck. If you were a guide running an illegal elk camp you wouldn't want to have it anywhere near one of the established trails. This trail looked like an old game trail that hadn't been used in years. It was perfect. The last thing you would want is for a tourist to stumble on your camp and this area was filled with tourists hiking on the many established trails.

PIS was like an old hound dog on a scent. Periodically he would stop and kneel down to look at something, or he would stop, scratch his beard and then move ten or fifteen paces into the woods around the trail and circle back toward the trail. Buck soon realized that this was how PIS maintained the sign. If he lost the trail he would move left or right until he could reestablish the trail. For the most part, the dog seemed to have traveled a fairly straight line. Several times over the next couple hours PIS would stop and point out where the dog had laid down to rest. Buck could hardly imagine how much the dog must have been hurting as it made its way back to the ranger's truck.

Buck was in pretty good shape for a fifty-eight-year-old man but after four hours of hiking over uneven ground, he needed to take a break. PIS, on the other hand, looked like he hadn't walked anywhere at all. He still wore his linen coat and his beret and he wasn't even sweating. Buck was mystified. It was early September but it was still extremely warm for this time of year. Buck was sweating profusely. PIS did agree to hold up so that Buck could take a breather and he didn't refuse the bottle of water and the trail mix bar that Buck had offered him.

Buck unfolded the topographic map and pulled out his hand-held GPS unit. He had been marking waypoints on the map as they had been traveling. PIS came over to look at the map with him. They had traveled in pretty much a straight line from the ranger's truck but what they both noticed was that they were not headed to Hunter Peak, at least not directly. If this trail continued, they were actually traveling to the west of the peak. Away from where most of the rescue units were searching.

"What do you think?" Buck asked.

PIS pondered the question and looked once more at the map. "If I had to venture a guess I would say that something distracted the ranger or she had some new information that we were not aware of. There are several trails that lead to Hunter Peak that she could have followed more easily than this trail, yet she chose to bushwhack through the trees. Very odd indeed," replied PIS.

Buck had to agree. He folded up the map, put it back in his pocket and they headed out again. Twice over the next hour PIS lost the trail in some rocky terrain and it took a little bit of time to reestablish the trail. Buck had spent that time listening to the other search teams reporting in. No one had anything good to report.

Buck and PIS had traveled for about another hour when PIS suddenly stopped and put his hand out so Buck couldn't move past him. At almost that same instance the radio crackled.

"Search team four to command. We have a serious problem, over."

"Go ahead search team four, this is command."

"Command we have a man down. One of the rangers stepped on what appears to be some kind of booby trap. He was impaled in the leg with a sharp stick that just popped out of the ground. He is bleeding badly and we need a paramedic."

"Search team four. Please begin first aid and try to stop the bleeding. We are sending in the paramedics. Please provide coordinates."

The search team leader gave them the coordinates and Buck pulled his map out of his pocket. The search team was in the grid next to the one he and PIS were working. Probably a little over a mile from their present location. Buck put the map back in his pocket and started to move in the direction of search team four but PIS stopped him again. Buck looked annoyed until he saw where PIS was pointing. Just above the surface of the trail, Buck spotted the monofilament fishing line. It was tied to a bush off to their left and was pulled tight across the trail.

"Booby trap?" Buck asked.

PIS nodded. "Yes. Be very careful. Let me see where this goes. Please stand back a couple paces."

PIS got down on his knees and slowly followed the line without touching it. Five feet off the trail and in fairly dense underbrush he stopped. The string was attached to a very rudimentary crossbow that had been anchored between two shrubs. The bolt was nothing more than a sharpened stick but with the tension on the line, it could have delivered a nasty surprise to whoever tripped it. PIS pulled a knife from his pocket, snapped it open with one hand and proceeded to cut the tripwire and disengage the bolt. He crawled back out of the underbrush.

"Could have been a bit of a nasty surprise for whoever tripped this," he said while handing the bolt to Buck. "It was low enough to the ground to cause some damage but I don't think it was intended to kill. Just wound."

Buck examined the bolt. "Crude but effective."

"How the hell did you spot the trip wire? I was looking at where you were pointing and I didn't see it until you touched it."

"Experience Agent Taylor. Someone does not want us to find this elk camp."

Buck pulled out his radio. "Command this is Buck Taylor. Please put the Sheriff on."

"Go ahead, Buck. This is Earl," replied the Sheriff.

"Earl, have all the search teams stop immediately. We just disarmed a booby trap along the trail we are following. There could be more out there."

"All search teams. You heard the man. Stop immediately until we figure this out. Buck, how do you think we should handle this?"

"We are certain we are on the dog's trail. Let us continue forward and clear a path and see where the trail takes us. In the meantime, I would suggest you pull everyone back to the parking lot. Right now, our trail is taking us to the west of Hunter Peak. We will call in as soon as we reach the end of the trail."

"Ok Buck. Stay in touch. All search teams, backtrack the way you went in and return to the parking lot."

Buck looked at PIS. "Let's keep moving. Slowly."

PIS nodded and started back down the trail.

Chapter Eleven

She had to park along the road leading to the Maroon-Snowmass trailhead parking lot. There were a lot of emergency vehicles ahead and it appeared that the entrance to the parking lot was closed. She had no idea what was going on. She had overheard a conversation at the restaurant that there was some kind of police search going on at the trailhead and she decided to come see for herself.

She decided to leave her car on the side of the road and walk down to the crowd to see if she could find out what was going on. She pulled the long brown wig down a little snugger on her head, pulled it back in a ponytail and put on her Denver Broncos ball cap. She climbed out of her car, grabbed her backpack out of the trunk and slung it over her shoulders. She looked just like all the other hikers that were walking down the road to the trailhead.

As she walked towards the barricade that was set up at the entrance to the parking lot, several disgruntled hikers came walking back from the barricade. Several people told her that the trail was closed until further notice. She thanked them as they passed, figuring that was what most friendly hikers would do.

She stepped into a crowd of hikers and day users who had gathered at the barricade and listened as the park ranger told the crowd that the authorities were in the process of looking for a lost hiker and the park would be closed until the search was concluded.

Most of the hikers took the information as gospel and turned to head for their cars. Some chose to stay and either grumble about the inconvenience or ask questions to try to get more information from the ranger. She stood quietly to the side of the group and listened. She had learned long ago that you got a lot more information from people if you stopped and listened and watched their body language.

As the other hikers conversed with the ranger, she heard his words but more importantly, she noticed his eyes. It was obvious to her that he was not being completely truthful. He was trying to be polite with the crowd but there was an underlying tension in his face and voice. Answering the same questions a dozen or more times gets old pretty fast but the ranger answered each query with a polite forced smile.

Satisfied that she was not going to hear anything new, as more hikers and curiosity seekers came and went, she turned and headed back to her car. Being the polite, friendly hiker, she was, she let those just heading for the barricade know that the trail was closed indefinitely. The other hikers politely thanked her before continuing on to the barricade to hear it for themselves.

She reached her car, put her backpack back in the trunk and stood for a minute looking down the road at the barricade. She knew the ranger was only being partially *truthful. It was obvious the trail was closed. So that was the truth. The missing hiker was another story. From the trailhead she could see the Pitkin County Search and Rescue mobile command center, so obviously, there was some kind of search going on. Typically, in small communities, when a hiker is lost or missing the Sheriff's office calls for volunteers but that was not the case here. Most of the volunteers she could see were uniformed searchers and she also noted a lot of law enforcement types. A lot more than you would see at a simple search and from the cars she observed the law enforcement folks had come from many different jurisdictions. She would need to think about this some more.*

She climbed into her car and just sat for a minute. Was it possible they had found it? Is that why all the cops were on the scene? In all the time it was there no one had ever stumbled onto it. Was it possible that someone spotted the newer lock? She had purposely taken an old looking padlock from her grandfather's garage so it would not be obvious to anyone looking that the lock was recently changed.

She started to feel a little nauseous and took a sip of water from the bottle between the seats. It couldn't be. She was just getting started. She had tried to be careful, just like she had been taught. She made certain she wasn't followed and she covered her tracks well. No, it was not possible. No one had discovered it in forty or fifty years. Why now? She started to shake and she wrapped her arms around her chest and squeezed. The shaking finally stopped.

She decided that she was just being paranoid and that the cops would not be waiting at her house when she got home. After all, how would they even know about her? She started her car, pulled off the side of the road and headed home. Even though she felt more confident that this didn't concern her and it was just a coincidence that something was going on in the same area, she had this little nagging bug in the back of her head. She would need to be very careful until she worked this all out.

Chapter Twelve

The trail was becoming more obvious as they moved forward. They were finding more and more dried bloodstains on the undisturbed undergrowth and PIS told Buck that with the amount of blood he was finding, they must be getting close to the end of the trail. He also had to stop once more and expose another booby trap. This time it was a shallow pit about a foot deep covered with a thin layer of sticks and leaves. Almost impossible to see, but it could have been quite effective. Buried in the small pit were a dozen sharpened sticks pointing up so anyone who happened to step into the pit would have had their foot impaled on any one of the spikes.

PIS spent a few minutes removing the spikes, which were buried a foot or so deep in the soil to keep them upright. At one point he commented about the fact that what they had encountered so far were very similar to the types of booby traps the Viet Cong used to set during the Vietnam war. Crude but highly effective.

Buck started to ask him about the comment but PIS just ignored him and finally stood up and said they should keep moving. Buck let it slide but wondered if he had just been privy to another little tidbit about PIS's life.

PIS moved down the trail with a little more urgency, or so it seemed to Buck. He seemed to be much more focused and they covered a lot more ground until they arrived at a small rise and PIS stopped and knelt down and touched something on the ground. Buck climbed up the little rise behind him, stopped to catch his breath and looked to where PIS had his hand. This blood spot was so obvious that even Buck could see it.

Without saying anything, PIS stood and moved a couple feet to his left and repeated the process. Buck looked and noticed the second large blood spot. PIS still hadn't said anything. He stood up and moved down the backside of the ravine where he found more dried blood. He stood and looked around the area. Then he looked at Buck. There was a seriousness in his eyes that Buck had never seen before.

"The dog was shot there." He pointed to the spot where Buck was now standing. Buck stayed silent. "It would appear he fell off the ridge in this direction and landed here." He pointed to another big blood stain. "There is a good blood trail leading back to the trail we came in on. I am amazed, that with the amount of blood that is here, that the dog was able to walk back four point four miles and get back to the ranger's car. He must have been in terrible pain."

Buck pulled out his hand-held GPS and looked at the data. They had traveled four point five miles. He hadn't told PIS how far they had gone but he hit the number almost exactly. Buck didn't know how PIS had known but he decided to keep that knowledge to himself. PIS was certainly an anomaly.

PIS climbed back up the small ridge and looked around.

"What do you think happened to the ranger? Any chance she might be still alive?" Buck asked.

PIS stood for a moment and Buck thought he saw PIS's eyes get a little misty.

"I don't think so." He pointed to the other large spot of blood on the ground a few feet to the right. "This is arterial spray. Notice the many small droplets. I believe the ranger was shot here." He slowly stood up. He pointed to a pile of leaves and sticks at the bottom of the ravine.

"I believe we will find the ranger under that pile of leaves."

Buck pulled his cell phone out of his pocket, clicked on the camera and took a couple pictures of the various blood stains as PIS pointed to them. He then put his camera away and looked at PIS. He nodded and they carefully made their way down into the ravine making sure to disturb as little as possible.

At the bottom of the ravine Buck took over and PIS stood back to let Buck do his job. Very carefully, Buck began to remove the leaves and sticks from the pile. Below the leaves and sticks, Buck found a layer of loose dry dirt. His heart sank. It was obvious, even to him, that the dirt was recently disturbed and he moved even more carefully.

Using his hand to brush away the dirt, the face of Susan Corey gradually revealed itself. Her eyes were still open and Buck could almost sense the horror she must have felt knowing her life was slipping away. The dark hole in her forehead and the lack of blood on her face told Buck that the kill shot had come almost too late. Buck figured Susan Corey must have been at the end of her life when someone put her out of her misery. He stopped and stared at her face.

Buck had seen a lot of death in his long career in law enforcement but he had never gotten jaded by it. He was still impacted deeply and seeing Susan Corey's lifeless face made him sit back for a moment and reflect on his own life. It also made him angry that this young woman's life had been cut short and he silently vowed to do everything he could to find and punish the person or persons who had done this.

PIS joined him and together they removed the dirt and debris from the rest of her body. PIS pointed to the bullet hole and the massive amount of blood that stained her green pant leg. Buck nodded and pulled out his camera again. He took pictures of the wounds and of her body as it lay and pictures of the debris that had been piled on her. He finally looked at PIS.

PIS said, "whoever shot her knew what they were doing. Shot her below her ballistic vest. She rolled down the slope ended up here and then the shooter shot her in the forehead. Such a terrible waste. I am truly sorry Agent Taylor."

Buck nodded. "Without your help, we might never have found her. Thanks for helping to bring her family closure. Now we need to call in the troops. This is now a crime scene."

Buck climbed back up to the top of the ridge and found that he had 2 bars of cell service. He decided not to broadcast the find over the radio, so he used his phone and dialed the Sheriff.

The Sheriff answered on the second ring. "Buck, does this mean what I think it means?"

"Yeah. Didn't want to broadcast it on an open frequency. We found Susan Corey. We are gonna need the Forensic Pathologist and the crime scene guys."

Buck told the Sheriff about what they had discovered. He pulled out his handheld GPS and gave the Sheriff the coordinates for the body and told him how to follow the trail from her truck. He would send PIS back up the trail to meet them halfway and he would lead them in the rest of the way. He asked him to send in a couple search and rescue guys to carry out the body when forensics was finished and he requested as many deputies as the Sheriff could spare. This was going to be one tough crime scene to process. He asked him to keep all the other law enforcement folks and rangers away from the scene.

The Sheriff mentioned that there were several Gunnison County deputies not that far from his location and he would request assistance from the Gunnison County Sheriff and have his deputies meet up with Buck to help work the scene. This deep in the mountains, jurisdiction lines sometimes get blurred and Buck told the Sheriff he would be grateful for all the help. The Sheriff would also be calling his homicide team.

Buck hung up and headed back to PIS and the body. He asked PIS if he would head back up the trail and meet the teams coming down. PIS slapped Buck on the back and headed up the ridge. Buck was now alone with the body and he said a silent prayer and asked the spirits of the forest to watch over her family.

Chapter Thirteen

Buck pulled a silver and orange survival blanket out of his backpack and used it to cover Susan Corey's body. He had also checked to make sure she still had her weapon, her radio and her cell phone. It was obvious that robbery was not a motive, so he quickly dismissed that idea and moved on to the next idea. Ambush. Was Susan Corey ambushed? And if so by whom? Buck was all too familiar with ambushes having barely survived an ambush while investigating a drug distribution network in Durango, Colorado a month or so back. If it hadn't been for luck and his friend Jessica Gonzales, the DEA Agent in Charge of the Grand Junction office, he would not be here today.

The Slattery brothers were prime suspects in a triple homicide Buck had been investigating in Teller County, when he was reassigned to the cartel investigation in Durango. Somehow the brothers had followed Buck to Durango and tried to ambush him in his hotel parking lot. Jess Gonzales was walking through the hotel parking lot on her way to meet Buck just as the shooting started. Buck and Jess had killed both brothers but Buck would never forget how close he came to getting killed that evening. He knew his late wife Lucy would not have been pleased.

He stopped and cleared that memory out of his head. Susan Corey needed and deserved Buck's full attention and he would not let her down. Buck stood up and looked around the area. The trees were not as dense in this part of the forest, as a lot of what they had passed through. The shot could have come from almost anywhere, so he needed to narrow that down a bit. He walked back up to the top of the ridge to the first blood stain. He looked down at the blood stain and noticed the spatter that PIS had first pointed out to him. Most of the spatter appeared to be on one side of the larger stain, so he decided to concentrate his initial search in that direction.

Buck walked back down into the ravine and headed in the direction he thought the shots might have come from. He noted one thing almost immediately. Whoever had buried Susan Corey's body had left almost no footprints. Whoever this person or persons were, they had skills. Buck moved carefully away from the body. He was still worried about additional booby traps, so he was very careful where he placed his feet. Remembering how PIS had used a circular pattern each time he lost the trail Buck followed a similar pattern. Every five feet or so he would stop and then move right and then left in a semi-circle around the body location.

Buck was just completing his fourth semi-circle when he heard some leaves and sticks crackling in the distance. Buck unsnapped the thumb break on his holster and removed his semi-automatic pistol. He slowly knelt down.

"Gunnison County Sheriffs!" a voice called out. "Coming in from the south."

Buck replied, "All clear. Come ahead." He rose and holstered his gun but kept his hand on the back strap. Just in case.

Buck spotted the two Gunnison County Sheriff's deputies coming through the trees, followed by two Gunnison County Search and Rescue members. He snapped the thumb break on his holster shut. Buck recognized Walt Jenkins. Walt was a corporal and had been with Gunnison County for about six years. The other deputy he didn't recognize.

Walt stepped up and extended his hand. "Buck Taylor, how the hell are you?"

Buck shook Walt's hand and Walt introduced him to deputy Jimmy Sanchez. Buck shook Jimmy's hand and then shook hands with the two rescue team members, Mike Brill and Connie Hancock, both of whom he knew quite well.

Walt walked over to the body and pulled back the corner. He stood there for a minute said a silent prayer and crossed himself. Walt was a devout Christian. He put the blanket over Susan Corey's face and looked around the area.

"Heck of a crime scene Buck. What do you want us to do?"

Buck explained about his semi-circle search pattern and that they were looking for the shooter's nest. He also reminded them of the possible booby traps. Walt told Buck that they had encountered a booby trap on the way up the hill.

"If Jimmy hadn't tripped over his own feet he would have gotten an arrow right in his backside," said Walt. "Luckily the arrow passed right over him and embedded itself in a tree. Who would have ever thought about booby traps in Colorado?"

Buck agreed and the four Gunnison searchers headed off to continue Buck's search pattern. Buck took the opportunity to take a breather and pulled a bottle of Coke and a trail mix bar out of his backpack. They had been going nonstop since this morning and Buck was beginning to feel his age. Finishing the Coke and the trail mix bar, Buck headed in the direction of his initial search to help the Gunnison County team. He was just coming up on the first searcher when he heard Jimmy Sanchez call his name.

Jimmy was about forty yards from the body and was looking at something on the ground as Buck walked up. He was soon joined by Walt Jenkins and they looked at what Jimmy was looking at. The spent shell casing was lying on the ground in plain sight. It didn't appear that anyone had tried to hide it, unless someone had missed it.

Buck pulled out his phone and snapped a picture of it. Walt pulled a clear evidence bag out of his backpack and handed it to Buck, who had already gloved up and he picked up the shell casing between his two fingers and placed it in the bag and sealed it. Buck signed his name to the bag and Walt placed it in Buck's backpack.

The group also noticed a large puddle of blood near the shell casing. From the way Buck read the scene, it appeared that whoever shot Ranger Corey was probably hiding behind this downed log and pretty much hidden from view. From this vantage point, Buck could clearly see the top of the ridge where Susan Corey was shot. But what was the blood?

Jimmy had moved off from the group and was following the blood trail that led to the little hideout. He called to Buck.

"I think I know what the blood is from."

Buck and Walt walked over to where Jimmy was standing. Jimmy was standing next to a huge pile of bloody guts.

Jimmy remarked, "I think someone gutted an elk here. It's not a fresh pile so I would say a couple days."

Buck and Walt agreed with his assessment. A picture started to form in Buck's mind. He explained his theory to Jimmy and Walt.

"My guess, at this point, is that someone was hunting out of season, possibly the illegal hunters that the ranger had been following. The hunters heard her coming and pulled the carcass over behind the downed tree and hid. Something the ranger or her dog did must have spooked them and someone shot her in the thigh. Shot the dog too but the dog managed to crawl away. Susan Corey wasn't as lucky. She fell into the ravine bleeding badly. Someone then shot her in the head, either to shut her up, or put her out of her misery or something."

Walt looked at Buck. "Man Buck, if that's the way it went down that is pretty cold. Using a kill shot on an animal is one thing, but to kill a person up close, that's something else entirely."

Buck just nodded. He tried to visualize what Susan Corey had been feeling at the time. Lying in a ravine feeling her life pumping out of her thigh and then watching as her killer stood in front of her and calmly points his gun at her and pulls the trigger. Whoever did this was going to pay. Buck made himself that promise.

Chapter Fourteen

She sits alone in the dark in her room. One small lavender candle burning in a small mason jar on her dresser. The night air is still unseasonably warm so she has the window open and she can hear the hubbub of mountain life as it passes by her home. Her parents had gone out to dinner as soon as she got home. They looked frazzled, even more so than usual. It has been hard on them, especially the last three years since she was away at college. They knew she would be leaving again very soon and she wondered if they hated her for her decision.

She had lived in Aspen all her life and for the most part, it had been a good life. Her parents were not rich and they didn't get involved in the Aspen social scene. They lived in the same little Victorian house on West Hallam Street that her grandfather bought in the nineteen fifties. She was the third generation living under the same roof and sometimes things got a little crazy.

Her father's father, her grandfather, had come to Aspen a few years after the end of World War II. He had been a soldier in the 10th Mountain Division as the war neared its end and had learned how to ski. Some of his fellow warriors were settling in small communities throughout the Colorado mountains and were working to build up the fledgling ski industry. He thought it might be fun to be a part of the movement.

His best friend, Gus Murphy, found a job with the recently formed Aspen Skiing Corporation and had offered her grandfather a job working as a mechanic on the ski lifts. Having been mechanically inclined all his life, her grandfather took to the job like a fish to water. As the years progressed, his life became more and more fulfilling and he felt he was living the American dream. He met and fell in love with her grandmother, bought the small Victorian house on West Hallam Street and raised a son there. It was a perfect life except that the demons were still working hard in the back of his mind.

The demons had always been there as long as he could remember and his time in the army had only deepened the lust they brought out. He had practiced his craft, as he called it, with great abandon as a young man. Many of the townsfolk around Lynchburg, Virginia thought he was odd and some actually feared him. He had grown up on a very rural farm outside Lynchburg. The family's water came from a pump and an outhouse served their more personal needs. To say they were dirt poor would have been an understatement. His father was a sharecropper and didn't even own the dirt under their meager house.

Life had not been easy growing up. He was constantly picked on when he was able to get to school, which was not often, and as things got worse his father would take to drinking and he was a terrible drunk. No one was safe from his rage especially his mother and younger sisters. Numerous times he had watched as his father left his middle sister's room and he heard her crying

inside. As his younger sister got older, the same thing
would happen to her. His mother would often come out of
her room with a black eye or a bruised lip. He wasn't
saved from his father's rage because he was a boy. His
father would belittle him all the time about not being
good at anything or not being a man. He would work him
from dawn til dusk and then if the mood was right would
beat him senseless for even the most minor infraction.

His escape often took him into unknown territory.
He took to following in his father's footsteps and started
abusing the animals on the farm. But it didn't stop there.
Many of the neighbors complained to the local Sheriff
about their pets disappearing. The Sheriff had visited the
farm numerous times but never found any evidence that
anyone on the farm was involved but the neighbors knew
the truth. What they had no way of knowing was how
deep the depravity went.

One afternoon one of the neighbors had
confronted him about a missing goat. He had seen the
goatskin hanging in a tree along the creek behind the
farm. The neighbor confronted him and his father with
the evidence and a fight broke out. By the time the Sheriff
arrived the neighbor was dead. His father, who was
covered in blood, tried to put all the blame on him but the
Sheriff didn't buy it. They were both arrested. His father
was convicted and died in prison a few years later. He
was convicted and given a choice, jail or the army. He
chose the army.

The army was a great place for him. They taught
him how to kill. A skill he honed with great enthusiasm.
He was so good at it that he was often the first soldier
called upon when a Nazi guard needed to be dispatched

silently. His knife became his friend and he used it most effectively when an enemy officer needed to be encouraged to talk. He was a skilled craftsman and his actions often turned the stomachs of even the most hardened soldiers.

He had been able to keep the demons under control for the first couple years after he moved to Aspen but they had become too strong for him to ignore. He needed to feed the demons but Aspen was a small mountain town. Missing people would be noticed. At first, he tried to feed the demons with animal sacrifices. He stayed away from family pets, too close to home, so he focused on wild animals which were in abundance in the forests around Aspen.

Killing forest creatures with his bare hands was certainly a lot of fun but it didn't satisfy the demons for long. He needed the sensation and the arousal that came from killing another human being. The incredible satisfaction it would bring as he felt life slowly slip away from someone who had been a living breathing person. He also missed the thrill of the hunt. Finding the right person and stalking them until just the right moment. He loved the challenge.

Her thoughts were interrupted by the commotion down the hall, so she stood, blew out the lavender candle and walked down the hall to her grandfather's room. Her grandmother was trying to get the very agitated man to calm down. Her grandmother looked up as she entered the room and her eyes pleaded for her granddaughter's help. Her grandfather had been getting more and more agitated lately. The past few decades had not been easy for the family. Since the accident that had left her grandfather a quadriplegic, he had been confined mostly to his bed but for the past five years, the Alzheimer's Disease had taken a terrible toll on his mind. He struggled to keep his sanity but his memories were all but gone and she feared that the demons were winning the final battle for what was left. She knew what to do so she sat down on the edge of the bed and started to hum a lullaby. It didn't matter what lullaby she hummed; it seemed it was the sound that would calm him down. Her grandmother took the opportunity to increase his morphine drip and he finally fell asleep. Her grandmother looked relieved. She sat for a few more minutes and then left his room grabbed her jacket and headed out into the night.

Chapter Fifteen

Buck and the others stopped their searching as they heard the first sounds of the parade of law enforcement personnel approaching the small ridge. Buck wanted to try to keep the crime scene as untouched as possible, so he headed back to the body just as PIS and the Sheriff came over the ridge. The Sheriff looked as solemn as Buck had ever seen him. Buck took a minute to review with the Sheriff what they had discovered and they planned out the perimeter of the crime scene. They would tape off the area from the top of the ridge, down into the ravine and over to where they had found the probable shooting location. The area was huge.

Since Buck was on scene as a courtesy more than anything else, he let the Sheriff take charge of the crime scene. He would step back and let the locals handle the investigation and would offer his services as needed. The Sheriff called his two homicide investigators over to where he and Buck were standing.

Moe Steiner was a twenty-year veteran of the Sheriff's Department. He was about five-ten and maybe one hundred seventy pounds. He had thinning hair and a large brown mustache. He was dressed in jeans, T-shirt and light jacket. His partner was Jane Fitzpatrick. Fitz, as she was affectionately known around Aspen, was a sixteen-year veteran and had been working homicide for almost ten years. The mother of three and grandmother of two she was five six and maybe a little overweight. She also had on jeans, a light flannel shirt and her dark blue nylon police jacket.

Buck shook hands all around. He had first met both investigators when he was investigating the missing heiress ten years ago. His only unsolved case. He knew them both to be exceptional investigators and extremely detail oriented. He had a feeling that this investigation, because of the location and the size, would be a challenge for both of them.

They had just begun discussing the overall crime scene when the Sheriff's two forensic techs, Claudia Gomez and Holly Flynn, crested the ridge followed closely by Dr. Emily Parker, the Forensic Pathologist for Pitkin County.

Colorado is one of about a dozen states that still use the Coroner system instead of the Medical Examiner system. The coroner for each jurisdiction is an elected official and that person did not have to have any experience at being a coroner or even be a medical professional. Anyone could run for coroner. The system was gradually evolving so that the coroner needed to complete a formal training program in death investigations but it was a slow process. Since unlike in the Medical Examiner system, the coroner did not have to be a doctor, each coroner would contract with a licensed Forensic Pathologist to handle any investigations that required an autopsy. These Forensic Pathologists were usually highly trained doctors, who in a lot of cases, split their time between several jurisdictions to keep costs down.

Dr. Emily Parker had been the licensed Forensic Pathologist for Pitkin County for five years. She had been a medical examiner in Los Angeles before growing tired of the rat race and had decided to relocate her family to the Colorado mountains. A graduate of Harvard University and John Hopkins Medical School, she was very highly regarded and the ultimate professional. Instead of working as a pathologist for several counties, Emily Parker had opened a family medical practice in Aspen, where you could still find her most days. At the time she wasn't sure if she wanted to go back into the medical examiner profession. That changed five years ago with the sudden death of her predecessor, Dr. Ross Malone, who died in a freak skiing accident on Aspen Mountain. Since Dr. Parker was already licensed as a pathologist, she took the job on, temporarily, until they could find a permanent replacement for Dr. Malone. The county was still looking.

She walked up to Buck and the Sheriff and extended her hand. Buck shook her hand.

"Nice to see you again Agent Taylor. I wish the circumstances were better."

Buck nodded. "Good to see you too Doc. Sorry for the long trek."

"No worries," she replied. She looked down at the body in the ravine. "Why don't you give me the tour since you found her. Ok with you Sheriff?"

The Sheriff told her it was fine with him but he wanted one of his homicide folks down there with them.

Fitz stepped forward and the small group started down the side of the ravine. Buck had worked with Dr. Parker several times before and knew that she would prefer to view the body first before asking for his report. She never wanted her first impressions tainted by the opinions of others. There would be time for that later. Buck and Fitz stood off to the side as Dr. Parker gloved up and knelt down next to the body.

While Buck, Fitz and Dr. Parker worked around the body, the Sheriff had a couple deputies tape off the area and he asked his forensic team to start working towards the body from the shooter's nest, for lack of a better term. Gomez and Flynn grabbed their gear and headed over to where the two Gunnison County deputies stood watch over the possible nest. Once there, they shook hands all around, gloved up and started working the scene. Walt Jenkins had grabbed the evidence bag with the shell casing in it from Buck's backpack and handed it to Holly and showed her where they found it. He told her that Buck had the pictures of the bullet insitu, as it lay, on his phone.

Walt and Jimmy Sanchez proceeded to walk the two forensic techs through what they had discovered during their initial search. They showed them the gut pile from the elk and indicated the direction the carcass had been dragged and finally hidden behind the downed tree where they found the shell casing. Gomez and Flynn worked the area as thoroughly as possible considering all the leaves and undergrowth and then started working towards the body. They needed to work fast as the light was starting to fade.

Chapter Sixteen

Dr. Parker carefully examined both bullet holes, took a liver temperature, and with the help of Buck, rolled the body over to look for exit wounds or other wounds that might indicate a struggle. The bullet that had penetrated Ranger Corey's forehead had exited out the back of her head and was buried in the debris under the body. It had made quite a mess coming out. Dr. Parker called over Claudia Gomez and asked her to carefully collect the skull fragments and brain matter and then see if she could locate the spent bullet.

The bullet that penetrated Ranger Corey's thigh had not exited and was likely buried in the bone. Dr. Parker would dig that out during the autopsy. Buck picked up Ranger Corey's pistol from the ground next to the body and dropped it into the evidence bag that Fitz was holding. He did the same thing with her radio and cell phone.

"Sheriff," Dr. Parker called. The Sheriff looked down from the top of the ravine.

"You can go ahead and have the rescue team bring down the body bag. Ranger Corey is ready to leave the scene."

She stepped out of the way as the rescue team came down into the ravine and placed the black PVC body bag next to the body. One of the rescue team members was an Episcopal minister and he knelt next to the body. As the rest of those in the area bowed their heads, he said a prayer for Susan Corey. He then made the sign of the cross and nodded to the rest of the team. The team gently lifted Ranger Corey and placed her in the body bag. Several deputies climbed down into the ravine and everyone pitched in to get the body to the top of the ravine. The trail was too narrow for vehicles, so the team would need to carry the body back to the parking lot. With permission from the Sheriff, they headed out. The light was fading fast.

Dr. Parker stowed her gear and removed her gloves. "Agent Taylor since you were the first on the scene I would like to hear your impressions." She pulled out her cell phone and clicked on the voice recording app.

Buck waited for Fitz to pull out her phone as well and then he began.

"PIS and I followed a very poor blood trail from the dog until we arrived at the top of the ridge above us." Dr. Parker looked at PIS who had been standing off to the side and out of the way and smiled. PIS nodded back.

"Once we arrived on the ridge, we found two larger blood spots, one from the dog and one from Ranger Corey. The dog's blood trail went off the ridge to the opposite side and we were able to follow it back to the trail we came in on. The other spot, which according to PIS appeared to indicate arterial spray, appeared to point in this direction. We followed the direction of the spray and at the bottom of the ravine we found a large pile of debris. I took photos of everything we did and found, from this point on, including the blood stains on the ridge. After removing the loose leaves and sticks, we found a layer of disturbed soil which we carefully removed and exposed Ranger Corey's face. The bullet hole in her forehead was obvious. We knew that the forehead wound was not the cause of the blood pool on the ridge, so we carefully exposed the rest of the body and discovered the wound in her thigh. After exposing and photographing the body and with the help of the deputies and rescue team members from Gunnison County, we continued to search the area. About forty yards out we found what appears to be the shooter's nest and we also found a gut pile a couple dozen yards beyond that."

Buck stopped to catch his breath and see if they had any questions.

"And your opinion Agent Tylor?" asked Dr. Parker

"My opinion is that Ranger Corey happened upon someone or more than one person who had illegally killed an elk. It appears they had been dragging the elk back in this direction when they heard Ranger Corey and her dog and hid the carcass and themselves behind the tree at the end of the crime scene tape. Either Ranger Corey or her dog did something that spooked the hunters and they shot her through the thigh. Missing her ballistic vest. Ranger Corey then rolled down into the ravine and was subsequently shot in the forehead and buried."

Dr. Parker and Fitz turned off their voice recorders.

"Thank you, Agent Taylor. Your assessment of the crime scene jives with my initial findings. The rest we will confirm during the autopsy."

Buck helped Dr. Parker and then Fitz back up to the top of the ridge and they headed towards the Sheriff. He was talking with his forensic techs as well as two of his deputies. The available light was fading and with the fear of additional booby traps the Sheriff had asked all his people to clear the crime scene before it got completely dark. He would leave two deputies to guard the crime scene and they would be relieved in four hours. He would continue this pattern until everyone returned to the scene first thing in the morning to continue looking for evidence.

The Gunnison team headed back south, with the deepest thanks from Buck and the Sheriff and Buck and PIS followed the rest of the group out of the woods.

"I would like to come back with you in the morning Agent Taylor, if that is acceptable? I feel I can be of use in tracking these evil doers."

"No problem PIS. We can meet where we met this morning. Let's say five AM. I'd like to get here before the crowd shows up."

"Very good sir."

The Sheriff's group, including Buck, the Doctor, PIS and the homicide detectives caught up with the rescue team carrying the body bag. The rescue team had stopped just shy of the entrance to the trail and one member of the team was in the process of unfolding an American flag which he then placed over the body bag.

He looked at the Sheriff who nodded and the somber procession headed into the parking lot.

The path from the trailhead to the waiting ambulance was lined with several dozen rangers, law enforcement officers and rescue team members who all now stood at attention and saluted as the body bag was carried past them. It seemed to Buck that even the forest creatures had stopped to show their respect. You could have heard a pin drop it was so quiet. The body bag was very gently placed in the waiting ambulance and those assembled began to head back to their various vehicles.

Miguel Vargas walked up to Buck and PIS who had moved off to the side of the trail. "I wanted to thank you personally for finding Susan Corey's body." He shook hands with both Buck and PIS. "I don't know how I'm gonna tell her son. They were extremely close and he is gonna be devastated. We're all devastated. It's been years since we've had a ranger killed in the line of duty. Susan Corey was one of the best."

Tears formed in his eyes and he turned and walked towards the ambulance. He would ride to the Aspen Valley Hospital in the ambulance with the body. He didn't want Susan Corey to have to travel alone. The ambulance pulled out of the parking lot followed by the contingent of officers, rangers and rescuers all with the emergency lights flashing. It was another incredible show of respect.

Dr. Parker stepped up and thanked Buck and PIS for their help. She told them she would perform the autopsy first thing in the morning and the Sheriff asked Detective Moe Steiner if he could attend the autopsy. Fitz would be back at the crime scene coordinating the search for evidence. Moe simply nodded.

The Sheriff said, "ok folks. It's been a long, sad day. Let's all meet up tomorrow morning and see if we can find the bastards who did this." They all headed for their cars and pulled out of the parking lot, checking out with the deputy who was manning the barricade.

Buck asked PIS if he could buy him dinner but as Buck expected PIS graciously declined so Buck dropped him off in Wagner Park. Buck then headed to a local deli, grabbed a sandwich and a couple bottles of Coke and headed for his hotel.

Chapter Seventeen

The younger one sat high up in the tree and watched the people below him. He had been watching when the older man and the crazy man with the funny hat had found the lady ranger. The Teacher was not going to be happy. Once they found the lady ranger the older man with the ponytail left and the other man stayed and started looking around. He was soon joined by four other searchers and together they found the hiding spot behind the downed tree.

Now he sat watching as more people arrived led by the older man with the ponytail. Some of them gathered around the lady ranger and others searched the area inside the yellow string. He would have to wait until dark before he would be able to climb down from the tree and run back to the cabin to let the Teacher know what he saw.

He was fascinated by the little boxes some of the people had. They would hold them out in front of themselves and then a light would flash. The first time he thought they were shooting the lady ranger again and this confused him but they also did the same thing behind the downed tree. He didn't understand. Maybe the Teacher would know what this odd behavior was all about.

As darkness started to settle into the ravine, he watched some of the people put the lady ranger's body into a black sack and then they took her away. The others soon followed. Maybe they didn't like being out in the woods at night. He always liked night in the woods. It was peaceful. The others made a lot of noise and sometimes he just needed to get away and he would find refuge in the woods.

He waited until almost full dark before he climbed down from the tree. He knew he shouldn't but he couldn't resist walking back to see where the lady ranger had been buried. Just before he got to the ravine, he was startled by the two men in dark clothes who were hiding up on the ridge. He froze. He knew how to walk in the woods like the Indians the Teacher used to tell them about when they would have story time. He knew they would never hear him, so he silently moved a little closer.

These people were dressed in black clothes and they carried funny looking rifles. They didn't look anything like the rifle he and the hunter had used on the lady ranger. He wondered why they were there. Could it be a trap? The Teacher had told them about the war and how the bad people would hide in the forests and then attack without warning. Were there others around? He hadn't spotted anyone else.

He sat for a minute and listened but they were very quiet. Maybe he should take out the big knife the Teacher had given him for being smart in his lessons and sneak up on them and put them down. He was so close to the one man leaning against the tree that he could stick him before he even knew he was there. Maybe the Teacher would reward him for protecting the others. He might get to use the rifle and become the new hunter. Then he remembered that the Teacher had been very upset that they had killed the lady ranger. He had told them that life was sacred and that killing people was wrong.

He was undecided as he watched the two men. He reached out and touched the handle of the small metal object that was wrapped in leather and hooked around the man's leg. The man jumped and looked around. The other man laughed and asked him if he was afraid of ghosts. The man continued to look around but he never saw the younger one who had scampered back a couple feet into the undergrowth.

It could be fun scaring the men in the black clothes but he knew he needed to get back to the mine and tell the Teacher. Slowly he backed away from the ridge and circled around the far side of the yellow string. He decided to take the long way back to the mine. He did not want to leave any kind of trail for the people to follow. He needed to protect the others.

An hour later he arrived back at the mine. Even though there was no light coming from the tiny hole in the mountainside he was able to find it without difficulty. The others were all asleep but the Teacher was sitting at the old wooden table drinking that foul-tasting liquid from the old bottle. He called it hooch and he wouldn't let any of them touch it. The younger one had taken a taste of the last little bit that was in the Teacher's old mug after he went to sleep one night and it burned his throat and belly as it went down. He never touched the foul liquid again.

The Teacher looked up from his cup. He had sad droopy eyes. He told the Teacher all about the people and about them finding the lady ranger. He also told him about the two men in the black clothes with the funny looking rifles. He waited for the Teacher to tell him he had done a good job of protecting the others but the Teacher just looked sadder and turned back to his cup.

The younger one knew better than to push the Teacher when he was drinking the foul-tasting liquid, so he silently walked away and climbed into his bed. He was soon asleep. The Teacher finished his drink and slowly lowered his head to the table. His last thought was that he hoped he could protect the others.

Chapter Eighteen

Buck and PIS arrived at the parking lot before dawn and checked in with the bored looking deputy who was sitting in his patrol car next to the barricade. He reported to Buck that all was quiet and that the third twosome of deputies had checked in about two hours before and he was expecting the second twosome to be walking into the parking lot any time now.

The morning was much cooler than the day before had been and Buck snugged his insulated Carhart jacket up against the breeze that came rushing down from the higher peaks. Fall was definitely in the air this morning but it didn't seem to bother PIS. He was dressed in the same clothes he had on yesterday and his linen coat was unbuttoned. Buck had never seen PIS sweat no matter how hot the weather got and he had never seen him look uncomfortable in the cold. His three-day stubble looked neatly trimmed. Just like always.

They headed down the trail leading back to the ravine. Buck had wanted to get there before the crowds showed up. He wanted to see if they couldn't pick up the killer's trail. Buck was always amazed to watch PIS in the woods. He looked so completely comfortable. The sun had barely started to lighten the sky and Buck needed a flashlight to see his way down the trail but PIS just forged ahead like he had walked this trail a thousand times. The conversation was kept to a minimum as they walked.

About a half hour into the trail they heard the second shift deputies approaching and Buck called out a greeting so they would not be surprised. Buck never liked the idea of surprising people with guns in the dark. The deputies stopped for a minute and exchanged pleasantries. Talked about how cold it had gotten overnight and told Buck about the earlier deputy who thought he felt someone touch his thigh holster. Scared the crap out of him and everyone had a good laugh.

Buck and PIS told them to have a good day and moved on. Buck stopped for a minute just after they left the deputies. He looked at PIS.

"Any chance what the deputy felt wasn't just his imagination?"

PIS thought about it for a minute. "What is it you Yanks often talk about, the killer coming back to the scene of the crime? That would be pretty ballsy I must say."

PIS and Buck continued down the trail until they arrived the ridge. The sun was just starting to come up over the mountains but the chill remained in the air. Buck called out to the two deputies on duty and announced themselves. Buck introduced himself to the two deputies. They were familiar with PIS. While Buck talked with the two deputies, PIS took a walk around the perimeter of the ridge. Curiosity about the deputy being touched got the better of PIS and he started examining the area for tracks or a disturbance of some kind. He found what he was looking for behind the big tree.

"Agent Taylor, a minute if you please."

Buck and the two deputies walked over to where PIS was standing. PIS knelt down next to the tree and pointed to a small depression in the leaves.

"Someone was definitely out here last night. I don't think the deputy imagined anything."

Buck and the deputies got closer and could barely make out a small boot print in the ground where PIS had scraped aside the leaves. Buck pulled out his cell phone and snapped a picture of the print.

"How can we be sure it wasn't from one of us yesterday?" Buck asked.

"From my recollection, none of us were near this tree. Besides, this print is way too small. Looks almost the size of a child's print or possibly a very small female." PIS responded.

Buck noticed the two deputies move their fingers a little closer to the trigger guard on their rifles and start to look around. Concern was definitely imprinted on their faces. Buck found his own hand sitting on the backstrap of his pistol. He slowly looked around the area.

PIS had stepped back away from the tree and was now down the opposite side of the ridge clearly looking for a trail. He gradually disappeared from view. The others stood their ground. In the distance, they could hear the rest of the investigators and searchers coming down the path.

As the Sheriff approached, he noted the concern and the tension of the small group on the ridge.

"Buck, what's going on?" he asked.

Buck recounted the conversation they had been having just before the Sheriff arrived. At this point, Fitz joined the group as did the two forensic techs. Fitz was the first one to speak up.

"You seriously think that the killer came back here last night and tried to sneak up on our deputies? For what purpose?"

Buck started to respond when PIS returned to the top of the ridge.

"The deputies definitely had a visitor last night and whoever it was, knew this forest very well and was very skilled. The trail disappeared back behind the tree and circled around the crime scene. This individual was out far enough that in most cases we would probably not have even looked for a sign that far out. If I hadn't been following the trail from the tree, I would never have seen it. Very clever."

The group looked at each other not sure what to say, so PIS continued. "I also think this person might have been sitting up in a tree yesterday afternoon watching what we were doing. Found a heavy impression under that big aspen just past the downed tree. It looks like someone dropped down off the lower branch."

"How can you be certain?" asked the Sheriff.

"I had checked that area under the tree right after we found the shooter's nest. Those impressions were not there yesterday afternoon. I lost the trail about a quarter mile from here, heading northeast."

Chapter Nineteen

The Sheriff was not happy. His first thought was that he had left two of his deputies out in the woods by themselves and that they could have been killed. His second thought was "Who the hell are we dealing with?" The perpetrator was in the woods within the past twelve hours. That was a big head start and they had a lot of ground to cover. He was going to need some reinforcements and everyone was going to have to be armed. This was not a job for the search and rescue team.

He called the group together. He explained his plan. The forensic team and Fitz would continue to work the scene under the watchful eye of two deputies. He would contact the Sheriff's in Eagle, Garfield and Gunnison counties and ask them to call out their SWAT teams and any deputies they could spare for a manhunt. He asked Buck to call his Director and see if he could remain on the investigation and then he and PIS would start scouting the area and see if they could narrow down the search area a little. He was still concerned about the booby traps they had found so far and that would hinder the search.

Buck took a minute to step away from the group and pulled out his phone. He was amazed that he actually had cell service this far back in the woods. He dialed the Director.

Kevin Jackson answered on the second ring. "Hey, Buck. You still in Aspen?"

"Yes, Sir. Things just got a little more complicated."

He went on to explain the most recent events to the Director and told him that the Sheriff would like him to remain on scene and help with the manhunt. He explained about the tracks they found this morning and about the booby traps.

"So you think that someone, possibly the killer, actually snuck up on the two deputies last night? To what end?"

"Can't say for sure sir. But it sure changes the dynamics of the investigation."

"Ok Buck. You stay. What do you need from me?"

"We could use a little help from the Grand Junction office. Whoever you can spare. Might also be wise to get some troopers down here. This manhunt is going to leave the county stretched pretty thin."

"Ok Buck. I will do what I can. In the meantime, you watch your ass. I came close to losing you once. I don't want to go there again." The Director hung up.

Buck put his phone away and went back to talk to the Sheriff. He told the Sheriff it was ok with Director Jackson that he stay and help. He also told him he had requested some help from Grand Junction and had also asked the Director to get in touch with the Colorado State Patrol and have some troopers fill in for his deputies around the county. The Sheriff thanked him for the idea about the troopers. He hadn't gotten that far in his thought process.

Buck pulled out his topographic map from his backpack and laid it on the ground. The Sheriff and PIS knelt next to Buck and Buck asked PIS to point out where he lost the trail. PIS took a minute to orient himself and pointed to a location about a quarter mile from where they sat.

"I think we should start at the shooter's nest and work out. We know where PIS lost the trail from last night but what bugs me is that we haven't found the trail to their elk camp. We know they killed the elk and dragged it as far as the nest. What we haven't found is where they went after that. I doubt they butchered it here. We would have found evidence of that. They had to continue dragging it out of here but to where?" Buck said.

PIS agreed. Buck looked to the Sheriff who nodded in agreement. He also agreed that Buck and PIS should try to find that trail to the elk camp. The Sheriff then pointed to three locations on the map. He was going to have his SWAT team follow Buck and PIS from the crime scene. He would have a couple of his deputies or reserve deputies meet up with the SWAT teams from the other counties and come in from three other areas. He would request that Gunnison SWAT approach from the Crested Butte Ski area and head north. One of the other SWAT teams would meet up at the Conundrum Creek trailhead off Route 15 and head southwest and the other team would start from Ashcroft off Route 15 and head northwest. They would all converge on where ever Buck and PIS ended up.

Buck agreed with the plan and the Sheriff asked his two SWAT deputies who had been the last team on the site this morning to accompany Buck and PIS. The Sheriff would have another deputy meet up with them later and bring them some sleeping bags and some supplies. He would start the SWAT teams out first thing in the morning. This should give Buck a chance to narrow down the trail. The Sheriff stood, shook hands with Buck and his team and told them to stay safe. He then headed back to the parking lot. He had a lot of calls to make and a lot of people to get organized.

Buck looked at PIS. "You good with this. I can't make you stay."

"No problem Agent Taylor. Happy to serve." PIS replied.

Buck grabbed his backpack and headed down the ridge to the shooter's nest. They needed to follow the elk. But first, they had to find it. That might be easier said than done. Either way, they had a lot of people who were going to be depending on them to get the job done.

PIS started working in a semi-circle around the shooter's nest. He surmised that since they had dragged the elk from the gut pile to the downed tree that they must have been heading in that direction when they encountered the ranger and her dog. He was both amazed and perplexed that whoever they were following was good enough to outsmart him. That didn't happen often.

PIS was out about a quarter mile from the shooter's nest and he was getting more and more aggravated with himself for not being able to spot the trail. Elk carcasses are not light and this one was being dragged across the ground. There had to be a sign. No one is that good. He stopped and looked back through the trees to the shooter's nest. He was on a straight line directly from the gut pile and though the nest. It had to be here. He slowly scanned the area and then he spotted it.

At first, he wasn't sure he was looking at it. It blended in almost perfectly with the surrounding area. He slowly walked forward scanning the area for booby traps as he went. The closer he got the more obvious it became. The undergrowth was denser than in the rest of the area. The sign wasn't much but to a trained eye; it was just enough. He stepped around the growth now noticing for the first time the cut ends of the branches. He stepped to the front of the mass and spotted the blood on the ground. He marveled at the cleverness of the camouflage. No wonder the ranger hadn't found this camp. It was practically perfect in its disguise.

PIS gave a short shrill whistle and waved to Buck and the two deputies who had been following farther back. He waved them over.

"Agent Taylor," he said as Buck and the deputies approached. "I believe we have found the hunting camp." Buck looked at the makeshift lean-to and the blood stain on the dirt floor. He was impressed with its simplicity. He looked around the area and even to his older tired eyes he could see the double track that went off to the Northeast. It was obviously a trail made by some kind of sled. A very heavy sled.

Chapter Twenty

She had discovered her grandfather's trophy box a couple months back and wondered about the significance of the baubles. She knew it was her grandfather's because no one in the family remembered the old cigar box that was hidden in a hole in the wall behind her grandfather's big Craftsman toolbox. She had mentioned it one night at dinner and no one reacted. Well, that's not exactly true. She thought she saw some kind of recognition in her grandmother's eyes but that disappeared as quickly as it arrived.

She waited until the family was asleep and entered her grandfather's room. He was sleeping soundly and she hoped that he might wake up in one of his, getting rarer, lucid moments. She hated to disturb him, so she started to leave his room when a low frail voice stopped her in her tracks.

She approached the bed and stood there with the trophy box held out in front of her. Her grandfather stared at the box in her hands and smiled. She hadn't seen him smile much since she had gotten home from college and it surprised her. He asked her to open the box so he could look inside.

She opened the box and held it so he could see inside. His heart monitor reacted almost immediately and she was afraid the change of tone from the monitor might wake someone else in the small house. She closed the box and pulled it away from him but his expression indicated that he wasn't done. She glanced towards his bedroom door to see if anyone might have heard them and then she reopened the box and he looked deep inside. She asked him what all these pieces meant. He smiled and asked her to remove the gold edged cameo necklace. She held it up for him to see and he told her that this was the first one.

She was a pretty runaway from somewhere up near Chicago. Her family life had been brutal, so she headed west to find her own way in the world. The Korean War was over and a lot of people were leaving their familiar homes to look for financial opportunities out west. The fledgling ski industry and lax laws were drawing people from far and wide and Aspen was no exception. The young woman had found work in a small diner just off the highway and she had found a room with several other young women. Her grandfather had befriended the young woman and they started seeing each other at night. Her grandmother never knew.

After a few weeks, she told him that she was tired of the cold and had decided to head to California. Her grandfather sensed an opportunity about to disappear so he told her he would drive her to the train in Glenwood Springs. He knew she hadn't told any of her friends about him, so he wasn't worried about getting caught. That night, as she slipped out of her rooming house, he met her up the highway and loaded her one suitcase in the trunk of his car. She was dressed in a long skirt, pretty white blouse and around her neck was the cameo neckless. A gift from her mother.

Instead of heading north up highway 82, he turned south and headed out of town. He turned down route 15 which at the time was just a narrow dirt road and found the old fire road that led to Conundrum Creek. She asked him where they were heading and he told her that he wanted to show her a beautiful sight before she left. He finally reached the end of the road, parked the car and reached his arm around her shoulders. The syringe bit deep into her shoulder and she started to yell but he put his hand over her mouth and held it there until the sedative had time to work.

The snow was not that deep on the old trail through the wood as he carried her over his shoulder. The old mining cabin was falling down but it wasn't the cabin he was interested in. Years before when he first arrived in Aspen he spent a lot of time exploring his new home and discovered the old cabin a mile or so down Conundrum Creek. It sat back about a quarter mile from the trail along the creek and was completely hidden from view. What interested him most about the cabin was the shaft the old miners had dug under the wooden floor of the cabin. The shaft went down about thirty feet and then opened into a large long tunnel. He found old broken down and decayed wooden shelves and a lot of old mining equipment.

When he first found the cabin he thought it would be perfect for his needs. He spent several weeks tracking down the owner of the property and discovered that the mining claim that the cabin sat on was owned by a man in Pittsburg who had almost completely forgotten about the old claim. Through a series of letters and telegrams, her grandfather was finally able to get permission to work the old claim and use the cabin.

He spent the next couple months cleaning out the space and installing the things he knew he would need. Along the walls, he bolted in chains and shackles for hands and feet. He purchased several kerosene hurricane lamps and built a bed with a straw mattress. The biggest improvement he was able to make in the machine shop at the ski resort maintenance shed. He fashioned a large metal hatch door that he installed over the old rotten wooden shaft door and put heavy duty hinges and a hasp on it.

The old miners had left an old kerosene stove in the tunnel that they had vented up through the ground a few feet behind the cabin. It would help to keep the chill out of the air and make it a more comfortable space to work in. He also placed his pride and joys in the tunnel. Over the years working at the ski resort he had managed to use the metal shop and had fashioned several beautiful knives and scalpels. Since he made them all himself, there was no record of him buying them. His space was finally complete and his body had tingled at the thought of what would soon be taking place in his secluded little world.

Her grandfather's voice seemed to grow stronger as he told her the rest of the story. He had carried the young woman to the cabin and had unlocked the trap door. He lowered her down the old wooden ladder and placed her on the bed while he fired up the kerosene lanterns and the old kerosene stove. Once the space got warmer, he stripped off all the young woman's clothes and tied her to the bed frame. She had a beautiful body, young and subtle. Her breasts were small but perky and she moaned through the gag as he repeatedly penetrated her. Twice he had to inject her with more sedative to keep her quiet. This was the first time he had ever had sex with someone other than his wife and he was surprised at how much he enjoyed it but the night was fading fast and he needed to get home before his wife woke up.

Now that he was totally spent he untied her from the bed and carried her over to the first set of shackles that he had bolted to the wall. Still naked, he hooked the shackles to her hands and feet. She had started to wake up and the fear in her eyes made him get excited all over again but he didn't have the time to penetrate her again. He was running out of time. He opened an old cabinet that was hanging on the wall and removed a leather bundle. He carefully placed it on the wooden table under the cabinet and unrolled it revealing his assortment of custom made knives.

He chose a thin four-inch-long scalpel from the bundle and admired it in the light from the kerosene lantern. He loved how the scalpel glowed under the yellow light of the lantern. He walked over to the young woman and held the scalpel so she could see it. She squirmed hard against the shackles and started to bleed where the metal shackles cut into her hands and feet.

Slowly and almost delicately he slid the sharp edge of the scalpel along her exposed abdomen. He had used this same technique on several high ranking German Officers during the war. They were a stubborn lot but eventually, they all talked. He didn't care if the young woman talked or not. This was not an interrogation. This was pleasure.

He could hear her screaming through the gag. He spent the next hour slowly slicing the young woman's torso, legs and arms until she finally passed out. She just didn't seem to have the stamina of the German Officers. It was almost disappointing. He walked over to the leather bundle on the bed and using an old rag, cleaned the blood off the scalpel and his hands. He got dressed and then walked back and turned off the kerosene stove and put his bundle back in the cabinet. If she was still alive when he returned he would finish the job but for now the demons were satisfied. He turned off the kerosene lanterns and climbed out of his workspace. He closed the hatch, made sure the padlock was shut and covered the hatch with the decaying floorboards.

The night had gotten colder and it had started to snow. He stood for a minute and just gazed at the beauty of the scene. He felt at peace for the first time in a long time. He walked back to his old car and headed home.

Chapter Twenty-One

She could feel the heat rising as her grandfather told her the story of his first civilian kill. She hadn't realized how sexually aroused she felt as he described the details of the kill. She felt embarrassed that she was feeling this way and didn't understand what was happening. Her grandfather knew exactly what was happening. He could sense that she had the same feelings he did when it came to taking another's life. He finished his story and looked at the vibrant pink color in her cheeks and the little beads of sweat that had formed on her forehead and cheeks.

He told her that he knew she was the one who would follow him. He could feel it deep in his soul. He told her that he would help her find her way along the path that had been taken from him so long ago. She stared in disbelief at what he was saying. She could never take a human life. She had never killed anything nor had the desire to do so. Or did she? His description of the kill had certainly stirred something deep inside her. Something scary but also something wonderful.

Her grandfather started to speak in dribble and incomplete sentences and then he slowly closed his eyes and went to sleep. The lucid moment had passed but she *had certainly learned a lot. She looked at the rest of the pieces of jewelry in the little box. Her grandfather just admitted to being a serial killer. One of the first in modern history, yet there had never been any hint that this was the case. She wondered how many more pieces of jewelry would have found their way into his little treasure box if he had not been injured so many years ago. She also wondered how he had kept the demons from destroying him since he was no longer able to feed their needs.*

She also wondered if her grandmother knew about his proclivities. She had definitely noticed the change in her grandmother's eyes when she mentioned the old cigar box she had found in the garage. Yet her grandmother never said anything about it.

She looked again at the trophies her grandfather had collected. She wondered about the people they had belonged too. Most of the jewelry appeared to be pieces that would have been worn by young women of the time. She wondered if she would ever be able to get their story from her grandfather. She would need to hurry. She was due back at school in early September. If she was going to act on the feelings that had been stirred up by her grandfather's story, she would need to do it quickly.

She closed the lid of the old box, leaned in and kissed her grandfather on the forehead and left his room. The house was quiet as a church cemetery and she was grateful. She headed back to her room and once inside closed the door and hid the trophy box in the back of her closet. She needed to understand the feelings that her grandfather's story had generated. Was it possible she was a serial killer too?

She had taken psychology classes at school and she understood that serial killers were psychopaths. She always believed they were evil incarnate and that they would stand out in society like freaks at a carnival. Even though she had never had the opportunity to see her grandfather in his early years, she never considered him to be odd. He had never spoken before of his craft. But now. His story had aroused something deep inside of her. Something she now both feared and found interesting and exciting.

Could it be true that he could sense in her the things that made him do the evil deeds he had told her about? It made her sick to her stomach and she ran into her tiny bathroom and vomited in the toilet. No, there was no way she could ever be the evil thing her grandfather had suddenly become in her eyes. But she was also envious of him. If the way she felt while he was telling his story was real, the sensation was amazing. She felt more satisfied, sexually, at this moment than she had with any of the college boys she had slept with over the years.

She knew she needed to pursue the feelings to see if they were real. She was afraid of what she might find and of what she might become but she needed to find out. She laid down on her bed, her head full of strange thoughts and feelings. She decided the first thing she needed to do was to try to find her grandfather's old cabin and see if the shaft was still locked up tight. She would check that out first and then decide on the next step. She fell asleep quickly.

Chapter Twenty-Two

Buck took pictures of the makeshift hunting camp with this cell phone camera and noting that he still had one bar sent the pictures along with the GPS coordinates he took from his hand-held GPS unit to the Sheriff and to Fitz. Fitz would have to bring the forensic techs down to the camp as soon as they were finished processing the crime scene at the ravine. Buck pulled a roll of crime scene tape from his backpack and with the help of one of the deputies ran the tape around the makeshift hunting camp.

Satisfied with the day's progress so far and with the light beginning to fade the small team decided to wait at the elk camp for the deputy bringing them in supplies and hole up there for the night. With the possibility of booby traps still out in the woods, Buck didn't want anyone getting hurt. At first light they would follow the sled tracks and see where they led. Buck also asked the Sheriff to have the deputy bring one more assault rifle with him. The idea that someone snuck up on the two SWAT deputies at the ravine had everyone a little jumpy.

While one of the deputies cleared the fire ring that someone had worked very hard to try and hide, Buck looked around the elk camp. There wasn't much to see.

The blood stains on the ground that had been covered up with leaves gave Buck the impression that the camp had been used for a long time. There were obvious signs that someone had been butchering animals but no evidence of tools. Whoever had cleared out of this camp had done so with a great deal of skill. There was not going to be much physical evidence for the forensic techs to find.

In the distance, Buck could hear the sound of a small high-pitched motor. He assumed the deputy bringing in their supplies was on a dirt bike or a small ATV, all-terrain vehicle. Just then, the driver came through the trees and stopped at the yellow crime scene tape. He had, in fact, been able to maneuver his small ATV along the trail they had left. That was actually quite an accomplishment considering there was not much of a trail to follow.

The deputy shook hands all around and then offloaded two backpacks and a couple sleeping bags from the small cargo cage on the back of the ATV. He had a Remington AR15 slung over his shoulder which he handed to Buck.

"Sheriff said you asked for this," the deputy said. "He also sent along some deli sandwiches for dinner, some water bottles and danishes for breakfast."

Buck was also glad to see that the Sheriff sent along a couple bottles of Coke. He would make sure he thanked the Sheriff.

"Sheriff wanted me to tell you that he has several deputies watching all the known trailheads on both Routes 13 and 15 and that the SWAT teams will head out at first light according to the plan you guys came up with earlier."

Buck thanked the deputy for the supplies and the information and the deputy climbed aboard the ATV and headed back up the trail. He wanted to get out of the woods before total dark. PIS had taken the food bag and was in the process of handing out sandwiches and water bottles. They each found a little piece of the forest and set their tired bodies down for a breather and nourishment.

The two deputies smiled at each other as they watched PIS open his backpack, remove his little tin and start to brew himself a small pot of tea. Everyone had heard the stories of PIS and his china tea set but few had ever seen it for real. Buck watched them but said nothing. Buck understood that for PIS this was a very private moment and he didn't want to interfere.

PIS looked up at the deputies as he took his first sip of tea from the china cup. "Even in the wilderness, gentlemen, we must remain civilized and there is nothing more civilized than a good cup of tea."

Everyone chuckled and dug into their meals. The sandwiches were excellent and as the sun set and the forest became darker everyone settled in for the night. It would be chilly tonight but the sleeping bags the Sheriff had sent them would be most welcome.

Buck rolled his sleeping bag out on a bunch of leaves and pine boughs he had cut and made himself a nice insulated platform to sleep on. He crawled into the sleeping bag and rested his head on his backpack. He had found a spot near the fire pit that gave him a small opening through which to look at the milky way above. This far into the forest the view of the Milky Way was incredible.

Buck looked up at the sky and thought back to the camping trips his family had taken when the kids were younger. After the kids had gone to sleep, he and Lucy would lie next to each other and stare at the stars. With no city lights to lessen the view, they were able to see billions of stars and even the swirling celestial cloud that flowed through the milky way. It was always magical, only this time it brought a tear to his eyes knowing that he would never be able to share another moment like that with Lucy. Buck closed his eyes and drifted off to sleep.

Buck had asked one of the two deputies to take the first watch. Everyone was concerned about having a repeat of the night before and did not want to face the possibility of someone sneaking up on the group.

The night had gotten cold as Buck slowly opened his eyes. He wasn't sure what had woken him but he sensed something was not quite right. He snapped open the thumb break on his holster and put his hand on the gun. He slowly looked to his left and noticed PIS lying flat on his back with his eyes wide open. PIS slowly turned his head toward Buck.

"We are not alone," PIS said in a whisper. Buck tensed and looked towards the two deputies. They both appeared to be sound asleep.

"Where?" asked Buck.

"Not sure. Could be maybe twenty yards out behind the lean-to. There might be two of them. Can't tell for sure."

"How do you want to handle this?" asked Buck

The fire had settled down into just a pile of hot embers and the forest was almost as dark as being inside a cave. PIS slowly slid out of his sleeping bag and still lying flat on the ground, crawled deeper into the woods behind them. Buck pulled his pistol out of his holster and slowly unzipped the sleeping bag. He would be ready to move if PIS needed help.

The deputy on the other side of Buck must have sensed something going on but Buck signaled for him to stay put. The deputy lowered himself back down on his backpack but Buck saw him pull out his service weapon and place it on top of his sleeping bag. Buck wasn't sure how long PIS was gone but his internal alarm clock told him it was about twenty minutes. Twenty very tense minutes.

Chapter Twenty-Three

PIS called out from somewhere behind the lean-to. "PIS coming in." Slowly he emerged from the right side of the lean-to. Buck and the first deputy crawled out of the sleeping bags, guns in hand. The other deputy suddenly woke up and wondered out loud what was going on. Buck grabbed a log off the pile they had collected earlier and dropped in on the fire. The embers caught the dry wood and the flames exploded adding much-appreciated light to the dark forest.

PIS stood next to the fire. "I could account for two of them. I think that was it. The first one was about thirty yards out behind a group of shrubs to the north. Had a very good view of our little camp. The second one was up a tree to the south. No more than fifteen yards. They must have heard me moving through the undergrowth because they moved off quickly. I will check for tracks in the morning."

The one deputy swore under his breath. Buck looked around. "Sounds like the same MO, modus operandi, from the other night at the ravine. You certain they are gone?"

PIS nodded and Buck and the two deputies holstered their pistols. No one was going back to sleep anytime soon. Buck was amazed at how easily PIS had been able to move around in the dark forest. The guy had some mad skills and even though Buck never asked specifically, he wondered where PIS had received his training. It certainly didn't come from being a homeless guy in Aspen.

The one deputy asked the question that everyone had on their minds. "What the fuck are we dealing with? What kind of criminal stays in the area of the crime and follows the police around?"

"Good question," responded Buck. "Not any kind of criminal I've ever encountered. Good thing is, we know they are still in the area and we know there are at least two of them."

Everyone agreed with Buck's statement but Buck felt uneasy. He wondered why the killers hadn't tried to run. What was keeping them in the area? Buck didn't have enough evidence to be able to answer that question, so he pushed it to the back of his mind. He would definitely figure out the answer before this was over.

Buck sat back on his sleeping bag and watched the fire. PIS walked over and sat down next to him. Buck noticed the perplexed look on PIS's face.

"What's got you bugged?" he asked.

PIS thought for a minute. "Either my skills are getting rusty, or we are up against people who have skills that far exceed mine."

PIS was quiet for a minute and Buck could see he was replaying the whole thing in his head. He finally spoke. "I was as quiet as a church mouse when I moved through the woods, yet they had me before I even got close to them and they were able to scamper off without me having any idea they were moving."

Buck sensed his frustration. PIS had skills in the woods that Buck could only marvel at. If PIS was concerned, then the people they were after were incredibly dangerous. They had already shown themselves to be cold-blooded enough to shoot a human being in the head at close range and they had proven they were not afraid to sneak up and observe armed law enforcement personnel.

Buck assured PIS that it wasn't his skills that were lacking. It was obvious that the people they were chasing knew the woods better than they did and they would just need to be a little more diligent. Buck sensed that they were getting close. They all needed to stay focused.

As dawn started to break over the mountains and the sky turned a pale shade of pink everyone in the camp felt a little relieved. They were now able to see around them and some of the concerns from the night before lifted. Each man packed up his sleeping bag and they each ate a danish for breakfast. PIS had disappeared into the woods as soon as it was light enough to see and he finally came walking back into camp.

"Agent Taylor, there were definitely two culprits last night as I had suspected. They both headed off in different directions but they met up again about a quarter mile from here. I also found the rest of the trail we spotted yesterday. They had done a bang-up job trying to hide it but the grooves from the sled were too deep to eradicate completely."

"Excellent, then we have a trail to follow." He looked at each man individually. "We need to stay alert. We know they are good at building booby traps and they are also not afraid to get close to us. Let's douse the fire and get moving. The SWAT teams will be starting soon. We need a target."

With that, the one deputy emptied a water bottle on the fire embers and stirred them around with a stick. The last thing they needed out here was a forest fire. PIS slung his backpack over his shoulders and started for the sled trail. The others followed a couple yards behind.

Chapter Twenty-Four

They had been following the men for almost an hour when the men finally settled in for the night. They had lit a small fire and then all slipped into their sleeping bags. The hunter had a good observation spot just beyond the lean-to and he had watched them all settle in. The younger one was on the other side of the camp up in a big aspen tree.

Once he was confident that the men were asleep, the younger one had silently climbed down from the tree and carefully snuck up to just outside their camp. He could hear the men softly breathing he was so close. At one point he was going to see if he could reach one of the rifles but the old man with the ponytail started to move around, so he thought it best to back off. He wasn't sure what he would do if he did get one of the rifles.

The men had rifles that didn't look anything like the old rifle the hunter used. Theirs were all black and had lots of things that seemed to be attached. The rifle the Teacher had given the hunter was just a wooden stock and a barrel. Nothing fancy but it did a good job on the animals they hunted.

The Teacher had told them all stories about a big war in the jungle and that he had used a rifle that was black and had things attached to it. It sounded just like the rifle the men were carrying. The younger one thought it would make a great prize to bring one of these back for the Teacher and the Teacher might reward him and let him use the black rifle to hunt with. Since the Teacher's hands shook really bad sometimes he didn't think the Teacher would be able to use the rifle anyway.

The men had remained quiet for quite some time, so the younger one moved back towards the tree he had been hiding in. The almost unperceivable clicking sound alerted him that something was wrong. The hunter had seen something, so he froze where he was. He glanced back through the trees just in time to see the old man with the ponytail slide quietly out of his sleeping bag and crawl into the woods. The old man with the ponytail made almost no noise as he scooted along the ground.

The younger one watched him for a minute. The old man with the ponytail had skills just like he and the hunter had. He had found their trails and traps. He wondered if the old man had been taught by the Teacher. The Teacher had told them that he had taught a lot of men during the jungle war how to survive in the woods. Maybe the old man with the ponytail was one of the Teacher's students. They would need to be careful if that was the case. He might know how to set traps like he and the hunter knew how to do and that could be dangerous.

The younger one knew he should head back to the safe place but he wanted to test the old man with the ponytail, so he started to move away from the men's camp. He would work his way back to the trail by making a big circle around the camp. He wanted to see if the old man with the ponytail would be able to track him so he decided to lead him towards one of the old animal trails that would take the men away from the safe place.

He made small noises as he went, crackling a leaf or snapping a small stick. He was having fun but then the old man with the ponytail stopped and looked at something really carefully on the ground and while still kneeling looked around. He then quietly set off in a different direction. The younger one wasn't sure what the old man with the ponytail had found but he was now heading back towards the hunter.

The younger one gave a soft, low-pitched whistle that he knew most people would never be able to hear but he knew the hunter would hear it. The low-pitched whistle was something momma had taught them all and it meant danger and for everyone to head back to the safe place. He continued down the old animal trail for a ways and then circled back around through the trees and headed home.

The younger one caught up with the hunter just down the trail from the safe place and then hid in the undergrowth and watched the trail for a while to make sure they had gotten away. Feeling confident that they had not been followed by the old man with the ponytail, they reset the booby trap on the trail and headed for the mine.

When they got back inside the mine, the Teacher was just starting breakfast for the others. They told him about the old man with the ponytail and that maybe he was one of the men the Teacher had taught how to survive in the woods. The younger one told him about playing with the old man with the ponytail and that he was as good as they were in the woods.

The Teacher listened to their story and looked concerned. His hands were shaking badly today and he was having trouble using the knife to put the jelly on the bread. The older girl finally took the knife and started making the sandwiches. They were running out of bread and some other things and they would need to plan a raid on one of the big houses.

The Teacher reassured them that everything would be ok and that once the men left the woods, they would sneak into the big empty house up by the ski lift and raid their food stores again.

The teacher sat down on the old chair and rested his face in his hands. The others went about their business of cleaning up the living area in the mine but the hunter sat down next to the Teacher and rested his hand on the Teacher's arm. The Teacher looked at him and the younger one and they saw the concern on his face. The Teacher told them to go back down by the cabin and make sure the traps were set just like he had shown them.

The hunter grabbed his rifle and the younger one went to the old box and took out some metal spikes and a hammer and a spool of old fishing line. The teacher led the younger one to the old green box and using the key from his pocket he unlocked the box and opened the lid. The younger one had never seen what was inside the old green box. The Teacher had told them never to touch the box and they never did.

The Teacher pulled out several old cardboard tubes with strings hanging out of one end. The tubes looked very old and they were covered in some kind of white powder. He also took out some metal tubes with wires attached to them along with a metal box with a T handle stuck in it. He put it all in an old backpack. He told the others to stay in the cave and that he, the hunter and the younger one would be back in a while. The Teacher slung the backpack over his shoulder and the three of them headed for the mine entrance.

Chapter Twenty-Five

Once outside and away from the mine the hunter and the younger one watched the Teacher as he very carefully slid one of the metal tubes into each of the cardboard tubes. He then took a big spool of wire that he had taken from the cabinet in the kitchen area and handed it to the hunter and the younger one. He told them to run the wire from the mine entrance back to the cabin. He needed six wire runs to different spots around the cabin and he pointed out where to run them. They took the spool and headed back towards the mine entrance.

The Teacher was worried. Many times, over the years, people had gotten close to the cabin or the mine entrance but this felt different and each time they had been able to either run them off with animal noises or simply hide in the woods or in the mine until they passed. These men were on a mission. He had seen determination like that during the war. These men were dangerous and he was convinced that they were only a scouting party. He was sure that sooner or later the woods would be crawling with people looking for his little family. The hunter had killed one of theirs and they were out for blood.

The Teacher had promised momma that he would do everything he could to protect the family and he had been successful for a long time. Now, however, he was worried that he might not have enough left to do the job. He was getting on in years and each day his hands seem to shake a lot more. He was also having trouble talking and doing even the slightest of chores. He was worried about what would happen to the family if he didn't wake up one morning. His thoughts went back to that day so many years ago.

He joined the army right out of high school and had found the family he never had before. His mom worked nights as a waitress at a local greasy spoon and his dad worked at the car plant in town. His dad was also a drinker and he had no problem beating on his wife and son when he tied one on, which seemed to be almost every night. The day after graduation he had headed for the army recruiting station and enlisted. The war in Vietnam was in full swing and he was able to leave for boot camp within two days of enlisting. He left that little west Texas town and never looked back.

Years of getting beat up by his father had given him an inner strength and he was able to handle everything the army threw at him. His test scores and his skills during boot camp got him noticed and he was offered a chance to become an Army Ranger. He thrived in this new environment and was soon proficient with every weapon the army had to offer and his escape and evasion skills put him at the top of his class.

He was in the middle of his third tour of duty in Vietnam when something inside snapped. Maybe it was too many close calls while on patrol, or maybe it was that he just could no longer stand seeing the kind of destruction and death that war caused or maybe he just got a conscience, but anyway, he had finally had it with war and killing.

His unit had come upon a small village in the Vietnam highlands that they believed was being used by the Viet Cong. They interrogated the local elder who denied it but his unit wasn't satisfied. To force the elder to talk they started shooting the civilians one by one. There was screaming and tears and then all of a sudden he lost control of the situation and his unit. He tried to stop the frenzy but by the time his men were finished, there was nothing they could do except set the village on fire and move down the road. He was grief-stricken and after brooding about it for a couple days, he swore to his men that he would see to it that they all paid for the terrible massacre.

A week later his unit was involved in a horrible battle for a valley that he cared nothing about and after three days of intense fighting, he finally had enough. Sometime during the third night of the battle, he slipped away from his tiny foxhole and silently disappeared into the forest surrounding the valley. For several weeks he used his escape and evasion skills to hide from enemy patrols until he finally crossed into Laos and eventually made his way to Bangkok in Thailand.

No longer in uniform and with long hair and a heavy beard he looked like some kind of homeless beggar. During his days in Bangkok he looked for ways to get out of the country and at night he would rummage through trash to find anything edible. Eventually, he found work on a tramp steamer with an Indonesian captain who didn't care about papers. He only cared about hard work.

For six months he sailed around the Indian Ocean before finally leaving the ship in Abu Dhabi in the United Arab Emirates. With money in his pocket he was able to fly to Spain and then on to Central America, eventually making is way across the US/ Mexico Border in New Mexico. Airport security at the time was pretty much nonexistent and no one ever questioned his driver's license. He assumed the army figured he had died in the battle for the valley and had never even looked for him.

He hitchhiked his way north through New Mexico and eventually found himself in Aspen, Colorado. He fit right in. The counterculture scene was in full swing and there were drugs and women everywhere. With his long hair and dirty clothes, he looked like everyone else but he found that he just couldn't deal with all the people. One day he headed back into the forest and after a few weeks of just being alone in his own thoughts, he stumbled on an old miner's cabin.

The cabin hadn't been lived in for years but it had good bones and he was able to use the scraps from the original cabin to fix it up, so it was livable. The miner, whoever he was, had tapped into a small spring so the cabin had running water and he also found the old mine a few hundred feet back behind the cabin. He spent the next several years fixing everything up so he had a rugged but comfortable home and more importantly he found the privacy he so badly wanted.

Before leaving Aspen, he bought an old M1 carbine from a pawn shop along with a box of 30 caliber ammo. He was a crack shot and had no problem making sure he had plenty of food to eat. All in all, he had a good life.

Chapter Twenty-Six

His thoughts turned to the morning he had found them. The snowstorm had been furious and had lasted three days and when it was over, there was probably three feet of fresh snow on the ground. The temperature had dropped way below freezing but the little miner's cabin was warm and cozy. He hated the idea of having to go out in the cold but his fresh meat supply was running low and he had decided before the storm set in that he needed to do some hunting to replenish his stock. The fact that the storm lasted three days only made his situation worse, so he put on his long underwear, every sweater he owned, which was only two, and his coat, hat and gloves and head out into the snow.

The day had dawned beautiful. The sky through the trees was a bright robin's egg blue and there wasn't a cloud to be seen. The fresh mat of snow on the ground was untracked and sparkled in the morning sunlight. He just stood in the doorway of his little cabin and admired the beauty that surrounded him. He closed the cabin door and headed out.

He found the old Ford station wagon on an old Forest Service fire road that hardly anyone ever used. The car was almost buried to its roof. The front wheels were sitting in a ravine off the side of the road. He thought it might be abandoned until he heard a faint cry coming from inside the car. Fearing the worst, he dropped the bundle of snowshoe hares he had shot and with his hands he started digging for the driver's door.

It was hard work and he was soaked to the bone and cold as hell when he finally cleared enough snow to open the driver's door. He would never forget the sight he found inside the car. The woman sitting in the driver's seat was barely conscious. She was wrapped in a coat and had wrapped herself up in a blanket, but it hadn't helped. Her skin was cold to the touch and he feared she was dead until she slowly opened her eyes. She stared at him and was able to mutter a short sentence. "Help my babies."

He looked behind her and couldn't believe his eyes. There, filling the back seat and the rear back facing seat where eight kids all wrapped in blankets with just their little faces visible. He was shocked. Most of them were barely moving and he knew he needed to do something before they froze to death. He had no idea how long they had been in the car but their situation was desperate. He told the woman he would go and get help but with a soft almost dying voice the woman pleaded with him not to bring the authorities.

He spent the next hour clearing the doors so he could get the kids out of the car one at a time. The whole gang of them were stiff and barely able to move but night was falling and he needed to get this little troop to his cabin before the temperature dropped even more. They would not survive another night in the woods.

Still wrapped in their blankets the kids helped each other as they struggled through the deep snow trying to follow the man's tracks. The woman, barely able to walk, managed to carry one of the youngest children and he had two of them in his arms besides the bunch of snowshoe hares. It took several torturous hours of trudging through the deep snow but his little troop finally reached the little cabin. He opened the door and ushered them all inside. It was going to be a tight fit but the closeness of their bodies would help them thaw out. Once inside they all crashed on whatever piece of real estate they could find and within a matter of minutes, the warmth of the cabin had everyone asleep.

He awoke to the smell of rabbits cooking in the big cast iron pot. Shaking the cobwebs out of his head, he remembered finding the woman and kids in the car in the woods and hiking back to the cabin. He raised his head from the table he had fallen asleep on and there, standing in front of his little wood stove, was an angel with a wooden spoon. The woman was taller than he thought she was the night before and she had the most beautiful long blond hair hanging down her back almost to her waist. For a minute he just sat there and looked at her.

She turned and was startled to see him looking at her. Her face glowed in the early morning light coming through the old lead glass window. She turned back to the stove and continued to stir the rabbit stew she had prepared. Gradually the children awoke and soon the little cabin was filled with more noise than he was used to. It was almost scary. He had lived alone for such a long time that having people around, especially this many, made him uneasy.

The whole gang gobbled down the rabbit stew like they hadn't eaten in weeks, which might have been the case and then everyone settled down and sleep overtook them once again. While everyone was asleep, he hiked back to the car and made several trips carrying what meager bits of luggage they had. He had hoped to find something in the car that would explain who she was and how she came to be stuck in the middle of the mountains in a snowstorm with eight kids.

Back at the cabin with their meager belongings he finally got some of the answers he was seeking. She told him that she had been driving through the mountains heading for a new start in California. She had family out there who were going to help her with her kids. She had taken a wrong turn after leaving Aspen and then the storm hit and she was completely lost. When the front tires went into the ravine, she knew they were in trouble so she wrapped everyone up in what she could and prayed for a miracle. God had sent him as an answer to her prayers.

She told him she was from Florida and that two of the children were hers from a failed marriage and the rest were either adopted or in foster care. She said she had permission from Florida to take the kids to California to a new life. He doubted the story right from the first minute she opened her mouth. He had interrogated enough prisoners while he was in Vietnam and he knew when people were lying to him. This woman was nothing but one big lie.

She never ever did give him a story he could believe but over the years he had finally stopped asking and they settled into a quiet life. The kids were growing and he found a new purpose in teaching them things, important things, like reading and writing but also necessary things like how to pick locks, set up traps and survive. The kids became very good at breaking into the huge mansions that had begun to spring up around Aspen over the years. Many of these were second homes for rich celebrities and business people and they were empty a good portion of the year.

They expanded the cabin to accommodate the entire gang and had also set up a second home back in the old mine. This was their safe place in case someone got too close to the cabin. They had used it several times especially recently as it seemed there were a lot more people hiking in the woods

Things went along fine until one morning two years ago when the woman woke up feverish and exhausted. She had tried to stand at the stove to cook breakfast but had passed out. Luckily, he was standing behind her and he was able to get her into the bed they shared. Over the next several days she woke up delirious and had very little idea of who anyone was. The Teacher, as the kids had been calling him, was beside himself with worry but he knew she would never let him go for help. On the third day, she didn't recognize him or the children. On the fourth morning she didn't wake up at all and her breathing was shallow and labored. She stopped breathing later that day.

In all the years they had lived in the same cabin the Teacher had never really gotten the whole story from her. He was able to glean that she had actually started out in West Virginia and that somewhere along the road she had decided to start kidnapping small children who were too young to know any better. She never told him how she chose the kids to kidnap or what she really intended to do with them and she never explained why their parents didn't come looking for them but over the years they had all become one big family and he finally stopped asking.

The children had chosen a beautiful spot above the mine for her grave. From there she would have a view of the entire area and they were very pleased with their choice. They had dressed her in a dress she had made that she always intended to wear for a special occasion but never had. She looked beautiful. The Teacher wrapped her in a blanket, carried her up the mountain to the grave site and slowly laid her in the shallow grave the oldest boys had dug. Each child had been told to find something special in the woods that they thought momma might like and they each placed their special treasure in the grave with her. The Teacher then shoveled the dirt back into the grave and then they all said the Lord's Prayer.

The Teacher knew that any chance of ever finding out her true story was now gone forever and he decided that the most important thing at this point was to keep his little family together. He had grown very fond of the children over the years and took great pride in teaching them the things they would need to know as their lives progressed. He also wondered what would happen if they eventually decided to leave the cabin. They were approaching that age where they would probably want more out of life than what was available in their little family group.

And now here they were setting up defenses and traps to protect their little family from the outside world. He had no doubt his children would be able to survive in the real world. He often would sneak into Aspen at night to steal food and other things they needed and he always tried to bring back a current newspaper or a new book to help them with their education. He was amazed at how smart the children were and how quickly they learned new skills. He was also amazed at how quickly and easily they learned to break into houses or stores without leaving any signs of having been there. Their survival skills, thanks to him, were top notch.

He had known for a while now that his days were numbered. He had read up on Parkinson's Disease in a medical book the children had stolen from a doctor's house and he believed that this was the ailment that was causing the hand tremors. He didn't think he had long to live but as long as he had a breath to take, he would do all he could to protect his family.

Chapter Twenty-Seven

PIS was very quiet as he scanned the ground around him. Once they found the first booby trap, in a spot that PIS had checked during his nighttime chase of their two followers, it was decided that Buck and the two deputies would stay several yards behind PIS. He had been able to disarm the trap but they didn't want to take any chances. Whoever they were chasing had been able to set up the trap in the dark, while being pursued by PIS.

Buck had spoken with the Sheriff by radio right after they had gotten on the trail. He finally had a decent signal and he was able to give the Sheriff their coordinates from his hand-held GPS unit. The Sheriff reported back that the SWAT teams were just starting to enter the woods and based on Buck's coordinates they should meet up in a couple hours.

"Sheriff please be sure to remind everyone about the booby traps. We have uncovered several more since we left yesterday." Buck said.

"You got it, Buck. Everyone has been told to be really careful. By the way, the guys from Gunnison are coming up on horseback so they may get there before the rest of the teams. You guys stay safe."

Buck wrapped up his radio call and they started back down the trail. PIS had moved ahead and Buck and the two deputies had lost sight of him. Buck wasn't sure where the feeling came from but his head told him to stop and he held up his fist. The two deputies knelt down and raised their assault rifles in a defensive position.

Buck had his assault rifle slung over his shoulder and he immediately pulled it around and took the same position as the deputies. They stopped, barely breathing and listened. All Buck could hear was the breeze rustling through the trees. Then the deputy, Manning, pointed to his ear and then pointed off to the left. Buck strained to listen. Then he heard it. There was definitely movement off to the left. Buck couldn't tell how far off but it was just within his hearing range.

Buck looked ahead for PIS but he still couldn't see him. Deputy Manning moved slightly to his left while staying in a crouch while Deputy Sanchez shifted to the right and covered the trail they had just come down with his rifle. They waited.

Buck had learned a little bit about the two deputies while they were eating their sandwiches the night before. Deputy Rick Manning had been with the Pitkin County Sheriff's department for about three years. He had been born and raised in the county and his Dad owned a gas station and convenience store in Carbondale. He was single and had served two tours in Afghanistan as a Marine before joining the department.

Deputy Michael Sanchez had been with the department about six years. He had been a standout bull rider in high school in Waco, Texas and had hoped to move into the PBR, Pro Bull Riders Association, after graduation but a bad trip on the back of a fiery bull ended with a career stopping knee injury. Unable to fulfill his lifelong dream to be a pro bull rider, Michael had spent a couple years just bumming around the western US before he settled in Dillon, Colorado. When he heard about an opening in the Pitkin County Sheriff's office, he applied and was surprised to be one of three people chosen for the three jobs available. Two years ago he married a local girl and they had a beautiful baby girl. His promotion to the county SWAT team had been a highlight of his life to this point.

Buck wasn't sure what to do at this point. He didn't want to move deeper into the woods because, with booby traps still a real possibility, this could be a trap to draw them in. He was just about to decide on a plan when he spotted a bright red spot coming through the trees. Everyone tensed until they spotted PIS.

Buck and the deputies stood as he approached and he stepped onto the trail and stopped to catch his breath. Buck looked at him with a questioning expression.

"Sorry Agent Taylor. Didn't mean to cause a stir." He caught his breath. "We were being followed again. Only one this time but close enough that I spotted him through the trees. I didn't want to lose him, so I broke off the trail and tried to circle around him."

"It looks like you didn't catch him. What happened?" asked Buck.

"Didn't need to. I think we are getting close." Replied PIS

"Well, what are we waiting for? Let's go get him!" said Deputy Sanchez.

"Hang on there young fella. This one is very crafty and it could be a trap."

PIS looked at Buck. "There is an old miner's cabin up ahead about half a mile. I didn't get too close but it looks abandoned. The person I was following disappeared into the woods behind the cabin." PIS went on to tell them that he had encountered two more traps while following the person of interest.

With booby traps still lurking in the woods, they would need to approach the cabin with caution. Since PIS was unarmed Buck suggested he remain back on the trail once they got close to the cabin. PIS just laughed and headed down the trail. Buck looked at the two deputies who both just shrugged their shoulders. Buck nodded in agreement and they headed off after PIS. This time they kept a little more distance between each other and Sanchez covered their rear.

The trail they had been following had almost completely disappeared when Buck and the deputies caught up with PIS who was now kneeling behind a downed tree. He pointed over the tree and Buck and Manning knelt next to him. Sanchez had taken a position behind another tree and was acting as lookout.

Buck spotted the little cabin about fifty yards off through the trees. It sat in a little clearing in the trees. Buck slowly scanned the area. As far as he could tell the little cabin appeared to be abandoned. But where had the person gone that PIS had followed? There were no visible trails leading away from the cabin.

Deputy Manning handed Buck a small pair of binoculars and Buck carefully studied the area around the cabin. It looked abandoned, just like PIS had told them but he had an uneasy feeling. They needed to clear the little cabin so they could continue trying to follow their person of interest. Buck had the two deputies move off the trail to the right and left. PIS reminded them to watch where they placed their feet and they both acknowledged that they understood. The two deputies would approach the little cabin from the sides while he and PIS approached the cabin head on. Once again Buck suggested that PIS stay back while he approached the cabin but PIS just smiled.

Buck started moving down what was left of the almost invisible trail and PIS followed a couple yards behind him. That was the agreement they had reached since PIS was unarmed. Both deputies had moved off the trail about twenty yards and were slowly working their way toward the cabin always keeping Buck and PIS in sight. Buck with his rifle up to his shoulder moved slowly at a slight crouch. Whenever he could, he would step slightly off the trail and hide behind an available tree. He continually scanned the area with his rifle as they approached the cabin.

The explosions caught them completely off guard. The first explosion went off just to the right of Deputy Manning and knocked him to the ground. The second explosion went off a few seconds later between the cabin and Deputy Sanchez who dove for cover behind a large aspen tree. Buck and PIS had just reached the cabin when the first two explosions occurred. Immediately after the second explosion PIS reacted and threw himself against

Buck driving him away from the cabin. They both hit the ground just as the front of the cabin exploded. The air was filled with flying pieces of wood and glass. Buck and PIS covered their heads with their arms and tried to bury themselves deeper into the leaves and the undergrowth. The sound was deafening.

Chapter Twenty-Eight

She had spent a good part of her summer vacation trying to locate her grandfather's torture chamber. She knew it was somewhere along Conundrum Creek but she was having a great deal of difficulty locating it. She didn't have much time to spend with her grandfather since she was working in a local restaurant, so she missed out on a lot of lucid moments. Those few times she was able to sit and talk with him he didn't make a lot of sense.

The last time she found her grandfather in a mood to talk he spent most of the time talking about his second kill. He had asked to see his treasure box again and she went and pulled it from the hiding space behind the big toolbox in the garage. He spent a lot of time looking at the small treasures but he kept coming back to a thin silver bracelet. He would stare at it for a few seconds, look at something else and then repeat the process as if drawn to it.

She knew better than to interrupt his train of thought, so she waited patiently until he was ready to tell his story. She took the bracelet from the treasure box for him, he stared at it and sat back against his pillow.

The young woman who owned the bracelet was from Maine. He couldn't remember the city but he sure remembered her. She was petite and pretty. He couldn't remember how old she was but she was old enough to drink and that was where he found her. She was on her way to Oregon to meet up with some friends from high school.

Her family didn't know she was in Aspen. She had told them she was going to Florida for spring break but she changed her mind at the bus station and decided to go to Oregon where her high school boyfriend was going to school. He found out that the boyfriend had no idea that she was on her way. She would be perfect. He discovered that the girl from Maine had no place to stay in Aspen and almost no money for food, so he found her a place to sleep in an old shed behind the maintenance shop.

Even though he was older than she was he liked the way she flirted with him. Her attention got him very excited. When he would visit her after work, she always seemed pleased to see him and she seemed to enjoy teasing him. He figured that the bright red lipstick was just for him. He told her about a hot spring located south of Aspen and that they could go there. Clothing was optional which didn't seem to bother her.

Telling his wife he had to work a night shift he met the girl at the shed and they headed for the old forest service road that led to the hot spring. Before they had even gotten to the spring, she had started to take off her clothes in the car. She reached over at one point and ran her hand along the zipper in his pants. He almost smashed into a tree along the narrow dirt road.

He pulled the car off the road and into the forest in a spot he had picked for its privacy. Once he stopped the car, she started to unbuckle his pants. He was more than ready as she straddled him in the front seat. He was so preoccupied that he almost forgot the syringe he had placed in the door pocket. She was so preoccupied that she never even flinched when he pushed the needle into her shoulder. They both exploded together and then she passed out in his arms. He pushed her off and got out of the car. Pulling up his pants he finished dressing and went to the passenger side door and pulled her out onto the ground.

The area was as dark as a cave but he had memorized the trail back to his little house of horrors and a half hour later he was unlocking the hatch under the floor of his little miner's cabin and lowering her down into the shaft. Once he got her down to the bottom of the shaft, he tied her to the bed just as he had done the first time and raped her for several hours until he was completely exhausted.

He then dragged her over to the shackles attached to the wall and bolted her in. He admired her naked body for quite a while before he got started. She was almost perfect. Once again, he opened the cabinet and removed his knife collection and after careful examination, he chose a ten-inch-long fillet knife.

He stripped of his clothes and approached the still unconscious young girl. He had read an article about an old Chinese torture technique called lingchi or death by a thousand cuts. The Chinese had used this technique to torture people prior to its abolishment around 1905. Basically, it involved using non-lethal cuts and slices to *ensure that the victim survived for a long period of time. He was excited to see how many cuts he could make on this young girl before she died. He wanted to wait for her to regain consciousness but he was getting excited, so he decided to begin.*

At some point early on the young girl woke up and the fear in her eyes only made his excitement greater. He realized that although he was enjoying the experience that he needed more practice in controlling his cuts. He felt that some were way to deep and after only an hour the young girl was bleeding profusely. He knew he should slow down and take his time but he kept getting more and more excited.

He was disappointed when the young girl finally passed out for good. He had been keeping count and had only gotten to two hundred slices. He would need more practice. He sat for a minute on the end of the bed and admired his handy work. He really liked what he saw.

He cleaned up his tools, got dressed and turned off the kerosene lantern. He was completely exhausted but excited by the prospect of practicing this technique some more.

She tried to ask her grandfather for better directions to the shaft but he just leaned his head back into his pillow and fell asleep. She found herself getting more and more excited as he described the technique. She wondered if she would have the strength to perfect what her grandfather had started. She put the bracelet back in the box and headed back to the garage to hide the box.

She felt very pleased with herself that she was giving her grandfather the chance to relive his life from so long ago. She hoped when he finally rested for the last time that he would feel good about his life. She was glad she could help him relive those memories.

She would need to continue her quest to find the hidden shaft and the old cabin on her own. She felt like she was getting close. She felt she was ready to follow in her grandfather's footsteps and maybe even develop a technique of her own. She wanted nothing more than to make her grandfather proud of her.

Chapter Twenty-Nine

The Teacher's hands were shaking so badly that he had to show the younger one how to insert the blasting cap into the dynamite instead of doing it himself. He stressed the need for total concentration. The dynamite had been in the mine for years and was very unstable. He told the younger one that one wrong move and he would blow them all up but the younger one was a fast learner and he was able to finish the prep work without incident.

The Teacher now led them out the front door of the cabin and showed them the locations he wanted them to place the dynamite sticks. Each one was buried slightly in the ground and covered with leaves, sticks and rocks. The hunter completed running the wires from the cave entrance to each location.

The Teacher showed them how to connect the wires to the blasting caps and then they headed back to the mine entrance. Once there, the Teacher went back inside the mine and returned carrying a metal box with a metal T-shaped handle sticking out of it. He explained that when the time came to protect the family, they needed to connect one wire from each set to the two little posts in the top of the box. Before connecting the wires, they would need to pull up on the T-shaped handle so it was ready to work.

The hunter laid out each wire run, in order of placement, on the ground just outside the mine entrance so they were ready. The Teacher then took the first set of wires and connected one wire to each post, tightening the two wing nuts down on the wire. He told them that when the time came they would need to push down on the T-shaped handle. That would set off the dynamite.

The Teacher wanted them to follow a specific order if they had to set off the explosives. Right outside first, followed by left outside, and then the one that was set inside the cabin door. If that wasn't enough they had a second set of explosives between the cabin and the mine and they were to follow the same procedure. He explained that this was a similar procedure to one that the US Marine mortar crews used in Vietnam during the jungle war. They would drop a mortar round into each of the four corners of a grid and then drop the fifth round into the middle. The idea was to cause the enemy to move from outside the grid into the middle and then drop a round right on their heads. He told them it was a very effective strategy. They both told him that they understood.

The Teacher also had them add a few more booby traps between the cabin and the mine entrance. He then cut down a few small aspen trees and had the hunter and the younger one stack them at the mine entrance to hide the door. He looked around the area between the cabin and the mine entrance. He had done everything he could to protect the family.

He told the younger one to head off into the woods and keep an eye on the men and he had the hunter hide in the large aspen tree that was about twenty yards away from the door and keep his rifle handy. He was hoping the men would get to the cabin, find it abandoned and keep going but he needed to be ready.

While the Teacher headed back into the mine to check on the others, the younger one headed off into the woods being careful not to trip over the wires that they had run along the ground. He was very proud that the Teacher had chosen him for this task. He was the best tracker in the family and someday he would be able to take the rifle and become another hunter.

The younger one caught up with the men about a half mile from the cabin. He stayed off the trail about fifty yards and hid amongst the trees and the undergrowth. He watched them for a while and then he suddenly realized that the old man with the ponytail was no longer with the group of men on the trail. Panic set in as he quickly looked around the area but couldn't find him. He decided to move to a different location.

As he quietly slipped through the woods, he almost ran into the old man with the ponytail. If he hadn't pulled back at the last moment and crawled under a downed tree the old man with the ponytail would have seen him for sure. He waited for the old man to pass and then snuck around the tree on the opposite side and headed back toward the cabin. The old man with the ponytail was very good and the younger one spotted him through the trees at the same time the old man spotted him.

The old man was moving straight towards him, so he ducked down into a small ravine and headed back in the opposite direction from which he was traveling. His path would take him away from the cabin but he needed to shake the old man. He stayed in the ravine for about half a mile then climbed out and circled around the trail the men had come in on and headed back towards the cabin on the opposite side of the trail.

He looked around but could not see the men. He felt good that he had been able to get away from the old man. He had gone a long way out of his way to escape the old man and he was worried that he might not get back to the cabin before the men got there. He made it to the mine entrance just as the men split up and started to approach the cabin. Two of the men moved off to the right and left side and the other man and the old man with the ponytail headed towards the cabin. They were all pointing their rifles in the direction of the cabin except for the old man with the ponytail. He didn't seem to have a gun. Maybe their group was set up just like the family. The men with the guns were the hunters and the old man with the ponytail was like him, the tracker.

The younger one took up his position behind the aspen trees they had cut and stacked at the mine entrance and pulled the metal box with the T shaped handle closer to the door. The Teacher had closed and bolted the mine entrance door to protect the others. It would be up to the hunter and the younger one to hold off the men. The younger one could barely see the hunter in the aspen tree but he knew he was there. Now they just had to sit and wait. Unfortunately, they didn't have to wait long.

Chapter Thirty

The first explosion almost bounced the Teacher out of bed. He had laid down on the bed to try to get rid of the headaches that seemed to plague his days lately. The others were doing their studies and were for the most part quiet. The explosion caused dust and bits of rock to fall from the ceiling of the mine and as he tried to stand up, the others screamed, scattered and hid under anything they could find.

The Teacher was disoriented for a moment and when he tried to stand up his legs gave out from under him and he crashed to the floor. He covered his head with his arms as bits of rock and dust rained down on his head. He looked around the mine to make sure no one had been injured and then was able to get his legs back under him and he headed for the mine entrance.

The second explosion caused him to stagger and bang into the mine wall. More dust and debris came down from the ceiling and he told the others to cover up. Some of them had crawled under the table and a few had crawled under the bed. They all looked confused and frightened.

He reached the mine entrance and was about to unlatch the door when the third explosion knocked him completely off his feet and his head slammed into the dirt floor of the mine tunnel. He reached up to his head and his hand came away covered in blood. His disorientation was back with a vengeance and he was having trouble figuring out where he was. His first thought was that he was still in Vietnam and that the base was under attack. He looked around for his weapons but he had none. He knew that wasn't right, so he must not be in Nam. His mind started to clear as two of the others ran up to him and tried to help him move so he could prop against the wall.

He was having trouble focusing and having troubling trying to figure out why there were kids sitting in the dark with him. Slowly his mind cleared and he started to remember. He could hear the others choking on the dust that had now filled the dark mine. He didn't understand what had happened. Could it have been a cave in farther back in the mine? He just couldn't get it worked out in his head.

All of a sudden his brain cleared enough and he remembered that he had been working with the hunter and the younger one and that they had set explosive charges around the cabin in case anyone got too close to the mine. It still wasn't making sense in his already fragile and now probably concussed mind. He knew he needed to help the others but he was having trouble getting his legs to work. He needed to get them out of the mine before they all choked to death.

It's amazing how sometimes one thing or event can bring about clarity. For the Teacher, that event was a series of gunshots coming from the other side of the mine entry door. He heard the first shots and realized that the hunter and the younger one were outside the mine and they were in trouble. He had left them to protect the others and he had gone to sleep. He needed to get to them to help them. It was his job to protect the others, not theirs. He had made a promise to momma. He had to do something.

He managed to get up on his feet with the help of two of the others and then he told them to run back and hide with the others. He found the latching bolt on the door and was just in the process of swinging the door open when he heard semi-automatic gunfire and lots of it. The men who were searching for them must have found them. Someone had blown the first three charges, probably the younger one and then the hunter had opened fire from his concealment spot in the big aspen tree. Now the men had opened fire on them both. He felt helpless and knew he needed to do something to help them.

Staying low he looked out of the mine entrance and spotted the younger one right next to the door. The plunger sat on the ground next to him and he was leaning back against the wall of the mine with his knees up against his chest and his hands covering his head. The Teacher had never seen him looked so frightened.

The Teacher crawled out the door on his belly and slid under the stacked aspen trees and wrapped his arms around the younger one. He held him as the bullets flew. While he held the younger one, he could still hear the unmistakable sound of the M1 carbine going off to his right. The hunter was making a valiant effort to defend their home but the semi-automatic fire he heard was withering. The hunter didn't stand a chance.

Staying low to the ground the Teacher half crawled and half ran towards the big aspen tree. He no longer heard the M1 carbine. All he heard was the semi-automatic weapons fire. As he neared the tree, he realized his worst fear. The hunter's body hung limply from the branch about eight feet off the ground with a lot of blood flowing from the bullet holes in his chest. The M1 carbine lay on the ground under his body.

With a lull in the rifle fire, the Teacher was able to reach up and pull the hunter's body down from the tree. He reached into the hunter's pocket and pulled out two more clips for the rifle. He ejected the spent clip and slapped in a new clip.

His mind was suddenly back in Vietnam and he needed to protect the men he had abandoned during the firefight. Feeling suddenly twenty-four again the Teacher jumped up, raised the rifle to his shoulder and charged towards the cabin. He had been able to get off two rounds before the first bullet hit him in the shoulder, but he didn't stop. He pulled the trigger twice more as he ran forward. The next couple rounds hit him square in the chest and he flopped back onto the ground.

He looked to his left and saw the younger one hooking up the next set of wires to the plunger. He had to stop him before he got killed too. The Teacher tried to turn on his side but the pain was intense. He held up his hand and tried to get the younger ones attention. He was too late. The explosion went off two feet from where he had hit the ground and he felt his body being flung into the air. The last thing he saw as he hit the ground were the bullets slamming into the younger one as he tried valiantly to get the next set of wires connected to the plunger. Then the lights went out and the Teacher was finally at peace.

Chapter Thirty-One

Buck was lying on the ground trying to catch his breath. PIS was lying partially on top of him. His first thought was, "this must be how all those quarterbacks felt when I pummeled them into the ground as a defensive back for the Gunnison High School Cowboys all those years ago."

Buck had been a standout high school football player and could have gone to almost any college he chose with a full scholarship, but he chose to join the army instead. With his teammate Hardy Braxton covering the left side of the line, they had broken just about every state high school record for defensive play. During senior year they had been called the "Wrecking Crew," and many of those records still stood today.

Buck had his arms over his head as debris rained down on top of them. He tried to shake the cobwebs out of his head but was having trouble focusing. He could feel blood dripping down his neck and his ears were ringing. He tried to move but he was pinned to the ground. Finally, the debris falling from the sky slowed and PIS slid off Buck. Buck looked over at PIS and noticed the pain in his eyes.

"You ok?" he asked.

"I think I caught a piece of shrapnel in my shoulder," replied PIS

Buck picked his head up off the ground and reached over PIS. Buck was amazed at what he saw. Sticking out of PIS's shoulder was a five-inch-long piece of wood. Buck slid closer. He didn't see a lot of blood but he knew this wasn't good. He told PIS not to move.

He was trying to get his radio off his belt when the first shots hit the wood that had fallen around him and PIS. He dragged PIS closer to the wood pile and then picked up his rifle off the ground. He needed to locate the sniper. He raised his head just slightly over the fallen logs but couldn't pinpoint where the shots were coming from. The remains of the cabin partially blocked his view down range. He rested his rifle on the top of a log and started to sight in through the scope when he heard rapid gunfire coming from both sides of him.

Deputies Manning and Sanchez were both behind trees and had engaged the sniper with withering fire. Buck looked through his scope in the direction they were firing and saw the bullets as they tore big chunks of wood out of an aspen tree about forty yards to their left.

Both deputies stopped firing and for the moment silence returned to the forest. Buck scanned the area with his scope. The movement from the right side was low to the ground. He had to look twice not certain he had seen any movement at all. As he watched the big tree, he spotted another person stand up and pull something out of the tree. Deputy Manning must have seen the same thing as he once again opened fire at the tree.

With his clip empty, Manning dropped the clip and was ramming a new clip home when a figure jumped up from the ground under the aspen tree and charged towards them. Several bullets hit the tree that Manning was hiding behind as the figure ran forward firing as he came. Buck and Sanchez returned fire and Buck saw the man falter and a red stain appeared on his right shoulder. Remarkably the man kept coming and was firing again. This time towards Manning who had regained his position behind the tree

Buck sighted in on the man the best he could and both he and Sanchez opened fire at the same time. Buck could see the bullets as they struck the man square in the chest and he flew backwards and hit the ground. Everyone froze for a minute.

Manning had come out from behind his tree and with his rifle raised had started to move towards Buck. Buck slowly climbed to his feet and kept scanning the area for any other danger. The explosion caught them both off guard and the dove for cover. Buck looked up just in time to see the body in the woods fly thought he air and land hard on the ground. He wasn't sure what had just happened but there was someone else out there with them and that someone still had explosives.

Sanchez looked up and something led his eye to a tight stand of aspen trees. The stand didn't look natural as the trees were too close together and from his location the trees looked more like they were leaning against something. He spotted movement behind the trees and fearing the worst he opened fire on the trees.

Buck, Manning and Sanchez held their positions and looked around carefully. PIS was now lying quietly against a fallen log from the cabin. Buck was amazed at how calm he appeared. Like getting stabbed in the back with a huge chunk of wood was an everyday occurrence. Buck put his hand on PIS's good shoulder and signaled for him to stay where he was.

Manning and Sanchez converged on Bucks position.

"Fuck Buck. What the hell just happened?" asked Sanchez.

Buck shook his head. "Got me. I feel like we've been in a war zone." He shook his head to try to clear the ringing in his ears.

The forest had been quiet for a few minutes and Buck suggested they head toward the big tree and see what they could find. The three men spread out and with rifles raised they moved slowly towards the tree. Buck was the first to reach the guy who had charged them. Kneeling next to body, he touched his two fingers to the side of the guy's neck and checked for a pulse. There was none which he pretty much figured after watching the guy get shot repeatedly and then blown up.

He picked up the rifle that was lying next to the body. An old M1 carbine. Buck hadn't seen one of those in years. It was a good rifle in its day and was still used by the military. He slung the rifle strap over his shoulder after checking the body to make sure there were no other weapons. He looked up as Sanchez waved him over to the big aspen tree.

He was almost to the tree when he heard a voice coming from his radio. He pulled the radio from his belt and keyed the mic. "Go ahead Sheriff," he replied.

"Are you guys ok? We heard explosions and gunfire. What's your status?"

Buck was just about to answer when he heard rustling in the trees coming from the trees to the left of where they had entered the little clearing. Buck, Sanchez and Manning immediately found cover and scanned the area.

"Buck Taylor. Gunnison County Sheriff's Office." Came a shout from the woods.

Buck stepped out from behind his cover and still with rifle raised called out.

"Come ahead. Slowly!"

The four Gunnison County deputies, all wearing camouflage, stepped out of the woods into the clearing and looked around. Buck lowered his rifle.

Walt Jenkins, with the Gunnison County Sheriff's Office, had been with Buck when they found Ranger Susan Corey's body. He walked up to Buck and they shook hands.

"Jesus Buck. What the hell happened? You guys ok?"

"Yeah, mostly," replied Buck. "Got one man injured."

Jenkins looked towards PIS. "Masters take a look. Masters has paramedic training." Deputy Masters headed towards PIS pulling out his first aid kit as he went.

Buck held up his hand to Jenkins and lifted the radio to his mouth.

"Sheriff, we are good. PIS has been injured and we are going to need transport. We are also going to need the Forensic Pathologist and Forensics. Gunnison County just arrived. Over." Buck gave the Sheriff the coordinates from his hand-held GPS and clipped the radio back on his belt

Deputy Sanchez yelled for Buck and ducked back behind the tree. Buck and Walt Jenkins headed for Sanchez while the other two Gunnison County deputies headed for the stand of aspen trees with Manning. As Buck approached, he saw Sanchez kneeling next to a body on the ground.

Sanchez looked up as Buck approached. "He's just a kid for Christ sake. We killed a kid." Sanchez had tears in his eyes.

Buck and Jenkins knelt next to him and looked at the body on the ground. Sanchez was right. Buck figured the kid couldn't be more than fifteen of sixteen. He had blond hair and blue eyes that were now clouded over in death. He had been shot multiple times. Buck put his hand on Sanchez's shoulder. Nothing he could say right now was going to change the way Sanchez was feeling.

Buck looked at Jenkins who just nodded. They headed over to where Manning and the other two deputies were standing and the scene was even worse.

Lying behind the stand of aspen trees was the body of another young boy. This one was probably no more than twelve or thirteen. Next to him on the ground was an old plunger for setting off explosives. The plunger looked to be a hundred years old and Buck was amazed that it still worked. Manning did not have tears in his eyes but Buck could sense that he was going through the same emotions that Sanchez was feeling.

Walt Jenkins tapped Buck on the arm and pointed to two sets of wires lying on the ground next to the body. "Looks like the kid wasn't finished."

"Yeah," replied Buck. "We better see where those go. Very carefully."

Buck headed off, following one set of wires, while Jenkins followed the other. They each found what they expected about forty yards from the body. The dynamite was very old and coated with white residue. Although he knew the dynamite was not connected to a timer, Buck also knew that this dynamite was probably very unstable. He found a stick and stuck it in the ground. He then pulled a piece of yellow crime scene tape from his backpack and tied it around the top of the stick. He walked over to where Jenkins was standing and repeated the process.

Chapter Thirty-Two

The Sheriff was following closely behind his SWAT team as they traveled along an old fire break that they had picked up on the west side of Conundrum Creek. Based on the radio report he received from Buck earlier in the morning they should be within a mile of Bucks current location. The two other SWAT teams were coming in from Gunnison County to the south and from the Maroon Snowmass trailhead to the west.

The first explosion stopped everyone in their tracks as it reverberated through the valley. The high peaks helped to amplify the sound but it also made it difficult to determine the direction from which the sound came. The second and third explosions did nothing to change that but that didn't lessen the concern the Sheriff felt. His SWAT team had already disarmed two booby traps, so there was concern with moving through the woods any faster.

The rifle fire immediately following did nothing to alleviate the Sheriff's concerns especially when the semi-automatic weapons opened up. "What the hell is going on?" he thought to himself. It sounded like a full-scale invasion was happening in his county. He grabbed the radio off his belt and called Buck Taylor. The lack of a response was not unexpected. Buck and his team were deep in the woods and he might be having getting out a signal.

He called the other two teams to see if they might have a better feel for which direction the sound was coming from. The Gunnison County SWAT team reported that they were about ten minutes from the location Buck had last reported and they were certain the shooting was coming from there. They told the Sheriff they would forego a little bit of safety and pick up their pace. The team coming from the trailhead was still too far away from Buck's last position but they would pick up the pace since they were following Buck's trail and assumed that all the booby traps along the trail had been exposed.

The shooting had stopped and the Sheriff was finally able to reach Buck. "Go ahead Sheriff," Buck replied.

"Are you guys ok? We heard explosions and gunfire. What's your status?"

There was a lengthy delay and the Sheriff started to get impatient. He was about to key the mic again when Buck responded. "Sheriff, we are good. PIS has been injured and we are going to need transport. We are also going to need the Forensic Pathologist and Forensics. Gunnison County just arrived. Over."

The Sheriff was not happy to hear the request for the Pathologist. That meant that somebody was dead. He keyed the mic and called his dispatcher. He asked the dispatcher to call the county Forensic Pathologist and his two forensic techs. He also asked the dispatcher to call the paramedics and activate the Pitkin County Search and

Rescue team. Finally, he asked the dispatcher to call Olaf Gunderson and have him bring a couple of his ATVs and a couple of his guides to the Conundrum Creek trailhead. Olaf had been a fixture in Aspen for longer than anyone could remember and he owned an adventure company. The trail the Sheriff and his team were on was somewhat decent for the most part and Olaf's experienced mountain guides should be able to maneuver their ATVs along most of it.

Finished talking to the dispatcher, the Sheriff put away his radio and directed his SWAT team to start moving towards Buck's last GPS fix. The Sheriff had no way of knowing how many people were dead but he was glad the shooting had completely stopped and that Buck sounded like everyone except PIS was ok. In spite of their most recent disagreement, he liked that old curmudgeon and he hoped he wasn't hurt too bad.

It took the Sheriff and his SWAT team another forty-five minutes to reach Buck's location. He stood at the edge of the clearing and looked around. In the middle of the field stood a smoldering pile of what he imaged was once a miner's cabin. The field was covered with debris. He spotted the two sticks in the ground with the yellow caution tape hanging from them and he directed his deputy who was trained as a bomb tech to carefully go have a look and see what needed to be done.

He spotted PIS propped against a log. One of the Gunnison County deputies was carefully taping around the huge chunk of wood so it wouldn't move. They would not attempt to remove the piece of wood until PIS was safely at the hospital. The Sheriff walked over and knelt next to PIS.

"You doing ok?" asked the Sheriff.

"Don't worry after me, Sheriff. Been hurt a lot worse than this," replied PIS.

The Sheriff looked at the Gunnison deputy and noticed him frown. He separated the back of PIS's shirt, that he had cut open to access the wound and the Sheriff could see scars all over PIS's back. It looked like someone had whipped him unmercifully at some point in his life. The Sheriff was stunned. There was so much they didn't know about this Brit. Maybe someday they would get the whole story.

He patted PIS on the shoulder and stood up. The deputy told him that PIS should be fine. He didn't think the piece of wood was embedded too deeply and PIS didn't seem to be in too much pain. He had even refused the painkillers the deputy had offered him. The tape job should hold the wood in place as long as they didn't jostle him too much. The Sheriff thanked the deputy and asked where Buck and the others had gone.

The deputy pointed toward a huge aspen tree and the Sheriff and his SWAT guys headed in that direction. Some noise to his right attracted his attention and he stopped. The rest of the SWAT team came through the trees along the trail that Buck had cleared. The Sheriff asked them to secure the area and start hanging crime scene tape around the entire clearing. The rest of the team was directed to grab some evidence flags and cones and start walking the clearing and marking anything they found that didn't look natural.

He headed off in the direction of the voices he could hear through the trees and stopped short as he reached a point where he was able to see the mine entrance. He could not believe his eyes.

Chapter Thirty-Three

Buck had asked the remaining Gunnison County deputies to search the area between the cabin and the mine entrance to make sure there were no other threats. He had checked the younger one for a pulse but found none which didn't surprise him. Sanchez was holding up ok. He kind of set in his head that maybe the bullets that had killed the two boys hadn't come from his gun. It gave him some solace even though he knew that he was one of the top shooters in the department, but with all three of them shooting, anything was possible.

Buck and Manning were standing to the side of the mine entrance discussing the safest course of action to enter the mine when they heard what sounded like coughing coming from deep inside the mine. They both raised their rifles and looked into the deep recesses of the pitch-black mine.

Buck gave a short shrill whistle to get the attention of the Gunnison deputies and waved them over to the mine. Deputy Sanchez had composed himself and joined the group by the entrance. The Gunnison deputies each had night vision goggles in their backpack, so Buck asked them to lead the way. Unfortunately, the dust was so thick in the air that the night vision goggles proved useless, so the deputies raised them off their eyes. With rifles raised and minimal light from Buck's flashlight and the flashlights on the rifles, they entered the mine entrance.

Buck noticed that the door they entered was a substantial piece of construction, definitely designed to keep people out of the mine. He wondered if the guy lying dead in the clearing built the reinforced door and also wondered what he was trying to hide behind it. Once inside even the flashlights had trouble cutting through the inky black darkness and dust that surrounded them.

Buck kept his flashlight pointed forward and followed behind the three Gunnison SWAT deputies who had separated and now walked down both sides of the tunnel hugging the walls as best they could. Manning followed Buck and Sanchez remained by the mine entrance door to cover their backs.

After what seemed like an eternity to Buck but was actually only a few minutes, the little troop entered what appeared to be a large room and they immediately crouched lower and moved to opposite sides of the space. Buck and Manning held their position in the tunnel and waited.

"POLICE. NO ONE MOVE!!" came a shout from Walt Jenkins. "We are armed and we will shoot!"

Buck could hear quiet movement along with sniffles and tiny coughs. The room was heavy with dust and even Buck coughed as they stood listening. Walt Jenkins moved back down the tunnel and moved next to Buck.

"We can see a couple people and they look like more kids. They are hiding under a table. Can't tell how many. What do you want to do?" asked Jenkins.

"Let's get as much light in the space as we can and see what we are dealing with. Be ready for anything," replied Buck.

"You got it," Walt responded. He keyed his mic. "Ok guys. Let's get all the flashlights turned on. Stay cool."

All at once three more flashlights lit up the space. The seven flashlights combined made a dent in the darkness and it was enough for Buck and the others to see four faces looking up at them from under a table. The faces appeared to be covered with soot. They looked scared.

While the deputies held their guns at the ready Buck moved into the room and knelt down next to the table. He told the kids to crawl out from under the table one at a time. At first, there was hesitancy, then finally one of the girls crawled out. She was soon followed by two more girls and a boy. Buck heard movement on the other side of the room and all guns turned that way. Two more girls crawled out from under a small bed that was pushed against the wall. To say the deputies and Buck were stunned would be an understatement.

Buck looked at the first girl who had crawled out from under the table. "Are there any more children in here?" he asked.

The girl, who looked about ten or eleven years old, looked around the space and then looked at Buck and shook her head no. Some of the kids were still coughing and Buck and the deputies were finding it hard to breathe themselves, so they pointed the kids towards the door and started walking.

Buck was the first one to exit the mine and was glad to see that Sanchez had pulled an emergency blanket out of his backpack and covered the young boy lying next to the mine entrance. He was followed by six children all of whom appeared to be around ten or eleven. Once outside, Buck and the deputies pulled some water bottles out of their packs and gave the kids a chance to get the dust out of their throats.

Buck noticed that each kid looked at the rescue blanket as they came out of the mine but no one said a word, they just looked sad and confused. Manning looked at Buck and Jenkins and signaled for them to follow him away from the kids. When they were far enough away for the kids not to hear, he said,

"What the hell did we just uncover?"

Buck looked back at the kids who were now sitting on the ground in a small group.

"Be damned if I know. One old guy and eight kids. I can't even imagine. I better radio the Sheriff and let him know what we found."

Jenkins nodded in agreement as did Manning and Buck pulled out his radio. He was just getting ready to push the mic when they heard movement at the front of the cabin and spotted the Sheriff and the SWAT team entering the clearing.

Chapter Thirty-Four

The Sheriff approached the group of kids sitting on the ground and just stared. He finally turned and headed over to where Buck and the others were standing.

"What the hell Buck?" he asked.

Buck shrugged his shoulders. "You got us. We were just wondering the same thing."

The Sheriff looked back at the kids and then back at Buck. Buck went on to explain about the explosions and the shootout. He excused himself from Manning and Jenkins and he and the Sheriff walked over to look at the dead kid by the mine entry. The Sheriff pulled the cover back just enough so the other kids couldn't see and then replaced the blanket. They next walked over to the aspen tree and Buck showed the Sheriff the body of the older boy. The Sheriff didn't say a word.

Their last stop was the body of the old man. The explosion had done a little damage to the body but it was the bullet holes in his chest that were what had killed him. The Sheriff stood for a long minute and then looked at Buck.

"I checked on PIS as we came in. He doesn't seem to be the least bit concerned that he has a chunk of wood embedded in his shoulder. I've got transport coming so we can get him out of here." He stood for a second as if deep in thought. "Honest opinion Buck. What do you think we have here? Is this some kind of cult or some weird sex thing or what?"

"I have no idea Sheriff. This is a new one on me. I've seen a lot of abused kids in my day but these kids don't look abused to my eyes. The way they held hands coming out of the mine, I almost get the feeling they are some kind of family."

The Sheriff looked at Buck. "Seriously? And who's this old guy, the father of these kids?"

"Possibly," said Buck. "But I don't think so. These kids all appear to be about the same age. The kid under the tree looks to be the oldest we have seen so far and the one by the mine entrance looks to be a little bit older than the rest. I doubt they are siblings in the typical sense."

"Fuck Buck. This is going to be a mess. I better let social services know. This is going to make their day." The Sheriff walked off pulling his radio off his belt as he went.

Buck took the opportunity and walked over to check on PIS. The Gunnison deputy who had been working on him explained that all things considered, PIS seemed to be doing remarkably well. Buck sat on the ground next to PIS and looked at him.

"I hate to be a bother Agent Taylor. Much ado about nothing," said PIS.

Buck looked at PIS. "You have a five-inch-long chunk of wood stuck in your shoulder. I don't think that's much ado about nothing."

PIS didn't say anything further, so Buck continued. "You pretty much saved my life back there. Thank you for that. How did you know the cabin was gonna go up?"

PIS smiled. "You are quite welcome even if all I did was push you out of the way. About the cabin. The pattern suggested an old tactic your US Marines used to use in Vietnam. The Marine mortar crews would drop their mortar rounds in a square pattern starting with the four corners. The enemy would move away from the corners into the center of the square and then the Marines would hammer the center with successive rounds essentially obliterating the enemy. It was highly effective."

Buck thought about it for a minute. "You think the guy we killed could be former military and might have spent time in Nam?"

PIS said he thought it was a good possibility. He hadn't seen the man before he was killed but based on the techniques it was possible. Buck wanted to talk to the Sheriff about PIS's thought, so he stood up patted PIS on his good shoulder and headed off to find the Sheriff. It was just about the same time as the final SWAT team group showed up.

Buck found the Sheriff and they both stood watching the Sheriff's bomb tech, slowly remove the blasting caps from the two sticks of dynamite that Buck had marked earlier. The bomb tech walked over and told the Sheriff that the dynamite was very old and even removing the blasting caps wasn't going to make the dynamite safe. He suggested leaving them where they lay and just keeping everyone away from them. The Sheriff agreed.

Buck told the Sheriff about his conversation with PIS. He also suggested they might run his prints through the military and see if there was anything to PIS's idea. The Sheriff agreed. He told Buck that the transport would be onsite in a few minutes along with the Pathologist and Forensics. He was planning to send the kids back first along with a couple deputies. PIS would go out with the kids so they could get him to the hospital. The Sheriff told Buck about the scars on PIS's back. Buck had no idea.

They heard the ATVs before they saw them. Olaf Gunderson had delivered in spades as ten ATVs drove into the clearing. Olaf waved to the Sheriff who waved back. Dr. Emily Parker walked up to Buck and the Sheriff followed by the two forensic techs, Gomez and Flynn. The Sheriff walked off with the two techs and left Buck standing with the doctor.

"Looks like we meet again, Agent Taylor," she said. "Do you always make a habit of being where the bodies are?" She smiled and Buck laughed.

"Seems so Doc. It's my curse I guess," he replied.

Buck asked her to follow him and he would show her the bodies. It would be getting dark in a couple hours and the Sheriff wanted to get everyone out of the forest by nightfall. They stopped at the older male's body first and the doctor knelt down and looked at the wounds. She noted the pieces of wood and debris that were buried in his back and side and Buck explained that besides being shot he had also been blown up. She looked at Buck with a confused look.

Buck suggested he show her the other two bodies and then he would be willing to answer any of her questions. He led the way to the boy under the aspen tree. She knelt down and gave the body a quick perusal. She stood up and her face said it all. Nothing needed to be said, so they headed for the younger boy over by the mine entrance. As they approached, she looked at the kids sitting on the ground.

Buck took her by the elbow and led her to the blanket that covered the third body. She pulled back the blanket and just stared for a minute. The age of the young boy was easy to see. The bullets that had killed him had done a huge amount of damage and she quickly counted about a half-dozen wounds. She looked up at Buck and then replaced the emergency blanket over the body.

"This is all so senseless. Was there no other way?" she asked.

"Sorry, Doc. We were under attack from several directions and we had to defend ourselves. We didn't know two of them were kids until it was all over. Everybody feels bad."

Just then a small figure appeared behind Buck and a soft voice asked. "Excuse me, sir. When will the Teacher be coming back?"

Buck and the doctor looked at each other. Buck knelt next to the young girl.

"What's your name sweetie?" Buck asked

"I'm Sarah. It's my turn to cook but I don't know what to make."

She was so calm, it was almost unnerving. Buck thought for a minute. "Is the Teacher what you call the older man?"

"Yes, sir. Will he be back soon?"

Buck thought carefully about his answer. "The Teacher is not going to be coming back. He was hurt badly and…"

"Is he dead?" she interrupted without batting an eye.

Buck looked at the Doctor and then back at Sarah. He decided to be straight with the young girl and see what would happen. The Doctor nodded.

"Yes, Sarah. I am afraid he is dead."

"Can we put him in the ground next to momma?"

Buck asked Sarah where momma was buried and she pointed to a trail that ran up the hill beyond the mine. He asked her if she would show them and she started to walk away. With Sanchez keeping an eye on the rest of the kids, Buck waved for the Sheriff to follow them and he and Dr. Parker followed the little girl up the trail.

About a quarter mile up the trail the little group with Sarah in the lead stopped at a small clearing that overlooked the valley below. The view was incredible. Sarah stopped next to a pile of stones and pointed. There was a wooden cross stuck in the rock pile. "This is where we put momma so she could visit god. Teacher said she would be happy here."

Buck, Dr. Parker and the Sheriff just stood for a minute and watched the activity in the clearing below. Finally, the Sheriff suggested they head back. The ATVs were ready to make their first trip back and they were burning daylight. Dr. Parker took Sarah's hand and they all headed down the trail to the ATVs.

Chapter Thirty-Five

Her grandfather's lucid moments were fewer and fewer as the summer progressed and even helping him look through the treasure box didn't bring out any more stories or more importantly the location of the mine shaft. She grew more and more frustrated thinking she was not going to be able to fulfill what she felt was her destiny. Time was running out.

She spent most of her free time when she wasn't working at the restaurant searching the area along Conundrum Creek. She even enlisted the help of some of her friends but to no avail.

Her luck changed just two weeks before she was scheduled to head back to Florida for school. Two miles from the Conundrum Creek trailhead she found what looked like an old seldom used game trail that she had promised to come back to but over the summer she had completely forgotten about it. It was a bright Saturday morning and the main trail was busy with tourists. She finally remembered the tiny trail and decided that this was the day she would follow it. Her frustration level and this strange sudden need had been building the last couple weeks and she felt like she was going to explode. If she didn't find the mine shaft soon, she might have to improvise which was never a good idea.

Over the summer, the little game trail had become even more overgrown and she actually walked past it twice that morning before she finally saw the faint trail as it snaked off deeper into the woods. Bushwhacking through the trees and the undergrowth, she walked for about a quarter mile before she found what looked like the remains of an old cabin. There wasn't much left, just some old logs in a pile. She could make out bits and pieces of what looked like old wooden shingles and also what might possibly be the remains of an old door.

Pulling on a pair of work gloves she brought along she started to move the logs and debris until she exposed what looked like part of an old wooden floor. Her excitement grew as she struggled to clear more of the floor. She tried to be as quiet as a church mouse so as not to attract the attention of any of the hikers using the main trail. Several back-breaking hours later she finally had almost the entire floor exposed and her heart sunk. There was no obvious trap door or loose boards and she sat for a minute and just held her head. All that work. Could she be in the wrong place? She knew this would probably be her last chance to explore before leaving for college and she felt terrible.

She was about to leave when she noticed one board that kind of stuck out above the others. The sun must have just cast the right shadow because she hadn't noticed the board earlier. Grabbing a thinner stick, she wedged the stick against the edge of the floorboard and applied pressure. It took several tries to get the stick to *finally catch and she almost fell over when the board popped loose from the floor. She dropped her stick and pulled up the board with her hands.*

She stood there for a moment and just stared. There, below the floorboard, was a rusted metal hatch. She almost screamed out with joy but then remembered all the hikers. She began carefully removing the rest of the floorboards until she exposed the entire hatch. It was just like her grandfather told her except for a lot of years of rust. She removed a small pair of bolt cutters she had taken from her grandfather's garage and set the jaws around the old lock, which it surprisingly cut through with almost no effort.

She stood for a moment and thought about what she was about to do. She had hunted for this place all summer and now it was hers. She also realized that once she opened the hatch and climbed down inside her life would change forever. Any smart person would call the authorities and have her grandfather arrested. He was a serial killer, possibly one of the first. He was also someone she had always looked up to. Could she possibly turn him in?

She thought about the two choices she could make. She could put all the floorboards back and walk away never to return, or she could continue on the path that felt more and more right and follow in her grandfather's footsteps. Did she really have it in her to take a human life? Unlike most of the serial killers she had read about this summer, she had a good life. She had never killed an animal. Hell, she never even thought about killing anything until she had discovered her grandfather's treasure box. Now it was all she could think about. The idea was enough to get her aroused.

She finally cleared all the thoughts out of her head and slowly opened the hatch. Her heart skipped a beat when the old rusty hinges made a loud squeak. She froze and listened for a minute hoping the noise hadn't attracted some unwanted attention. She made a mental note to bring some oil from her grandfather's garage and oil the hinges.

Looking down into the dark void, she spotted the old metal ladder hanging against the side wall of the shaft. It looked like it had hardly any rust on it. The smell emanating from the shaft was not at all unpleasant and just smelled dry and old. Pulling her flashlight out of her backpack, she turned it on and scanned the bottom of the shaft, which looked a long way down. She was hoping she wouldn't find the shaft filled with spiders or rats or even snakes but the floor of the shaft just looked dusty.

Gathering up her courage, she set her foot on the first rung of the ladder and, using the door for support, she started to climb down into the tunnel below. She reached the floor of the shaft without incident and scanned the tunnel before her with the flashlight. The tunnel was roughhewn with an occasional brace supporting the roof but to her amazement, the tunnel was only about ten feet long before it opened into a chamber that was exactly as her grandfather had described it.

There against one wall was an old wooden bed. The mattress was old and was covered with an old horsehair blanket. She had to stop for a minute as she visualized her grandfather having sex with the women he brought here. She couldn't picture her grandfather as a rapist, so her mind made the image more pleasant than it probably had been. She spotted the shackles on the opposite wall and could still see faint brownish stains on the dirt floor. She assumed that must be blood and she suddenly felt unsure of her path. Her stomach twisted into a knot and she felt like she wanted to vomit but she forced it back down and continued her search.

The old cabinet was hanging on the wall above a very old wooden table and she opened the cabinet. The leather roll was still neatly tied as she picked it up and placed it on the table. She unrolled the bundle and stepped back. The various knives her grandfather made shined bright in the light of her flashlight. They looked brand new. She picked up one of the thin scalpels and was amazed at how sharp it still was. It was as if time had stood still since the last time her grandfather was here. She put the scalpel back and carefully examined some of the other knives.

A sudden thought occurred to her and she put down the knife and pulled a pair of blue nitrile gloves out of her backpack along with a clean white rag. She wiped down the handles of the knives she had touched and carefully rolled them back up in the leather bundle and returned it to the cabinet. She closed the door and wiped the small knob on the cabinet. She would need to be careful from here on out.

She looked around the chamber and spotted another tunnel running deeper into the mountain. Following the tunnel, she came to another chamber a little ways back. This chamber contained several stacked beds with very rickety frames. She assumed this must have been where the miners would have slept but as she got closer, she noticed the lumps that were lying on each bed. She pulled back an old oilcloth cover which pretty much fell apart in her hand and jumped back startled

Stacked on the bed were two mummified bodies. They were brown with age and appeared to be women. She quickly recovered and checked the other beds. The bodies were stacked on top of each other several to a bed. They all appeared to be naked. She counted fifteen bodies which seemed odd. Her grandfather's treasure box contained sixteen trinkets. She wondered where the sixteenth body was. She spent a few minutes examining the bodies without touching them and she could barely make out lots of tiny cut marks in the now withered skin.

She had never asked her grandfather how he had disposed of the bodies after he was finished with them. The sight before her put an end to any speculation. The answer was he didn't, which is most likely the reason he had never been suspected of a crime. No bodies were ever discovered, so no crime was committed. It made sense.

She threw what was left of the oilcloth tarps back over the bodies and left the chamber. She found the old kerosene stove and the lanterns as she was walking back through the first chamber but she had no idea how to work them so she decided she would bring down a couple lanterns. She could make improvements to the space when she came home from school for her next break. She climbed up the ladder remembering to wipe the rungs clean of her fingerprints. Once back above ground she closed the hatch and wiped the old hasp.

She had been carrying with her the entire summer an old padlock that she found in her grandfather's garage and she hooked it through the hasp. She figured an old lock would draw less attention than a new one if someone found the hatch. She carefully replaced the floorboards and then covered the floor with the debris she had removed earlier. Satisfied and very excited she headed for the trailhead and her car.

Chapter Thirty-Six

Once the Sheriff felt confident that there were no other threats in the area, he released the SWAT teams. Each group headed back in the direction they came. The mood was somber and there was very little conversation as they departed the scene. The kids had been taken out, along with PIS, on the first ATV run. The ATVs had returned a little bit ago and were waiting for Dr. Parker to release the bodies so they could transport them back to the trailhead and the awaiting ambulances.

The Sheriff spent a few minutes in conversation with Buck and then with a hearty handshake thanked him profusely for his help the past couple days. The forensic techs had taken Buck's rifle along with the rifles of Manning and Sanchez. They would now be evidence. Manning and Sanchez would be placed on paid leave until the investigation into the shooting was over.

The Sheriff asked Buck to stop by the Sheriff's office as soon as he could and write out a statement. Since Buck was not going to be part of the investigation, the Sheriff released him and he and the two deputies started the long walk back to their cars which were up at the original trailhead.

As they approached the original crime scene, they ran into Moe Steiner and Jane Fitzpatrick. They had hiked back to the scene of Susan Corey's death one last time and were getting ready to head back to the trailhead when they heard all the explosions and shooting. The SWAT team passed them a while before and they started to follow in the same direction. The Sheriff had called Fitz a little bit ago and asked them to head his way.

Fitz waved to Buck as they approached. "Crazy day, huh?" she said.

Buck and the deputies filled her in on what had transpired. Moe had opened his notebook when the conversation began and he was carefully taking notes as the conversation progressed. Buck told them about PIS's conjecture that the older victim might have had military training possibly from Vietnam and Moe made a note to contact the military. He also told them about the gravesite that the young girl Sarah had told them belonged to momma. Fitz pulled out her phone and dialed a number.

Gary Cummings, the elected Coroner for Pitkin County, answered his phone on the second ring. He exchanged pleasantries with Fitz and then Fitz asked him if they were able to exhume a body that was buried in the woods without an exhumation order. Gary explained that since it was part of the investigation, they should have no issue but that he would issue an exhumation order anyway just in case. She would be covered. Fitz thanked him and hung up.

Buck wished her and Moe good luck and told them to call if they needed anything and he and the two deputies continued up the trail. There was very little conversation as they walked. Sanchez still seemed to be having issues with the death of the two boys. It was true that they were killed while trying to kill Buck and the deputies but he was still having a hard time dealing with it.

When they finally reached their cars, Buck thanked the two deputies for all their help and told them to call if they needed anything. He held Sanchez back a minute and reached into the glove box of his car. He handed Sanchez a business card for Susan Lewis, Psychologist.

"If you need someone to talk to, give her a call," Buck said. "She is really good and she helped me a lot after the shootout in Durango. Tell her I sent you."

Sanchez looked at the card and was about to say something when he hesitated and put the card in his pocket. "Thanks, Buck. I might give her a call."

They shook hands and Sanchez headed for his car and a couple days off. Buck slid into his car after putting his gear in the back of the Jeep and just sat for a minute and enjoyed the quiet. He had mixed feelings about not being involved in the investigation but he also knew that Steiner and Fitzpatrick were very good at their jobs and he had no doubt they would get to the bottom of it.

He thought about the kids for a minute and what a strange situation he had walked into. He would check on them in a couple days and make sure they were good. He pulled out his phone and called his boss.

Kevin Jackson, the Director of the Colorado Bureau of Investigation, answered almost immediately.

"Hey, Buck. I was ready to file a missing person's report on you. You ok?"

"Yes, sir. It's been a hard couple days," Buck replied.

The Director, no surprise to Buck, had been kept apprised of the entire chain of events by the Sheriff and told Buck he was proud of him. He was also sad that it was Buck that was the one to find the body of Ranger Susan Corey

Buck filled the Director in on the latest events and the Director listened carefully. He told him about the explosives and about the shootout and the two dead kids and about the other kids they found in the mine. When he was finished there was a long silence on the other end of the phone.

Finally, the Director said. "Two dead kids, that's rough. You going to be ok, or you need to talk to someone? And another shootout. Is there something you're not telling me?"

"No sir," replied Buck. "My head is on straight. Besides, I still have the number for the Psychologist you had me see after Durango. Things are really good."

Buck changed the subject. "I am going to stick around here for a couple days. I need to fill out a statement for the Sheriff and be available for the shooting investigators. May get in a little fishing while I am here."

"Ok. Call if you need anything." The Director hung up.

Buck was an avid fly fisherman and he tried to get in a little fishing whenever he could. Besides the statement he needed to give the Sheriff he also wanted to head over to the hospital to check on PIS. He started the car and pulled out of the lot.

Chapter Thirty-Seven

PIS had just come out of surgery when Buck arrived at the hospital. He was in recovery and still a bit groggy when Buck badged his way past the charge nurse and walked into the room. PIS looked up and smiled when he saw Buck.

"Agent Taylor, how good of you to come by."

Buck stood by the side of the bed. "You look pretty good for a guy just had surgery. They taking good care of you?"

"Surgeon says I should be able to get out of here in a day or two. The piece of wood only penetrated about three inches and it didn't hit anything vital. Going to be sore for a while."

"Good to hear," said Buck. He shook PIS's hand. "You need anything you call me. I owe you." PIS just nodded his head and then sunk back into the pillow and closed his eyes. Buck left his business card on the table next to the bed and walked out the door. His next stop was the Sheriff's office.

He left the hospital, turned left onto Route 15 and turned right onto Main Street. He reached the Sheriff's office in about five minutes and pulled into the parking lot. He walked into the office presented his ID to the desk officer and was buzzed through. He headed down the hall to see if the Sheriff had gotten back from the crime scene yet.

The Sheriff was sitting behind his desk. He was talking to a deputy who was seated in one of his visitor's chairs but he waved Buck in. The deputy stood up, nodded to Buck and walked out the door. Buck took a seat.

"Statement could have waited til tomorrow Buck."

"That's ok. Want to get it down on paper while it's still fresh in my mind," replied Buck.

They spent a few minutes discussing the events that had transpired and Buck told the Sheriff he had visited PIS at the hospital and not surprisingly he looked like he was hardly bothered by the whole thing. They chatted about PIS for a few minutes and speculated on the source of the scars they had seen on his back. He certainly was an interesting fellow.

The Sheriff stepped around his desk and shook Buck's hand. He thanked him for his help and led the way to the conference room down the hall. He found a pad of paper and a pen and told Buck to take his time. The Sheriff walked out and closed the door. Buck started writing and by the time he was finished, two hours later, he had written a small novel. Buck prided himself on details and he double and triple checked his statement before he stood up to find the Sheriff.

The Sheriff was on the phone, so Buck set the pad down on his desk and turned to walk out. The Sheriff held the phone against his chest and called after him.

"Funeral procession for Susan Corey is tomorrow afternoon. We are starting from the hospital parking lot at 1 PM. The family is not planning a church service, so the procession will head from here to the cemetery in Glenwood Springs for a graveside service. Thought you might like to be there."

Buck thanked the Sheriff and headed for his hotel. He needed a shower and a bunch of sleep. Buck was surprised that it was so dark when he walked out the front door of the Sheriff's office. He hadn't realized he had spent so much time writing his statement. He swung by a local deli that was still open, grabbed a sandwich and a bottle of Coke and headed for his hotel.

Buck had just opened the door to his hotel room when his phone rang. He recognized the number and answered the call.

"Hey, dad. Are you ok?" asked his oldest son David.

"Hey, David. Yeah, I'm good. A little tired. It's been a long couple days."

"I just ran into a couple of the Gunnison County SWAT guys in the bar and they said you were involved in another shootout. For real?"

Buck took a few minutes and gave David the Reader's Digest version of the events of the last couple days. About the hunt for Susan Corey and then the hunt for her killers and finding a family of children living in the woods south of Aspen with an old guy. He also acknowledged that there was, in fact, another shootout.

"Must have been rough finding out you guys shot two kids. Not sure how I would have reacted."

"Yeah," replied Buck. "The one deputy, Sanchez, took it pretty hard. Gonna take a while to put this one behind us."

"Listen, Dad. You need anything you let me know. And you better call Cassie and fill her in. Her team was heading to a fire along the Arizona/New Mexico border but she might have seen something about the shooting on the news. I haven't seen the news story yet but according to the SWAT guys they mentioned that you found the ranger's body.

They said their goodbyes and Buck hung up the phone. He really didn't want to listen to Cassie, his middle daughter, tonight but he knew she would be pissed if he didn't call. Cassie had quit law school a couple years back and took a wildland firefighters job with the Helena Hotshots out of Helena, Montana. Much to her mother's dismay, she had thrived in her new job. Right up until her death, Lucy still didn't like the idea of her daughter willingly putting herself in danger. It was bad enough that her husband faced certain danger all the time in his job.

Buck dialed Cassie's number. Cassie answered on the fourth ring.

"Hey, dad. Everything good? We are just getting ready to head into the woods. What's up?"

"Hi, kiddo. I just wanted you to hear it from me first and not the news. There was another shootout today. I am ok."

Buck gave her the same quick version of the story he had just given his son. When he was finished, there was silence on the other end of the line and he wondered for a second if he had dropped the call.

"Did you shoot one of the kids?" she asked.

"Won't know for a couple days. There were three of us shooting and we were pretty much shooting blind. The people shooting at us were well hidden."

"Ok. I've got to run but I will call when we come out of the field. Please be careful. I don't know if I could handle losing you too." Cassie hung up and Buck just sat there for a minute and looked at the phone. Cassie had been very close to her mother and she had taken her death hard even though they had all been expecting it for over five years. When it finally happened though, it still hurt and Cassie was still grieving, as were they all. Buck's whole world revolved around Lucy. She really was his soul mate.

Buck stripped off his clothes and jumped into the shower. The water felt good and he could feel a little life drifting back into his sore, tired body. He dried off and was getting ready to crawl under the sheets when his phone rang. He looked at his watch. Any time his phone rang this late, it wasn't good.

Buck answered his phone. "Buck Taylor."

"Buck. It's Earl Winters. Hope I didn't wake you but I may need your help with something."

Chapter Thirty-Eight

Buck listened carefully as the Sheriff explained the reason for his call this late. A young couple were heading back to their car after hiking along Conundrum Creek and had stopped near an old collapsed mining cabin to have dinner and they noticed a terrible smell like rotting flesh or spoiled meat drifting around the cabin. The took a cursory look around the clearing but couldn't find anything.

The smell was enough to run them off and they headed back to the main trail. They ran into a couple of the Sheriff's SWAT guys in the parking lot and told them what they had encountered. The two SWAT deputies followed them back down the trail to the turnoff for the side trail and smelled it almost immediately.

They followed the trail up to the old cabin and after looking around they noticed a couple loose boards and when they pulled up the boards, they found what appeared to be a locked metal hatch. The deputies reported that the smell was really bad near the hatch. Since it was getting pretty dark, they GPS marked the location of the cabin and escorted the young couple back to their car.

The Sheriff told Buck that he was able to catch Judge Franklin before he went to bed and the Judge was in the process of signing a search warrant for the hatch.

"Buck, my guys are going to be focused on the Susan Corey investigation for a while. I could use your help with this. If it doesn't turn out to be anything you can bug out but I would like some experienced eyes on this till we know what we are dealing with."

"No problem Sheriff. I know where the trailhead is. I can meet your guys there in say fifteen minutes." Buck was about to hang up when he had a thought. "Sheriff, can you get someone from public works to bring a small generator and a couple work lights to the site? Might help if we are going underground."

The Sheriff thanked Buck and hung up. It looked like Buck wasn't going to get any sleep tonight. He knew he should call Director Jackson and let him know what was going on but he decided to wait until they knew what they were dealing with before he made the call.

Buck put on clean jeans and a clean T-shirt, clipped his gun and badge to his belt and headed out the door. The Conundrum Creek trailhead was about a ten-minute drive through town, so he jumped on Main Street and headed southeast until he reached Route 15. He turned south on Route 15 and a few minutes later turned right at the turnoff for the Conundrum Creek trailhead. He pulled into the space behind two Pitkin County Sheriff's cars.

Buck climbed out of his car and walked around to the rear and opened the hatch. Just to be on the safe side, he slipped his ballistic vest over his shoulders and zipped it up. He put fresh batteries in his flashlight and added three more clips for his 45-caliber pistol in their respective pouches. He added his nylon CBI windbreaker and his CBI ball cap. He locked the rear hatch and headed to the small group of deputies assembled just at the entrance to the trailhead.

Buck shook hands with the four SWAT deputies. Sergeant Jamie Winters, the Sheriff's daughter, would be the lead officer on this little excursion into the unknown. She apologized for dragging Buck out after what he had been through but she appreciated his help. Buck nodded and suggested they get moving.

It took about an hour in the dark to get to the almost hidden turnoff for the cabin. Without the GPS Buck doubted they would have ever found it in the dark. Buck stopped for a minute and checked the air. There was definitely a foul smell in the air. The SWAT officers led the way and they all commented on the smell as they got closer to the cabin. Buck had a lot more experience than the young SWAT officers and he was willing to bet good money that they were going to find a dead body. The smell was unmistakable.

The old cabin was just as the Sheriff had described. The old timbers were laying every which way and most of what lay on the ground was rotten from years of being in the weather. Even the remaining floorboards had seen better days and Buck saw where the first deputy on the scene had pulled up one of the floorboards. The metal hatch lay below the floorboards, so Buck and the deputies removed the debris and pulled up the remaining floorboards.

Once they exposed the metal hatch, Buck took a few pictures of it from different angles with is cell phone camera. The hatch was covered in rust and still appeared to be sound, so Buck didn't think the metal had rusted through. The smell was intense. Buck took a picture of the padlock while it was still locked. It was definitely not a new padlock. It reminded him of the padlocks his father used to lock up his tool boxes.

Satisfied with the pictures he switched over to video and asked the deputy with the bolt cutters to cut the lock and remove it. Buck videoed the entire process. Buck stepped back away from the hatch and snapped open the thumb break on his holster. He rested his hand on his gun. The SWAT deputies raised their weapons to the ready position and Jamie Winters removed the padlock and lifted the hatch making sure she stayed out of the line of fire from her team.

The smell was overwhelming and one of the younger SWAT officers disappeared into the woods and threw up his dinner. Everyone stood back to try to let the air clear. Buck took a small jar of Vick's Vapor Rub out of one of the pockets in his ballistic vest and rubbed some under his nose. He passed the jar around and the SWAT officers followed suit. It helped but not as much as he had hoped. He was glad that he hadn't put on a good pair of jeans or T-shirt. These were definitely headed for the trash once they were finished. Buck had learned over the years that you can never get dead guy smell out of your clothes. He also knew it would take five or six showers to get the smell out his hair and nose.

Jamie looked at Buck and asked. "Should we wait for the lights from public works or should we go in with flashlights?"

"Let's not wait," replied Buck.

Jamie removed a portable electronic gas monitor from her backpack, attached it to a length of rope she carried and lowered it into the shaft. It would be a bad thing to walk into a mine full of methane gas. She watched the monitor as it reached the floor and then pulled it back up. Nothing so far. Just to be safe, she had her guys pull out their full-face gas masks and once snug she stepped onto the top rung of the ladder and climbed down into the dark. She was followed closely by her team. Buck would remain topside until they had cleared the mine.

Chapter Thirty-Nine

The bar was packed and she had been nursing the same beer for most of the evening. Two of her girlfriends were heading back to college on Monday and tonight was girl's night out. The noise from the crowd and the laughter at their table made it hard to concentrate but she was running out of time and she needed to find the perfect subject.

She had never been able to discuss with her grandfather how he chose his victims. What little she did know didn't help. She knew he chose women who were traveling alone or women who wouldn't be missed, but how did he know. There were well over two hundred people in the bar tonight and she was having trouble focusing on one or two who might make the cut.

Getting asked to dance every couple songs didn't help either and her girlfriends kept getting on her case about not drinking. She still had doubts that she would be able to do this. She was still struggling with the fact that she didn't have any of the signs that came with being a serial killer. She had spent time over the summer in the library reading everything she could find on serial killers and she didn't seem to fit the profile.

Of course, the more she thought about it, her grandfather didn't fit the pattern either, at least the part she knew about him. She wondered how far he would have gotten and how many women he would have killed if he hadn't gotten into the accident that night. The story the family always told was that he was coming home from visiting a friend in Glenwood Springs.

According to family lore, there was a terrible rain storm that night and the roads were slick as glass. In those days, the late fifties early sixties, very few vehicles were available with four-wheel drive, especially in family cars. Her grandfather had been coming around a sharp corner, lost control on the slick road and the car flew off the road and crashed down into a creek bed before flipping over several times and wrapping around a tree. Her grandfather hadn't been found for several days until a county road crew noticed the damaged guardrail on the side of the road.

By the time they were able to get him out of the car and into the hospital, he was, for all practical purposes, dead but the doctors believed that the cooler temperatures had actually slowed his body down enough to keep him from bleeding to death. Her grandmother, her dad and his brother Stewart had raced to the hospital as soon as the Sheriff called.

The county had mounted a search for him but the weather was so poor that for several days the searchers couldn't stay out more than a couple hours. He was lucky the road crew had noticed the guardrail, or he wouldn't have made it. What her grandmother found at the hospital that night was a broken man. The doctors weren't sure he would survive more than a few days but he surprised everyone and lived another fifty or so years.

His body was broken almost to the point of not being recognized. He had broken his back in several places and the doctors were certain he would never walk again. Of course, they weren't sure he would ever wake up, so they weren't concerned about his being able to walk. That time would come if he survived. The story was he was in a coma for several weeks and when he finally woke up, he was a quadriplegic. He had completely lost the use of his arms and legs. Her grandmother had been devastated.

She never doubted that her grandmother loved her grandfather but she imagined there must have been times when she would have preferred that he had died in that accident. Her grandmother had spent the rest of her life being his twenty-four hour a day caregiver. She never saw her grandmother complain.

So here she sat in a crowded bar trying to wrap her head around her grandfather's life and what his legacy might have been had he survived to continue his craft.

She was just about to give up her quest and order another beer when she spotted a tall, good-looking young man who had just entered the bar with some friends. She could feel the excitement build in her very private areas. She wasn't sure if the urges she felt were to make him her first victim or just to have sex with him.

She wondered how she would be able to do it. If she drugged him how would she get him to the old cabin? There was no way she could carry him that was for sure.

She hadn't really considered that part of her plan. This changed everything.

If she invited him into the woods to see something, go skinny dipping in a hot spring or just to have sex she might not be able to overpower him when the time came. If he fought back, she would lose. She had never been very athletic. Suddenly she needed a new plan. She thought about how hard this serial killer stuff was going to be. So many decisions had to be carefully made and evaluated to make sure one didn't get caught.

She turned back to the conversation going on at the table and she danced a few more dances. Then suddenly in a moment of clarity, she had a thought. Maybe she was looking in the wrong direction. Female serial killers were not all that common but if she chose a female victim instead of a male that would throw the whole thing out of whack. If the authorities did discover her little torture chamber, they would start looking for a man. This could work. She would most likely be able to overpower a woman at least until she got good enough and developed her real technique. With all she needed to learn she needed to make the first kill as easy as possible. She still didn't even know if she could do it.

The initial problem solved she still had to think about how to get her victim to the cabin. She decided that this first time she would try to lead the victim to the cabin before she completely passed out. The hot spring thing might work. She could find a woman to befriend. Someone who had a little too much to drink and might need a ride home. No one would notice one woman helping another woman who was a little tipsy. It's what women do to avoid predators.

She had been able to score some ruffies from a guy she had dated for a while. She had no idea why he had them but it didn't matter. He needed money and he sold her a small bag without any questions. Ruffies were typically called the date rape drug but the reality was that only a very small percentage of rapes were actually attributed to being drugged. Most rape victims were either drunk or under the influence of some more common drug. If she could slip her victim a ruffie away from the bar or even down by the cabin, she wouldn't have to worry about getting the body there by herself.

Chapter Forty

The SWAT team assembled at the bottom of the ladder and immediately assumed a defensive posture. Sergeant Winters signaled the team to move forward and with rifles at the ready position and flashlights on they moved down the tunnel side by side. As they entered the first larger chamber, they broke off to either side of the tunnel and covered the room with their lights.

Two of the SWAT members moved down the right side of the room and two moved down the left. Sergeant Winters and her teammate had just reached the old broken-down bed when she heard a yell from the other side of the room followed by.

"HOLY SHIT!!!"

And "what the Fuck!!"

She turned towards the sound and saw, in the lights, what had caused such a reaction from her teammates. The body appeared to be hanging from some old shackles that had been mounted to the wall. It was blackish-purple and bloated so as to be almost unrecognizable. Sergeant Winters stepped over to her teammates while the fourth SWAT member cleared the rest of the room. She looked the body up and down.

Even with their masks on, the smell was almost overpowering. The skin was already starting to slough off the bones and in another couple days the body would have ended up in a lump on the floor.

She lowered her rifle and pointed to the cut marks that covered the body. They were coated in dry blood and were starting to spread open as decomposition caused the body to expand. There was a dry pool of blood under the body that had mostly disappeared into the dirt floor.

Suddenly the room was bathed in light and the three SWAT members almost jumped out of their skins. The other team member who had cleared the room had discovered a couple battery operated lanterns on an old wooden table and turned them on. That was when they noticed the victim's eyes. They could almost feel the fear that this person had experienced. It was utterly ghastly.

Sergeant Winters directed two of her members to continue searching the tunnel that they could now see at the opposite end of the chamber from where they had entered. She and her other teammate began searching the body chamber. She spotted the old cabinet hanging on the wall over the table with the lanterns on it and opened the door revealing a rolled-up leather bundle. She left it where it was. She would let Buck or the forensics team do the honors. Her job was to secure the space.

A voice came over her radio. "Sarge, you need to come back here and see this."

"What is it Eddie?' she responded

"Not sure I can describe it. You better come take a look."

She closed the cabinet and her and her partner headed down the tunnel following the lights from their flashlights. They had gone a few yards down the tunnel when they saw another room and the faint light of her team's lights. She entered the room and stopped in the doorway unable to believe what she was looking at. Her teammates had removed some old deteriorating covers from some old rickety beds and there on the beds were a whole shit load of mummified bodies. All appeared to be naked and all appeared to be female.

"What the hell did we just walk into?" she asked no one in particular.

One of her teammates responded. "Looks like one of those old Egyptian tombs they show on the Discovery Channel."

She couldn't agree more.

"Ok. Don't touch anything else. Let's go back the way we came. This is a crime scene and we need to clear out."

She left the room and headed for the ladder followed by the rest of her team. Once up the ladder they all quickly removed their masks and tried to breath clean air but the air around them still smell like dead guy. They moved away from the hatch and Buck followed. He gave them a minute to catch their breaths.

"Ok, Sergeant. What did you find down there?"

"Not sure Buck. There is a fresh body hanging up that looks like it was tortured unmercifully and we found a room full of mummified bodies. Looks like all women and looks like they were all tortured as well."

"Alright. Let's tape off the area and prepare for a long night. I called the Sheriff a little bit ago and asked him to have the public works guys bring out an exhaust fan and one hundred feet of flexible air duct besides the lights and generator. See if we can get rid of some of the smell. I need to call the Sheriff back. He is not going to be happy."

The Sheriff was still at his desk. It had been a long couple days and he had a bunch of paperwork to still get through. His cell phone rang and he looked at the number.

"Fuck, Buck. I guess I ain't gonna get much paperwork done tonight, am I?"

"Sorry, Earl. This might be as bad as it gets."

Buck went on to describe the scene that Sergeant Winters had described to him. The Sheriff listened quietly. Buck asked the Sheriff to call Dr. Parker, the Forensic Pathologist, and also have the fire department bring out some Scott Pack breathing tanks. The Sheriff asked Buck about forensics. His forensic techs were still at the other old mine gathering evidence and so were Fitz and Steiner. He was spread pretty thin.

"You want me to call Denver and see if they can spare me to work this with you guys?"

"Sure would appreciate the help. Thanks, Buck," the Sheriff replied.

Buck hung up from the Sheriff and dialed the Director.

A very sleepy voice answered the phone. "Buck, don't you ever sleep?"

"Sorry to wake you sir but it's important."

"It always is when you call. Ok, I'm awake. Let's hear it."

Buck described the scene, just as he did with The Sheriff along with the Sheriff's request for help. Although Buck had statewide jurisdiction, it was always the policy of the Colorado Bureau of Investigation to work with local law enforcement only when they requested help. Buck had for the most part always abided by that time-honored tradition. When he finished, the Director gave a low whistle. "I assume you are thinking serial killer? Should we call in the FBI?"

Buck replied. "I'd like to hold off until we know more. The Sheriff's team is spread pretty thin. I'd like to roll the forensics team from Grand Junction and also bring in Paul Webber to give me a hand. He did really good on the Montrose thing."

"Ok, Buck. I will call Stan and have him roll everyone. Anything else?"

Stan Greenheck was the Agent in Charge of the Grand Junction office of the CBI and technically Buck's direct boss. However, over the past couple years, Buck had been working more for the Director and the governor than he had for Stan and it always bothered him, but Stan was always good natured about it because Buck got results and he was Buck's boss. That was good for him.

"Yes, Sir" Buck replied. "Do we have any Forensic Pathologists on standby that we can call? Dr. Parker out here is already up to her hips in dead bodies and I am sure she would appreciate the help."

"I will start making calls   Looks like we are going to be waking up a lot of people. How do you always get involved in shit like this?"

"Just right place, right time I guess. Thank you, sir." Buck hung up his phone.

Chapter Forty-One

The public works crew and the fire department arrived while Buck had been on the phone with the Director. Sergeant Winters and her team were helping them set up the generator and two of her guys went back down into the mine to string up some temporary lights. The smell in the area around the shaft had dissipated a little and it was easier to breathe.

Buck's phone rang and he answered. "Hey, Paul. Sorry to get you out of bed."

"No worries Buck. Don't usually get a call from the Director at three o'clock in the morning. He filled me in but I wanted to check with you before I left Grand Junction to see if there was anything else you needed from here?"

"Thanks, Paul. No, I think we have everything covered. Get here when you can but don't kill yourself. We aren't going anywhere anytime soon. Oh, and Paul. Wear your oldest clothes. Something you won't have a problem throwing away when we are done."

"That bad, huh?" Paul replied.

"Yeah. That bad. See you soon." Buck hung up. It was time to head down into the mine. Buck was glad he wasn't claustrophobic. This would be a bad week to have that problem. Buck walked over to the two firemen who had brought in the Scott Pack breathing apparatus and they helped him put on one of the tanks. Buck was familiar with the system and had used one on several occasions.

Buck checked his cell phone battery to make sure he had enough juice for pictures and climbed down into the shaft. His first mental note was to have forensics check the hatch cover side walls and ladder rungs for prints. He stepped foot on the dirt floor and was pleased to see that the lights were working just fine.

Sergeant Winters stepped foot on the floor next to him and told him to follow her. She proceeded down the short tunnel and into the first chamber. With the lights on, it wasn't nearly as foreboding. Buck asked her to hold up as he took out his cell phone and took a couple overall pictures of the chamber. They then proceeded over to the body.

Buck took multiple pictures of the body, insitu. What Sergeant Winters had described was even more gruesome under the lights. The body was completely naked and obviously female. Both hands were shackled to the wall and her feet were shackled as well. The body was covered with hundreds of slices, some deeper than others. The number of very shallow cuts was amazing and varied in length from a small knick to one across her stomach that must have been a foot long.

"You ever see anything like this before?" asked Sergeant Winters.

"No, but I have read about it. It's an ancient Chinese method of torture. Can't recall the Chinese name for it but it translates to something like death by a thousand cuts."

"You must read some really weird books," she responded

Buck laughed. It actually helped to break the mood a little.

"Ok, Sergeant. Let's see the rest."

Sergeant Winters showed him the bed, which he photographed from several angles and then she opened the cabinet to reveal the leather roll. Buck took pictures of the roll and then carefully removed it from the cabinet and laid it on the old wooden table. While he did that, he also took pictures of the LED lanterns that were on the table. They appeared to be fairly new.

Buck switched his phone camera to video and asked the Sergeant to open up the roll. She carefully untied the two leather strings and unrolled the bundle. She stepped back as Buck panned his camera along the length of the bundle and then he put his phone away.

"Oh my god!" exclaimed the Sergeant.

"Yeah," replied Buck. With his gloved hand he picked up one of the scalpels and brought it closer to his face mask. "Beautiful workmanship," he said.

He placed it back in the bundle and stepped aside as the other two SWAT members pulled the flexible duct past him. He heard the exhaust fan fire up and almost immediately the air seemed to get better. Buck lifted off his facemask and took a breath. He could work in here now without the Scott Pack. He lifted it over his shoulders and set it on the ground turning off the airflow. Sergeant Winters did the same thing.

Buck left the bundle laid out on the table and followed the Sergeant down the next tunnel. They stepped into another small chamber and sure enough, there were four rickety wooden bunk beds and on each bed were several mummified bodies. Buck pulled out his phone and photographed each bed and then a couple overall shots of the room itself. He slowly walked around the room stopping at each bed and looking carefully at each body.

Even through the mummification he could see that these women had all been tortured with the same method as the newest victim in the other room.

Sergeant Winters voiced the question he had been forming in his mind.

"It looks like these women all died the same way as the woman out front but these bodies look positively ancient. Can't be the same killer, can it?"

Buck looked at her. "Excellent question, Sergeant. I would think not but the methods look very similar." He turned around and headed back to the front chamber. Dr. Parker had just entered the room and was looking at the body hanging off the shackles. She looked at Buck.

"Remind me the next time you come to town to take a vacation, ok?" She smiled and Buck and the Sergeant laughed. He knew she was partly serious.

They followed the same path as he and the Sergeant had followed earlier and returned to the front chamber. Dr. Parker looked depressed. She had never performed an autopsy on a mummy before and now she had fifteen of them. She told Buck that CBI Director Jackson had called her on the way over and told her he was flying in several experts on mummies from the Museum of Nature & Science in Denver. He also had two more Forensic Pathologists in route and they should be here in a couple hours.

"Alright," said Dr. Parker. "Let's start with the newest body."

She and Buck gloved up and she approached the body. Dr. Parker was very thorough as she probed the body, carefully examining every cut mark. After about forty minutes she stepped back and removed her gloves.

Chapter Forty-Two

She had spotted the girl about an hour before, while she was dancing with that hunky Rusty Grover. The girl was moving past the empty tables and sneakily drinking what was left in the empty glasses. She could see the girl was getting pretty loaded.

The girl was cute, with shoulder-length blond hair pulled back in a ponytail. She had a faded blue streak in her hair on the right side. She was wearing a pair of ripped jeans, an old sweater and sneakers that had seen better days. The girl made it through several empty tables before the bouncer came and spoke a few words to her and escorted her out the front door and into the street.

She excused herself from the group and headed for the restroom but veered off and after checking to make sure her friends didn't see her leave, she walked out the front door. The night had gotten a lot cooler than it had been a few hours ago and she shivered as she pulled her jacket tighter around her.

She wasn't sure if she was really that cold or if her nerves were kicking in. Was she really about to do this? She still had doubts about her role as a killer. On some level, it felt right but on other levels, she wondered if she *was just doing this because she was fascinated by her grandfather. She always looked up to him and finding out he had killed several women in his younger years didn't change her opinion of him.*

She got into her car and pulled out of the parking lot. She had no idea where the girl had gone, so she started driving up and down the streets and alleys. She had only gone through two alleys when she found her behind one of the hotels looking in the dumpsters and then staggering down the alley.

The girl looked a little startled when she pulled up next to her and rolled down the window. She asked the girl if she would like to get some real food and as it penetrated through her booze fogged mind, the girl told her that she would like that. The girl climbed into the passenger seat, put her head back into the headrest and fell asleep.

She stopped at the all-night convenience store and bought the girl a burrito and a bottle of water. She slipped the ruffie into the bottle of water and shook it up to make sure it dissolved. The girl was still sound asleep, so she headed for the trailhead. This might be easier than she imagined.

She pulled into the trailhead and pulled the car as far off the road as she could. Next, she walked around to the passenger side of the car and opened the door. She shook the girl a couple times until she started to wake up. She told the girl that she had food for her and a place to stay but she needed to get out of the car and walk with her.

The girl took the burrito, unwrapped it and started to eat like she hadn't had food in a couple days. She washed the burrito down with a big swig of water. The girl half stumbled out of the car and she held her by the arm and started down the trail. She wasn't sure if it was the ruffie or the booze but the girl just stumbled along with her like a little-lost puppy. There was no conversation.

By the time they reached the old cabin, the girl was almost incoherent and proceeded to pass out. She had to drag her limp body the last twenty feet to the shaft. She unlocked the padlock and opened the hatch. She stopped for a minute and listened to the sounds around her. She didn't hear any people, which was just as she expected. She grabbed the coil of climbing rope that she had left at the top of the ladder and ran the rope around the girl's chest. She put on her gloves and lifted the girl over the edge of the hatch. Even though the girl couldn't have weighed more than a hundred pounds it surprised her how difficult it was to lower her and the roped slipped through her hands and the girl fell the last fifteen feet down the shaft. She hit the ground hard.

She stepped onto the top rung of the ladder and started down pulling the hatch closed as she went. She reached the bottom and stepped onto the ground. The girl was still unconscious, so she untied the rope and dragged her to the chamber. Once there she stripped off the girl's clothes and threw them in a corner.

She had trouble holding the limp girl in place and hooking up the shackles, and by the time she was finished, she was sweating. She stood back and looked at the girl hanging against the wall. Her body was fairly thin and *she had small pert breasts. She looked like she hadn't eaten well in quite some time.*

She walked over to the old bed and slowly undressed while watching the girl. She laid down on the bed and tried to get herself excited but it just wasn't happening. Maybe it was the nerves or maybe, unlike her grandfather, there just wasn't a sexual component to her needs. She decided to just get on with the cutting.

She opened the cabinet and pulled out the old leather bundle. Once untied, she rolled it out on the table and pulled out a thin scalpel. She walked over to the body and stood for a minute. She was trying to figure out how to begin.

Her first slice was very tentative and the scalpel barely drew any blood. She was almost disappointed. The second slice was across the girl's stomach and that one drew a lot of blood. The girl twitched. After a few more slices she finally figured out just how much pressure to exert and she began to make progress.

By the time the girl started to wake up, she had lost so much blood that she wasn't able to offer much resistance. She tried to scream through the gag but nothing came out. The girl's eyes showed the fear she was experiencing and it made her cut even faster as she watched the life slowly leave the girl's eyes. The ground at her feet was covered in blood and she stepped back and admired her handy work.

She had been keeping track and she had gotten to almost five hundred slices before the girl died. She was proud of her accomplishment. Not bad for a first-timer. She used a container of water she had brought down earlier to scrub her scalpel and wipe the blood off herself. Surprisingly there wasn't much.

She put the scalpel back in its place in the bundle, rolled up the bundle and placed it back in the cabinet. She walked back to the old bed and put her clothes back on. She once again looked at the girl. She was pleased and she felt no remorse. As a matter of fact, she didn't really feel anything. Maybe she did have the killer gene in her like her grandfather. She checked to make sure she hadn't left anything, turned off the lanterns and climbed back out of the shaft.

Morning was still a few hours away, so she locked up the hatch replaced the floorboards and the debris and headed for her car. She felt very tired. Killing someone slowly, was hard work. She might have to pick up the pace on the next one.

Chapter Forty-Three

Dr. Parker stepped back from the body and leaned against the table under the cabinet. "Death was probably from massive blood loss. I counted roughly five hundred slices of varying depth and length. The autopsy will tell more but I think the cut along her throat might have knicked the artery. But even if it didn't, she wouldn't have lasted much longer than she did. Based on the decomp I'm gonna guess she has been down here about a week, maybe a week and a half."

"Can you tell anything about the killer from the cuts?" Buck asked.

"Not really. There are a few cuts that look like they might have been tentative. Possibly the first couple slices. What surprises me is that there are no signs of resistance in the cuts. It looks like she didn't fight back or try to twist out of the way. I will bet we find some kind of drug in her system when we get her on the table."

Dr. Parker told Buck it was ok to remove the body. She was going to go see if she could do some preliminary work on the mummified bodies in the other room. Buck asked Sergeant Winters to have the paramedics come down and take out the fresh body. She told him that his forensic team had arrived from Grand Junction and they were carrying in their equipment. And also that Paul Webber was upstairs. Buck thanked her and asked her to send everyone down. He would wait for them here so that Dr. Parker wasn't alone.

The paramedics and the firefighters were the first to climb down the ladder and some of them openly gasped when they walked into the chamber and saw the body hanging there. The paramedics pulled out a poly body bag and laid it on the ground in front of the body. The firefighter using a cordless side grinder proceeded to cut through the shackles and they gently lowered the body onto the body bag and zipped it up.

Paul Webber and the CBI forensics team entered the chamber. They were all wearing one-piece white Tyvek overalls with their hoods up, Tyvek booties, surgical masks and nitrile gloves. Buck watched as they each stopped and looked at the body as the firefighters and paramedics lowered her onto the body bag.

"You ok Paul?" Buck asked. Paul looked a little green.

Paul answered hesitantly. "Yeah. I'm good. Been a while since I saw a body like that. Wow."

Buck walked Paul and the forensic team through the mine just as he had Dr. Parker. He pointed out areas he definitely wanted printed and swabbed for DNA. They ran into Dr. Parker in the second chamber. She had had one of the SWAT officers help her move the bodies very gingerly off the first bed and was kneeling next to the three mummified bodies taking pictures. She looked up as Buck and his team entered the already crowded chamber.

Buck introduced her to Paul Webber and the forensics team. She would be spending a lot more time in this chamber, so they needed to strategize so as not to be tripping over each other. Until the bodies were removed completely from the mine, Dr. Parker was in charge and she would direct the forensic team to gather evidence she felt was important while they also followed their own procedures. It was going to be a very long day for everyone.

Buck could see that Paul Webber needed some fresh air, so he suggested they head topside. Once outside the shaft, Paul took off his mask and unzipped his jumpsuit.

"Oh my god Buck. What the hell have you gotten us into?"

Buck was just about to answer when his phone rang. Buck looked at the number and answered the call. "Yes, sir Director?"

"Hey, Buck. I think I have everyone you need headed your way. Can you fill me in?"

Chapter Forty-Four

Buck described the scene inside the mine to the Director while Paul stood next to him and listened. Buck told him about the condition of the fresh body and about the mummified remains in the back chamber. He told him about the knife set they had discovered. He thanked him for getting the team assembled so quickly and especially for the help he had summoned to help Dr. Parker with the autopsies.

The Director asked Buck to speculate on the scene. Buck never liked speculation. He preferred to have the facts in front of him, but he knew that anything he told the Director would stay within a very small circle.

"Well, sir. It looks like we have two different crimes here. We have what appears to be some very old multiple murder serial killings and then a much more recent kill, carried out in what appears to be a very similar manner. We have no idea how long the mummified bodies have been here but we know that the most recent murder occurred within the last week to week and a half. No way at this point to know how the two crimes are related but from my very cursory observation I would say they definitely have a relationship."

The Director listened as Buck spoke. He interrupted only once with a question which Buck answered as best he could and then he told Buck to stay in touch and call if he needed any help. Buck hung up his phone. He was just going to talk to Paul as the Sheriff entered the clearing followed by several people who looked like grad students and an older gentleman wearing a safari hat.

"Buck, ran into Professor Frederick Standish in the parking lot. These young folks work with him." Buck introduced himself to the Professor and his team. The Professor shook his hand.

"Pleasure to meet you, Agent Taylor. I am a Professor of Archeology at the University of Colorado Boulder and these young men and women are some of my top grad students."

The Professor was probably in his fifties but appeared to be very fit. He wore green cargo pants and a safari shirt with his sleeves rolled up. He and each member of his team carried a backpack. They all looked like they came ready to work.

The Professor continued. "When Director Jackson called me this morning and described what you had found I was intrigued, to say the least. He expressed the urgency of the situation, so I gathered up my team and headed right out. We'd like to get to work right away."

Buck asked Sergeant Winters to escort the Professor and his students back to the rear chamber to help Dr. Parker and they all disappeared down the shaft. The Sheriff followed them down the ladder.

Buck hadn't noticed that the sun had come up and he looked at his watch. He needed some sleep but there was a lot to do. "Paul, I need you to head over to the county clerk's office and the tax assessor's office and see if you can figure out who owns this cabin. If it was part of a mining claim, the path might get a little convoluted but see what you can find out. Second, take some pictures of the lanterns on the wooden table. They look brand new. See if you can find out who in town sells that brand and then see if maybe someone has security footage of the purchase."

Paul zipped up his suit and replaced his hood and mask and headed back down into the mine. Buck found his backpack and pulled a warm bottle of Coke out of the mesh sleeve on the side. He took a long drink and sat down for a minute on the pile of logs that used to be a cabin.

The Sheriff climbed out of the hatch and walked over and sat down next to Buck. The sun had cleared the mountains and it was shaping up to be a beautiful fall day. The aspen leaves around the cabin were starting to turn yellow and the contrast to the green of the pine and spruce trees was a magical sight. The summer had been unusually wet and that meant that along with the yellows there would also be a large amount of red and orange colors this year.

Buck was thinking about the times that he and his late wife Lucy used to sit on the handicap dock at the park in Gunnison and look out over the Gunnison River at the aspens on the other side. Lucy always loved the fall colors. Buck wiped a tear from his eye. He missed her very much.

"You ok, Buck?" The Sheriff asked.

"Yeah," Buck replied. "Well, what did you think down there?"

"Not sure what to think. I'm worried that we have someone trying to imitate a bunch of killings from a long time ago. Scares me to think we might have a serial killer in our little town. Was also wondering if I should call the FBI and get them involved.?"

Buck looked at the Sheriff. "Let's hold off on the FBI until we know more. I will take care of them. You have enough on your plate right now. How is Fitz coming with identifying the old guy at the other mine?"

The Sheriff filled Buck in on the investigation so far. The Doctor had pulled the two bullets from Susan Corey and the state crime lab had determined that they came from the old guy's M1 carbine. The woman's remains had been unearthed from the mountaintop grave but they were waiting on Dr. Parker to perform the autopsy. So, nothing on that front yet. Moe Steiner had taken pictures of all the kids along with DNA swabs and fingerprints and he was running them through every system available both state and federal looking for any matches to missing kids. He mentioned that Fitz had been having trouble getting any kind of response from the military on any possible ties the old guy had to one of the services.

Buck stopped the Sheriff and pulled out his phone, looked up a number and dialed.

"Hey Buck, how are you brother?" answered Jess Gonzales, the Agent in Charge of the DEA's office in Grand Junction.

"Doing great, Jess. Good to hear your voice," Buck replied.

Jess gave Buck a little rundown on where things stood with the Durango investigation and Buck gave her a quick debrief on the shooting of the ranger.

"We all heard about the ranger getting killed. Heard you were involved. You got a drug angle on this one?" Jess asked.

"Sorry, Jess. No drug angle but I need a favor for Sheriff Winters over in Pitkin County. His homicide folks are looking into a possible military angle on the old guy that was killed and his investigator is not getting much help from the military. You did such a great job getting us the info on the Green Beret in Durango I was wondering if you might be able to push someone to help the Sheriff?"

"For you Buck, anything. Let me make a few calls. Can you text me the contact info for the lead investigator?"

Buck said he would and they chatted for a few more minutes. Buck hung up the phone and immediately pulled up Fitz's contact info and texted it to Jess.

"Thanks, Buck. I appreciate that," said the Sheriff. He looked at his watch.

"I need to run. The procession for Susan Corey starts in less than two hours. See if you can make it." The Sheriff stood up, shook Buck's hand and headed down the trail. Buck had almost forgotten about the procession for Corey. He would need to make some time to be there.

Paul Webber came out of the hatch and took off his mask. He had pictures of the lanterns and he also had digital fingerprints from the girl in the front chamber. He had gotten them from the forensic tech and told Buck he was going to swing by the Sheriff's office and run them through AFIS.

Buck stood up, grabbed his backpack and told the deputy who was now manning the crime scene entrance that he would be back in a while. They both signed out with the deputy and then he and Paul headed down the trail towards their cars. Buck needed to shower before he went to the service for Susan Corey. He stunk of dead guy and he didn't want to offend anyone. He told Paul where he would be and they parted company in the parking lot. Buck headed for his hotel.

Chapter Forty-Five

The funeral procession for Ranger Susan Corey pulled out of the hospital parking lot and turned onto Main Street. The procession was led by a Pitkin County Sheriff's patrol car with lights flashing. It was followed by a Colorado Parks and Wildlife Department pickup truck full of flowers that had been delivered to the coroner's office over the past couple days. The pickup was followed by the black hearse bearing the flag-draped coffin carrying the body of Susan Corey. Behind the hearse was the Sheriff and then a contingent of over one hundred cars and emergency vehicles from Pitkin County as well as several of the towns and counties surrounding Aspen.

Buck pulled out of the parking lot as the last emergency vehicle passed in front of him. He had gotten back to the hotel and taken three showers to try to get rid of the smell. He wore his cleanest pair of jeans and a clean T-Shirt. He hadn't expected to be here this long, so he hadn't packed anything more than the three-days supply of clothes in his GO bag.

The procession traveled along Main Street and then continued on as Main Street turned into Highway 82. Buck was amazed at the outpouring of love and support as they traveled through town. All along the sides of the road people were standing and waving American flags. Even after the highway had begun, there were crowds of people on the road. Susan Corey was getting a heroes send-off. Something she very much deserved.

As the procession crossed the line between Pitkin and Garfield Counties, several Garfield County Sheriff's patrol cars and emergency vehicles joined the procession. The procession turned off Highway 82 and proceeded up Grand Avenue to the Rosebud Cemetery. The procession stopped behind a black limousine and everyone exited their vehicles and lined up along both sides of the pathway leading to Susan Corey's grave.

Buck felt a little underdressed with all the spit and polished class "A" uniforms that were lined up on the walkway, so he walked behind the honor guard and stood off to one side. Miguel Vargas, the Chief Ranger for the Glenwood Springs office of the Colorado Parks and Wildlife Department stepped up onto the path. He was dressed in his class "A" uniform, forest green pants and short jacket, tan shirt with green tie and his green "Smokey the Bear" hat. He was escorting an older woman and man whom Buck figured must be her parents. Behind him, a female ranger, also in Class "As" escorted a young man in a dark suit. This must be her son.

The flag-draped casket was carried by six CPW Rangers and followed the family. Everyone along the path stood at attention and saluted as the casket went by. Buck placed his hand over his heart. Buck was surprised as a shadow crossed his side and he turned to find PIS standing next to him. His right arm was in a sling and he was dressed as always, except today instead of a bright red cummerbund and ascot, PIS was wearing a forest green cummerbund and ascot. He stood alongside Buck and placed his hand over his heart.

To say Buck was surprised to see the Brit was an understatement. He just had surgery yesterday and here he was looking like his old self, except for the sling. Buck also noticed that the hole made by the piece of wood that had pierced his linen coat was sporting a brand new black patch.

The casket reached the grave site and everyone along the path filled in around the family who were sitting in the front row. Miguel Vargas gave a moving eulogy and several rangers from her office also spoke about Susan Corey. A local chaplain continued with the service. Buck gathered from the service that Susan Corey was not really a religious person. It was a beautiful service under a clear blue Colorado sky but it didn't have much of a religious tone to it.

The chaplain finished the service and the six Rangers who had been part of the honor guard folded the American flag and presented it to Susan Corey's mother. In the distance a bugler played taps. The family stood and headed back to the limo and Vargas announced that there would be food and drinks available at the CPW office. Buck and PIS silently followed the crowd and Buck offered PIS a ride to the CPW office, which he accepted.

Once in the car, Buck looked at PIS. "Surprised to see you here today. Did you escape from the hospital?" he asked PIS.

"Doctor said I was a miraculous patient and that I could leave whenever I was ready. Couldn't stand being locked up inside that long. The sheriff was nice enough to give me a ride up here. It was quite a moving procession."

Buck agreed and they headed over to the CPW office for refreshment. In the parking lot of the CPW building was a huge white tent, so Buck and PIS headed that way. Once inside they each grabbed a sandwich and a bottle of water and began milling about. Buck was amazed at how many people showed up and PIS was amazed at how many of those people Buck actually knew.

Buck and PIS walked over to the table where the family was sitting and Miguel Vargas stood and introduced Buck and PIS to Susan Corey's parents and her son. He mentioned that they had been instrumental in finding Susan and her parents thanked them profusely. Buck was a little embarrassed but PIS was his jovial self and had launched into a lengthy conversation with the family. Buck stepped away and signaled for Miguel to follow him.

Away from the table, Buck asked Miguel how the son was holding up. Miguel explained that even though his grandparents lived in Pueblo, they had agreed to move up here and stay in Susan's house until Jimmy graduated next year. Buck knew that a fund had been set up for the boy asked Miguel how they were doing with raising money. Buck had donated money this morning before he left his hotel room.

Miguel said. "Craziest thing. A lawyer showed up at the bank in town that was handling the donations and gave the bank a certified check for one hundred thousand dollars. He also had a letter telling the bank that a college fund had been set up in James Corey's name at a bank in the Bahamas and that the bank would cover all of Jimmy's college expenses for a four-year degree to any college Jimmy chose to attend. The bank manager had been totally floored but he checked it out and both the check and the account in the Bahamas were real."

"That's amazing. No idea where the funds came from?" asked Buck.

"Not a clue. Jimmy has a guardian angel someplace." Miguel shook Buck's hand. "Thanks for everything you did for Susan. You ever need anything you give us a call. We owe you." He walked back to the family and sat down at the table.

Buck watched as PIS shook hands with Jimmy and his grandfather and gave his grandmother a big hug. He shook hands with Miguel and headed back to where Buck was standing. Buck had an idea running around in his head but it didn't want to land. Buck had watched PIS interact with Jimmy Corey and he wondered silently, if it was possible, that the money and the college fund somehow came from PIS. "Nah. How was that even possible? After all, this is PIS we are talking about. But then again, who was PIS, really?"

Buck and PIS headed back to Buck's car. Once inside, Buck told PIS about his conversation with Miguel and about the money. PIS never reacted. He just said how nice it was that someone was looking out for the young man, then he closed his eyes and went to sleep. Buck woke PIS as they pulled into the parking lot of the hospital and PIS thanked him for the ride and stepped out of the car. Buck watched him walk through the front door to the hospital. He pulled out his phone and called Paul Webber.

Chapter Forty-Six

The thrill of the kill had started to fade. She had gone home that night and slept like a baby. The next morning, she still felt wired. The response hadn't been sexual but the kill had still excited her. She felt better and better about her technique as the night wore on. She really got an adrenalin jolt when the girl woke up and realized what was happening to her. If only it had lasted. The cut she had made across her neck must have hit the artery. She thought she was shallow enough but there was a little spurt of blood that wouldn't stop. She would have to remember that for the next time.

She had been hoping there would be a next time before she had to leave for college but it was not meant to be. She had been back to the bar every night after work, since the first kill and this would be her last night in town and she had not been able to find the next victim. She finished her drink and told her friends at the table that the next round was on her. Instead of waiting for the waitress, she walked up to the bar.

The woman behind the bar was the owner. She hadn't really met her but this was where she and her friends hung out all summer, so they got to know who was who. The bartender/owner walked up and asked her *what she needed. She gave her the order for three beers and laid a twenty-dollar bill on the bar.*

The bartender/owner came back with three beers and stared at her for a minute. She was beginning to feel a little self-conscious when the bartender/owner finally spoke.

She had admired the necklace she was wearing and wondered where she had found such a pretty piece? She told the bartender/owner that she had found it in a pawn shop in Florida. The bartender/owner looked at it a little closer and then said something that chilled her to the bone.

The bartender/owner told her that she had once had a neckless very similar to that one but that she had lost it when she was involved in a car crash many years before. The neckless had belonged to her grandmother and she had borrowed, well actually stole it, when she ran away from home. She had been in a crash just outside of Aspen and the necklace had disappeared. No one at the hospital remembered seeing it.

She asked the bartender/owner if she remembered anything else about the crash but she said that she must have fallen asleep after she was picked up hitchhiking on the highway and when she woke up in the hospital several days later, she couldn't remember anything about the crash. The police told her that the man who picked her up was probably going to die and that she was very lucky to be alive.

She left the twenty on the bar, picked up the three beer bottles and walked back to her table. She was too stunned to even talk. Luckily her friends were doing enough talking, so they never noticed.

She had taken the jade necklace out of her grandfather's treasure box. She had admired it since she found the box and she decided that it would be one thing to remember her grandfather with. He had been slipping in and out of consciousness for the past couple weeks and the family was not holding out much hope. Since it was her last night in town and she was certain no one would have any idea where the necklace came from, she decided to wear it out. How in the hell could she have ever guessed that someone would recognize the necklace? What a huge cluster fuck.

She needed some air, so she excused herself and walked out the front door and stood on the sidewalk. The air was fall crisp and it felt good. Her thoughts turned to the woman at the bar. She didn't remember anyone ever mentioning that there was a passenger in the car with her grandfather the night he crashed. Is it possible this woman was in the car with her grandfather? How could that have gotten missed in the family stories? More importantly was it her necklace that was in her grandfather's treasure box?

She put her hand up to her open mouth. "Oh my god." This woman was supposed to be her grandfather's sixteenth victim. That's why there were sixteen mementos in the box but only fifteen bodies in the mine. He was on his way to the mine to kill her when the crash occurred. But why had no one ever mentioned a second person in the car?

The bartender/owner did not appear to know who was driving the car that night. She had no recollection of the accident. Her grandfather must have already drugged her when he crashed the car. She didn't know what he used as a sedative but whatever it was, it had to be fast acting and very powerful. Powerful enough to induce amnesia?

She felt a strong chill run up her spine and then in a moment of clarity, she struck on an idea. One that would hopefully keep her focused while she was away at school. She would finish what her grandfather had started that fateful night so long ago. She would take care of his sixteenth victim. She would need to devise a very good plan for this kill. It would take time and it would need to be perfect. The bartender/owner was no slouch. She ran a bar. She would probably be tough to deal with and she had a pretty good build, even after so many years. She pictured the woman in her younger days and understood why her grandfather had chosen her. She was probably a real looker in her day, because she was gorgeous now.

This was awesome. What better way to honor her grandfather than to finish his journey? She felt her excitement build just like it had the night of her first kill. It was a shame. If she only had more time. But that's ok. She would be back at Christmas. She would start working out the plan in her head and by Christmas, it would be perfect. She just knew it. Her grandfather would be so proud of her.

She stepped back into the bar and shook off the chill from the night air. Her body was warm and tingling. She sat back down at the table where her friends were still *talking away and took a sip of her beer. She looked over the top of the bottle and stared at her next victim.*

The next morning her father and mother packed up the car and drove her to Denver for her flight back to Jacksonville. She hugged them and stepped into the security line. She wrapped her hand around the jade necklace and said a silent prayer that her grandfather would live long enough to see her complete his final act. She smiled as she went through security and waved goodbye to her parents.

Chapter Forty-Seven

Buck left the hospital parking lot, turned right onto Main Street and pulled into the parking lot for the Sheriff's office. He entered through the front door showed his ID to the officer at the front desk and was buzzed into the back. He found an empty desk in the bullpen, sat down and pulled his laptop out of his backpack.

The first step in any murder investigation is the creation of the murder book. This was pretty much the entire investigation in one place and would include interviews, forensic reports, autopsy reports and crime scene photos. It was also a chronological listing of how the investigation has progressed.

Over the years, Buck finally caught up with the rest of the world and started to use the murder book template in his laptop. In the old days, everything was done with paper and pencil. The problem was, that there was only one book and anyone who needed access had to go to wherever the physical book was located. This was tough since Buck was very rarely in the same place for long. The laptop made it simple since it was always with him and it also gave instant access to anyone who needed to either review something or add a report.

Buck started with the title page and entered the name of the community and the date. The File automatically opened a new case number and that number would be everyone's source of reference for anything related to the case. His next task was to build the chronology of the crime.

Buck was very meticulous about his investigation notes and between the chronology and the case summary he spent over two hours sitting. He got up to stretch his legs and walked over to the soda machine in the corner and bought another Coke. His third of the day, so far. He found a couple boxes of cold pizza in the refrigerator and grabbed two slices and popped them into the microwave. "Hell of a lunch," he thought, as he walked back to the desk he had been using.

Buck pulled out his cell phone and connected the micro USB cable to his laptop and downloaded all his crime scene photos. He spent the next two hours reviewing each picture and attaching a label to them before placing them in chronological order. His final task, for the moment was to enter the emails for everyone involved in the case and send them an alert that the file had been uploaded and was now available for use. He closed his laptop and went to see if Fitz or Moe Steiner were in the office.

He spotted Moe Steiner walking back from the central printer and followed him back to the office he shared with Fitz. He was just about to ask Moe if they were making any progress on identifying the old man from the cabin when Fitz walked in followed by a tall sharply dressed black man with close-cropped hair. He wore civilian clothes but his military bearing was obvious.

He had on a nylon jacket with a patch on the front right and ARMY CID emblazoned in white letters on the left.

Fitz introduced Buck and Moe to Major Richard Cranston. They shook hands all around. Moe suggested they get out of the cramped office and move to the conference room down the hall. Once seated around the conference room table, the Major opened the computer bag he had slung over his shoulder and pulled out a file. He slid the file over to Fitz and sat down.

"First I would like to apologize for taking so long to get back to you. Didn't realize the urgency until I received a call from headquarters in Washington. I was told this was a top priority," said the Major. Buck silently thanked Jess Gonzales.

The Major continued. "The fingerprints you uploaded caught us all off guard." He pointed to the file. "They belong to First Lieutenant James Michael Forester. Lt. Forester has been listed as missing and presumed dead since 1968. He was awarded a bronze star posthumously for bravery during the battle from which he disappeared. Although an extensive search had been made after the battle, his body was never found. He has been in our POW/MIA registry since that time, until today."

Fitz read through the file and slid it over to Buck. Buck had seen his fair share of military files just like this one as an Army MP. He quickly scanned the file. Lt. Forester had entered the Army in 1965 as a ninety-day wonder. Basically, he went from civilian to army officer with only ninety days of training before he was shipped off to Vietnam. It was said during the Vietnam war that the lifespan of a fresh Lieutenant was about sixteen minutes. Forester had beaten the odds and had been involved in several large-scale operations while in country.

Buck closed the file slid it to Moe and looked at the Major. "Why are you here Major? I am sure the Army has better things for a Major to do than to drive all the way from Denver to Aspen to deliver a simple file. Could have sent the file by email. What's not in the file?"

Fitz and Moe looked at Buck and then at the Major. They weren't sure what was happening. The Major looked at Buck and pulled another file from his computer bag and slid it over to Buck. Buck opened the file and started to read. He finished and slid the file to Fitz and Moe.

The Major sat back in the chair and said. "Lt. Forester and his unit were being investigated for an attack on a village just south of the DMZ. This was right after the My Lai massacre and the army was very sensitive to having its units running amuck and killing civilians. Lt. Forester and several of his soldiers were slated to be arrested within a day or two of the battle they were in. No one outside CID had been told of the arrest, so we doubt he ran because of it. The information that was gathered during the investigation was that Forester tried to stop the carnage and he threatened to have the men responsible brought up on charges. Our sources indicated that he took the massacre to heart and was extremely depressed that he had not been able to stop it. Our first assumption when we couldn't locate him was that he might have been fragged by his own men. We could never prove it, so we were back to, he was either killed during the battle, taken prisoner or he finally had enough and just disappeared into the forest. Until your fingerprint inquiry came though, we just weren't sure. Now we are."

The Major sat quietly. Buck looked at Fitz and then Moe. He said to the Major, "what is the Army's interest in this moving forward.?"

The Major thought for a minute. "We have a conflict. He was cleared of all charges and awarded the bronze star. He is also now a deserter, possibly a kidnapper and if I read your report correctly, was involved in a shootout with police. He is an MIA who has been located and should be treated as a hero but the circumstances make that almost impossible."

Buck closed his eyes and scratched his forehead. "Unless Fitz or Moe disagree, all indications are that he was protecting the children he was with. How he got those children is still under investigation but you are correct, he is still a deserter and as a former soldier myself, I cannot see the army giving this man a military burial. My feeling is that the body will remain with us until the Army can notify any existing relatives and if they choose to take the body, that will be up to them. I would suggest the army remove his name from the POW/MIA registry and close his file."

Moe and Fitz had nothing to add. Buck had spoken from his heart and he felt the Major agreed with him. The Major handed his business card to Fitz. "We are already in the process of making the notification. If no one claims his body, please give me a call. No matter what happens I will see that he gets a decent burial even if not necessarily a military funeral."

The Major stood, shook hands all around and Fitz led him down the hall to the main entrance. Moe and Buck discussed the Major's visit and came to the same conclusion. They weren't sure what the Army was looking for but they didn't find it here. Fitz had returned to the conference room and they spent a few minutes discussing both cases thus far.

Moe had been bringing back a report from the printer when he had first encountered Buck and he showed the report to Buck and Fitz. The report came from the State Crime Lab in Pueblo. The bullets that had killed Ranger Susan Corey had come from the M1 Carbine they had found at the old cabin. Now they just needed to figure out who pulled the trigger.

Buck was beat and he said goodnight and headed for his car. He couldn't remember the last time he slept.

Chapter Forty-Eight

Paul Webber spent most of the day behind the counter at the Pitkin County Clerk's Office going through book upon dusty book of property ownership records trying to pinpoint the owner of the old mine and cabin. Not all of the mining claims were digitized, so it was pretty much all hand work. He was able to find the general location of the cabin on the county plat map but after that, his trail hit a lot of roadblocks trying to identify individual mining claims in an area that had several dozen claims.

With the help of several of the nice ladies in the Clerk's Office, he was finally able to narrow down the claim to just a couple and then finally he hit pay dirt, as the old miner's use to say. He found the original claim for the land under the cabin and spent the rest of the day following sale after sale until he finally got to what he believed was the last purchase.

He felt good about what he found since the last time the mining claim changed hands was in the early 1940's. The claim had not changed hands since. Now he was working his computer trying to locate the person who had last purchased the claim. He was just about to give up for the day when he found a motor vehicle registration for one Marvin Bishop Jr. He had been searching for Marvin Bishop and this was the closest he had gotten.

The only problem was that Marvin Bishop was fifty years old. He couldn't possibly have purchased a mining claim in the 1940's but perhaps his father or grandfather had. He was able to run a reverse directory search and found a number for Mr. Bishop. Marvin Bishop lived in Castle Rock Colorado. Actually, based on his address he lived in Castle Pines, a very exclusive gated community just south of Denver and full of huge mansions.

Paul dialed the phone number he had found and was pleased when the call went through. The call was answered by a woman with a heavy Spanish accent. "Hello, Ma'am," he said. "I am looking for Mr. Marvin Bishop. My name is Paul Webber and I am an Investigator with the Colorado Bureau of Investigations."

"Dr. Bishop is not home right now. Could I take your number and have him call you back?" she responded. Paul gave her his cell phone number and told her it was urgent that he speak with Dr. Bishop as soon as possible. She promised to pass on is number and hung up.

Paul hoped his next task would be a bit easier but as he dove back into the internet, he soon realized that it was probably not going to be. It seems that half the outdoor stores in Aspen carried the lantern they had found in the mine. Plus, it was also available online through Amazon.

Paul decided to let that search wait and he pulled the picture he had taken of the victim's face and decided to hit some of the bars and restaurants in town and see if anyone had seen her. He needed to get something to eat anyway, so this would be a great opportunity

Since he had been cooped up all day in the musty archives, he decided to do his search on foot. He left the Clerk and Recorder's Office, crossed Main Street and headed south on Galena Street. His destination was Wagner Park but he stopped along the way to grab a deli sandwich and a bottle of water. Once sated, he continued on his journey.

Paul worked his way through the homeless people in the park and was getting frustrated. The picture he had was not the best sample of what someone looked like and the more squeamish in the park turned their heads away when he showed it to them. He finally found a small group of young men and women sitting together at a picnic table and approached them with the picture.

As each person looked at the picture, one young girl mouthed "Oh my god," and covered her mouth with her hand. It was too late. Paul heard her and he asked her to look at the picture again.

"Do you know this girl?" Paul asked.

The girl looked at the picture again. "It looks like Blue, but she left town a couple weeks ago." Paul asked her to look at it again. Then one of the young men in the group asked to see it again and he agreed with the young girl.

"What do you know about this girl, Blue?" Paul asked.

The group didn't really know much. She had shown up in Aspen a couple weeks back and was only around for a little while before she left. One young man said he thought she came from some a small town in North Carolina or someplace back east. The group kind of agreed. She wasn't all that talkative and she stayed mostly to herself. The girl who first identified her said she use to spend a lot of time in the alley behind the Jackpot Bar.

Paul spent a few more minutes talking to the group and then thanked them and headed for the Jackpot Bar and Grill. Halfway there his phone rang and he answered. "Paul Webber."

"Uh, hello Detective Webber. This is Dr. Marvin Bishop. My housekeeper said you left an urgent message. How can I help you?"

"Thanks for calling back Dr. Bishop." Paul went on to explain the reason for his call and that he was trying to reach a Marvin Bishop who owned a small group of mining claims in the Aspen area. Dr. Bishop thought for a minute and then told Paul that it was possible that his father had once owned some worthless mining claims but he would need to talk to his father and look through his father's papers.

Paul asked him to please do that and then asked for his address and asked if it would be possible for him to come by tomorrow and meet with Dr. Bishop's father. Bishop explained that his father had suffered a stroke about five years back and he couldn't guarantee if his father would be able to have a conversation but that the detective was welcome to come by at around noon. His father was best in the mornings.

Paul thanked the Doctor and hung up. He felt good about his progress, so he continued walking to the Jackpot.

Chapter Forty-Nine

The Jackpot Bar and Grill had been an Aspen institution for years. It was dark and smelled like old beer and vomit and it was one of the most popular places in town for the younger set. They had live music five nights a week during the summer and the food was marginal at best. Paul walked through the front door and almost gagged but he squared up his shoulders, stepped up to the bar and asked to speak with the manager.

The bartender looked him up and down. "Maggie Stevens. This is my place. You a cop?"

Paul pulled out his CBI ID card and held out his hand. "Paul Webber, Colorado Bureau of Investigation." Maggie shook his hand. She had a firm handshake. Paul also noticed that she was a very attractive woman. He figured she must be in her fifties but he would find out he was wrong.

Maggie Stevens was actually in her seventies. She told Paul she had owned the bar since the early 1970's. She bought it with her ex-husband. Paul asked her how long she had been in Aspen and she told him that she had been involved in an auto accident in 1964 and spent several months in the hospital in a coma. She went through several months of rehab and when she was finished, she decided to stay in Aspen. Over the years she worked in several bars until her and her ex husband were able to buy the Jackpot.

"What can I do for CBI?" she asked.

Paul explained the reason for his visit and asked her if he could show her a picture of the person he was looking for. He told her the picture was a little disturbing. He opened up the gallery app on his phone and held the picture up for Maggie to see.

"Girl doesn't look too good," commented Maggie. She looked closer, and then she yelled across the floor for the big guy who was setting up a podium at the front door. Boomer was her lead bouncer and she showed him the picture.

"This look like the girl you threw out of here about a week or so ago?" she asked him. He looked closer at the picture. "She looked much better that night than she does in this picture, but yeah, sure looks like her. Found her wandering around from table to table finishing off anything that was left in the glasses after people left the bar."

"Anyone pay any particular attention to her while she was here?" Paul asked.

Boomer thought for a minute. "Not really. She was pretty much by herself until I sent her packing."

Paul thanked Boomer and Maggie and walked back out into the clean mountain air. He stopped a few more young people as he walked down the sidewalk but he wasn't able to get any more information on the woman they called Blue. He was a little discouraged but he had made progress. He headed back to his car, but first, he wanted to stop off at the Sheriff's office to see if anything came back on her prints.

He walked through the front door of the Sheriff's office, presented his ID to the desk officer and was buzzed through the locked door. He found the young woman who had helped him send the prints through the AFIS system and asked her if anything had come back on his prints. Nothing yet.

He sat down at the empty conference room table and dialed Buck. Buck had just gotten out of the shower and was getting ready to put his head down when his phone rang. He checked the number and answered his phone.

"Hey, Paul. What's up?"

Paul filled him in on the conversations with the young people in the park and the conversation with the owner and the bouncer at the Jackpot. He told him about what he found on the mining claim and his conversation with Dr. Bishop. He told Buck he was going to drive over to Denver in the morning to interview the doctor and hopefully his father. Buck told him he had done a good job and to let him know how things went in Denver. Buck was going to meet up with Dr. Parker and the archeology team and see if they were making any progress. He was also going to check with forensics and the crime lab. He reminded Paul that the murder file had been uploaded and to make sure he recorded the information from his multiple interviews.

Buck disconnected the call. He pressed speed dial one and heard the Director's phone ringing. The Director answered and Buck filled him in on the progress so far. He told the Director what an excellent job Paul Webber had done with tracking down the mining claims and getting somewhere on the girl's identity.

He also told the Director about the visit from the Army CID agent. He relayed the conversation as best he could remember it and then voiced the same question to the Director.

"I just can't figure out what the Army was after today. I got the feeling that maybe they wanted us to clear this guy so they could honor him. Seemed a little weird."

The Director agreed and then asked Buck a question he hadn't thought of yet. "What's the possibility that this guy Forester has friends or relations in high places?"

Buck thought for a minute. "Hadn't thought of that possibility. I'm going to suggest to Fitz that they take a little bit deeper look into their suspect. Thanks, Director."

The Director hung up and Buck dialed Fitz's cellphone. When she answered, he told her about his feelings about the army's visit and suggested she look into Forester's background a little deeper now that they had his military file. They talked for a few more minutes and then she hung up. Buck finally crawled into bed and shut off the light.

Chapter Fifty

Paul Webber turned off Highway 287 onto Happy Canyon Road and pulled up to the main gate for Castle Pines. He presented his ID to the guard at the gate and gave him the address he was seeking. The guard walked into the guard shack, made a phone call and returned to the car. He handed Paul back his ID, gave him directions to the address and opened the security gate.

Paul missed his turn once and managed to circle back and find the home of Dr. Marvin Bishop Jr. Dr. Bishop lived on a quiet cul-de-sac. The house, although not as large as Paul expected, was set back amongst the trees. He could see a nice view of the mountains from behind the house as he pulled into the driveway.

Grabbing his computer bag, Paul walked up the sidewalk and rang the doorbell. The door was answered by an older Latina wearing a lavender maids uniform.

"Mr. Webber?" she asked. "Please come in. The doctor is waiting for you."

Paul stepped into a beautifully appointed entry foyer with marble tiles and light wooden millwork. He followed the housekeeper to an open door where she stepped aside and directed him in. Dr. Marvin Bishop Jr. rose from his desk and met Paul with a strong handshake.

"Is it Agent or Detective Webber?" he asked.

"Paul will be just fine Doctor and thank you for seeing me so quickly." Paul sat down in one of the leather guest chairs across the desk from Dr. Bishop.

"I only hope you haven't driven all this way for nothing. My father seems to be having a fairly good morning but I am not sure how much he will be able to answer. He suffered a stroke five years ago and we brought him back to Colorado from his home in Pittsburg. His memory skills are a little off and he has very little use of his left side."

Paul told the Doctor that anything that might help would be appreciated. The Doctor handed Paul a stack of legal documents and explained that these were all the documents he could find related to his father's dalliance with buying up mining claims in the Colorado Mountains. It seemed that his father had seen the writing on the wall when it came to World War II and he thought the country would need plenty of gold and silver if it entered the war. He thought he would get rich.

Marvin Bishop Sr. had, over the years just prior to World War II, purchased eleven small mining claims in the Colorado high country. All sight unseen and all pretty much worthless. Dr. Bishop explained that his father had never been to Colorado prior to five years ago after he suffered his stroke. He was just always fascinated with the old west and wanted to be able to say he was a part of it. A law firm in Denver, that specialized in mining claims, handled all the purchases.

He went on to explain that his father had joined the army, as every able-bodied man had done after Pearl Harbor and had seen action as an Army Engineer. Once the war was over, he had returned to Pittsburgh and began a career as a Mechanical Engineer until he retired in 2000 after the death of his wife.

Paul had listened intently as Dr. Bishop spoke and made a lot of notes in his little notebook that he always carried. He now looked at the papers that Dr. Bishop handed him. The Doctor was correct. There was not much new information in the stack. He pulled out the documents for the claim he was interested in and looked through the pages. He had gotten pretty much the same information from the Clerk and Recorders Office in Aspen.

"Would you like to meet my father now, Paul?" asked the Doctor.

Dr. Bishop stood up, as did Paul, and they walked down a hallway to a room off the kitchen. Dr. Bishop knocked and opened the door.

"Dad, you have a visitor," he said as they entered the room. Paul looked around the room and the first thing he noticed was a larger version of the mountain view he had seen from the driveway. He also noticed that other than a hospital-style bed there was very little medical equipment in the room. The Doctor was standing next to a leather recliner.

The gentleman sitting in the recliner was quite old. He was wearing a white button-down shirt with a red, white and blue striped bow tie. He looked very dapper.

"Dad," said the Doctor. "This is Paul and he would like to ask you a few questions about some of your old mining claims. Would that be alright?"

Paul stepped up to the recliner and shook a very frail, almost translucent, hand. There was a noticeable droop on the left side of Marvin Bishop's face but his eyes were bright and shiny. Paul sensed there was still a lot of Marvin Bishop behind those eyes.

Paul sat down in the chair the doctor had brought over.

"Mr. Bishop. Thank you for seeing me today. I only have a few questions if that's ok?"

Marvin Bishop responded with a garbled answer and Paul looked at the Doctor who translated that it was ok and to please proceed. Paul showed Marvin Bishop a picture of the old cabin from his phone and asked him if he recognized the building. Marvin Bishop shook his head no. The rest of the conversation didn't go much better. Marvin Bishop confirmed what his son had said, that he had never even been to Colorado prior to 2000. Paul was able to make out some of his words but a lot of what Marvin Bishop said was garbled and Paul could see the frustration building in Marvin Bishop.

Paul was looking through his notes. He asked Mr. Bishop if he had ever leased his claims to anyone or allowed anyone to work the claims? Bishop said something that he couldn't make out. Dr. Bishop moved next to his dad and asked, "Dad can you repeat what you just said?"

Marvin Bishop looked frustrated but he repeated what he had said. Paul looked at the doctor who shrugged his shoulders. It had sounded like Marvin Bishop had said, "wicked smilley."

"Dad, we don't understand what you are trying to say."

The Doctor looked at Paul. "I think he is getting tired. We should let him rest. I am sorry you came all this way for nothing."

Paul stood up and gathered up his papers. He followed the Doctor back to the door when they both turned, startled by the noise. Marvin Bishop was using his good right hand and was banging furiously on the metal tray table next to his chair. He kept repeating the same thing. "Wicked smilly." Dr. Bishop rushed to his side and tried to calm him down but he kept banging and trying to communicate.

Paul knelt down on the other side of the recliner and in a very soft voice said. "Mr. Bishop, did you let someone work this claim after you bought it?"

Marvin Bishop stopped banging and smiled at Paul, who dug into his computer bag and pulled out a blank piece of paper and a wide tip black marker. He put it on the tray and slid the tray closer to Mr. Bishop. He took the cap off the marker and placed the marker in Mr. Bishop's good right hand.

Very slowly and with an engineer's precision, Mr. Bishop started to write on the paper. The Doctor looked at Paul and Paul just smiled. It took a few minutes and then Mr. Bishop reached out and handed the marker back to Paul. Paul put the cap back on the marker and picked up the paper. "Richard Smiley."

Paul shook Mr. Bishop's frail hand and thanked him for his time. He put the paper in his computer bag and followed Dr. Bishop out the door, gently closing it behind him.

Dr. Bishop looked at Paul. "How did you know what he was trying to say?"

"I didn't," said Paul. I just had a feeling he was trying to tell us something important. My dad, after his stroke, always tried to write down things he wanted to say. Thought it was worth a try."

"Well thank you for your patience and I sure hope this helps your investigation."

Paul thanked him for his hospitality and walked out the front door. He put his computer bag in the trunk of his car and pulled out his phone. He called the CBI office in Grand Junction and asked for Agent Ashley Baxter.

"Hey Bax, it's Paul," he said when she answered the phone.

"Paul. What's up? Thought you were with Buck?"

"Right now I'm in Denver. Have you got a few minutes to do a computer search for me?" He gave her the information he had gotten from Marvin Bishop and told her he would be back in Aspen in couple hours and if she found anything to call Buck.

He disconnected the call and dialed Buck's number but the call went straight to voicemail. He left a message telling Buck what he had found in Denver and that he had Ashley Baxter running it down on the computer. He hung up, started the car and pulled out of the driveway. Today was a good day.

Chapter Fifty-One

Buck stopped by the hospital to check on PIS only to find out that PIS had checked himself out of the hospital late the night before. He thanked the nurse and walked out of the hospital, got in his car and headed for the Conundrum Creek trailhead.

He was just pulling into the parking lot when his phone rang. He looked at the number and answered the call.

"Hi, Max. What's up?"

"Hi, Buck. How's my favorite cop?" she said.

Maxine Clinton was the head of the State Crime Lab in Pueblo. A former Biology Professor, Max had been running the lab for the past twenty years. She was about sixty-four years old, slightly overweight and had been married to her husband for just about all her adult life. Buck had seen Max converse fluently and eloquently with college professors and business leaders and he had seen her drink just about every cop she ever met under the table. She was a bourbon girl and proud of it. She considered Buck Taylor one of her closest friends and Buck felt the same way about her.

"Doing good Max."

"Are you working with Jane Fitzpatrick on the Aspen shooting?"

Buck explained that although it was not directly his case, he was still helping out when and if he could. Max told him that she used an open order for an overnight DNA test to run the DNA from the female that had been buried. The Director had originally approved it for the investigation into the drug cartel in Durango but she hadn't used it because that investigation had moved so quickly. She knew this case in Aspen was a top priority, so she went ahead and authorized the test.

That's what Buck liked about Max. She wasn't afraid to step up and make decisions. "Did you get any results?" Buck asked.

"You bet. I just emailed them to Fitz but since it was your DNA test I wanted to let you know I had used it." She gave Buck a quick rundown. "DNA belonged to Corrine Everheart. She's a real piece of work. She has a juvenile record that will need to be unsealed. She has an impressive arrest record for someone who was only thirty-five when she fell off the planet and disappeared. Drugs, gambling, prostitution, assault and oh yeah, kidnapping. She was only out of lockup for five months when she left West Virginia and was never seen again."

"Nice work Max. I will follow up with Fitz later today. Thanks."

Max ended the call the same way she had been doing for years. "God will watch over you, Buck Taylor. You are a good man. Stay safe." She hung up.

Although Buck hadn't been to church since he received his confirmation, he always appreciated Max's little blessing. It wasn't that he didn't believe in god. He wasn't sure what he really believed in. He didn't like organized religion but he never held that against anyone. A lot of people prayed for his wife during the five years she fought metastatic breast cancer but in the end, Lucy still died. Although he was mad at first, he soon realized that in order to be mad at god he first had to believe in god and he just never got there. He always felt there were forces in the world that he couldn't explain and he always thanked the river spirits whenever he had a chance to do some fly fishing. He just didn't have a place for one god in his life. He never held Max's beliefs against her. He always figured that it couldn't hurt if she believed he was worthy.

Buck stepped out of his car, grabbed his backpack and started down the trail. The day had dawned a little overcast and there was definitely a chill in the air. The leaves were changing colors and almost every day it seemed there was more gold in them thar hills. He enjoyed this time of year. Fall was Lucy's favorite time of year and they had enjoyed many fall walks together on the trails around Gunnison before she was no longer able to walk without a cane. The walks had stopped completely when she needed a wheelchair to get around. Then it was just little jaunts on the concrete sidewalks in the park along the river. Even after all this time he still missed her every day.

Buck reached the old mine cabin just as Professor Standish and his archeology students were taking down their tent and packing up their tools. He had passed a couple firefighters on the trail who were carrying out the last body bag. Professor Standish stood with his hands on his hips looking around the site. He spotted Buck as he entered the clearing.

"Morning Professor. Looks like you guys are wrapping up. How did it go?" Buck asked.

"Oh, good morning Agent Taylor. We had a fascinating time. It isn't very often we get to use our archeological procedures on a modern site. We learned quite a bit."

Professor Standish went on to explain to Buck the procedures they had followed and some of their preliminary finding. He mentioned that much of what they had uncovered would need to be verified in the lab but he spoke with a very nice woman at the State Crime Lab and she was making sure his tests had top priority.

Buck saw how excited the Professor had gotten and he listened intently but he needed a few answers, so he interrupted the Professor's debrief.

"Professor, is there any way from your exam to determine if this was the work of one person or several?" The Professor asked one of his students to bring over his laptop and he fired it up and opened to a series of photos. Buck moved in for a closer look.

The Professor pointed his pen to some of the pictures that contained very detailed images of some of the cut marks and slices. He pointed out some similarities and also some incongruities as he called them. Then he stepped back.

"Based on what we were able to see it is our opinion that all these bodies were killed in the same manner by the same person."

"Any idea how long ago? I'm guessing this cabin has been around since the late 1880's but obviously, the hatch appears to be newer."

"Quite right, Agent Taylor. We did a little research and determined that the screws in the hatch were most likely purchased sometime during the 1950's. We are having one of the welds tested but we feel confident that it will show about the same age. The wooden furniture in the mine is from the early 1900's, as is the old kerosene stove."

"How about the bodies, Professor?" Buck asked.

"The lab tests on the skin and the carbon dating will probably corroborate our findings but we would estimate that based on several factors the bodies were killed and left in the mine sometime during the mid-fifties to early sixties."

Buck thanked the Professor and asked him if he could email him a preliminary report of their findings as soon as possible. The Professor said that would not be a problem and he should have something ready first thing in the morning. He took Buck's business card with his email address on it and headed off to join his students in their packing.

Chapter Fifty-Two

Buck put on a pair of nitrile gloves, slung his backpack over his shoulder and climbed down the ladder into the mine. He noticed the blue fingerprint dust on the ladder and he reminded himself to check the murder book and see what evidence the forensic team had sent to the lab.

He stood at the entrance to the first chamber and scanned the area. He had been over the space several times himself and he knew the forensic team had gone over every square inch with a fine-tooth comb but Buck had found over the years, that no matter how thorough the teams were, sometimes things got missed. It was even more important now that there was no one in the space and all the evidence had been removed.

The space looked different. The bed frame was still there but the old straw mattress had been removed as had the little wooden cabinet and the leather roll of knives. He noted that the team had also removed a significant amount of dirt from under the old shackles. He assumed they would be looking for a DNA match but he figured if they found one it would have to be a modern connection since DNA hadn't even been discovered in the mid-fifties. He continued to scan the chamber.

Finding nothing else, he moved down the tunnel to the back chamber, where the mummified bodies had been found. Here too, the old straw mattresses had been removed. He pulled his flashlight out of his backpack and shined the light under all the bed frames and along the ceiling. Nothing much to see here.

Buck was turning to head back to the ladder when he had a thought. He had no idea how far back into the mine the forensic team had gone. He knew the SWAT deputies had done a cursory check just to make sure there were no other bodies around but he wasn't sure if the tunnel had been thoroughly searched. He turned on his flashlight again and headed down the tunnel.

The beam of light from his flashlight was barely holding its own as the darkness of the mine tunnel surrounded him. Buck had never been claustrophobic but the darkness in the mine was blacker than anything he could remember and it filled him with dread. Shaking off the closeness of the dark he continued down the tunnel until he came to the end. He panned his flashlight around the tunnel.

There was nothing to see at the end of the tunnel. Whatever work had happened here happened a long time ago. He had no idea what he was even looking for. Maybe just a clue to who had been the last person to do any kind of work in the tunnel.

He could barely see the light from the back chamber as he turned and started back down the tunnel the way he had come. He was swinging the flashlight beam back and forth and almost missed it on the first pass. He took a step back and moved the flashlight slowly over a small pile of debris that was pushed up against the wall.

A glint from something shiny caught his eye as the flashlight passed over the pile on the third pass. Buck knelt down and started to slowly move the debris around. He spotted a flat metal object about the size of a quarter and picked it up. Although it was slightly rusted and dirty Buck recognized it immediately. It was a partially rounded square with two red swords crossed over a blue background and the banner across the top said "Mountain". This pin belonged to a member of the 10th Mountain division. He also knew right away that this pin was a lot younger than the mine.

Buck pulled a small plastic evidence bag out of his backpack and noted the date and time. He also set it back on the ground where he found it and took several pictures with his cellphone. He placed the pin in the evidence bag, sealed it and signed his name across the flap.

Buck continued his search of the tunnel but found nothing else of interest and finally headed for the ladder. Once outside, he closed the hatch and removed the Sheriff's padlock from the hasp.

Buck called the Sheriff and he answered on the second ring. Buck told him what he found in the tunnel and they discussed what the pin represented. One issue the Sheriff brought up was the fact that there were several men who lived in the county who had once been part of the 10th Mountain Division. Many of the men who trained with the 10th, essentially America's first skiing soldiers during World War II, were involved in the startup of America's recreational skiing industry. A lot of former soldiers had settled in Aspen, Vail and Steamboat and had been the driving force in opening skiing up to the masses. The Sheriff personally knew of at least 10 former members who lived in the county. He would have one of his deputies put together a list for Buck.

The Sheriff also asked Buck if he could stop by the office when he had a minute. There were two investigators from the Arapahoe County District Attorney's office who wanted to interview Buck about the shooting involving the two kids. The County Attorney had requested an outside agency handle the shooting investigation especially since two kids had been killed.

Buck told the Sheriff he was on his way and that he could also have the Public Works guys come get the generator, the lights and the fan. He asked the Sheriff to see if they could weld the hatch shut so no one could enter it.

Buck hung up and checked his messages. Paul Webber had called with the name of a person of interest. There was also a call from his youngest son Jason, just checking in to make sure he was alright. He had heard about the death of the ranger and about Buck's involvement. He didn't mention the shooting, which Buck was glad of. Jason was much more sensitive than his brother and sister and he took everything to heart. He had been very close to Buck's wife Lucy and he still seemed to be struggling with her death.

Buck called Jason, got his voice mail and left a message telling him that he was fine and he would call soon. He grabbed his backpack, slung it over his shoulder

and headed for the car. He felt good. The pin in his
pocket was their first solid lead.

Chapter Fifty-Three

Buck pulled his car into the Sheriff's office parking lot and turned off the engine. He sat for a minute and then pulled out his cellphone and dialed Hank Clancy, Special Agent in Charge of the FBI's Denver office. Hank answered on the second ring.

"Buck Taylor. How the hell are you?"

Hank had been an integral part of the investigation of a Mexican drug cartel trying to set up a distribution network in Durango that Buck had headed. With the help of several local, state and federal agencies, they eventually broke up the cartel's operation and, in the process, made the largest drug bust in history. Hank, in spite of being a FED, was good people and he and Buck had a good working relationship.

Buck and Hank chatted a few minutes about the results of the drug bust in Durango and where things stood with the investigations that continued as a result of their raid. He then took a few minutes to fill Hank in on this new serial killer investigation in Aspen. Hank listened carefully and asked a few questions.

"So, the real reason for my call is to see if the FBI has any record of a serial killer operating in Colorado in the late fifties early sixties?"

"Geez Buck," said Hank. "You don't want much do you? I will admit that I am intrigued. Fifteen mummified bodies in a mine shaft. How crazy is that?"

"Yeah," replied Buck. "I've never run across anything like this before. New one on me."

"I'll bet the Sheriff is just thrilled?" said Hank.

Hank went on to explain that multiple murderers were not called serial killers back in the fifties and sixties. That wouldn't happen until the early seventies. He told Buck that it was unlikely their records had been digitized that far back but he would have one of his clerks start researching and see if they had anything that might help. He asked Buck to keep him informed and if he needed the FBI to get involved, to just give him a call. Buck hung up.

Paul Webber was just starting up the stairs to the front entrance to the Sheriff's office when he spotted Buck walking across the parking lot. He waited at the top of the stairs.

"Hey, Buck. Did you get my message?"

"Yeah," replied Buck. "Sounds like making the drive to Denver was worthwhile."

Paul filled him in on the visit with the Doctor and his father as they walked through the doors, showed their ID's and were buzzed through. Buck set his backpack down on the conference room table and grabbed a seat.

He removed the 10th Mountain Division pin in the evidence bag from his pocket and laid it on the table.

While Buck opened his laptop to the murder book page, Paul examined the pin.

Buck looked up from his laptop. "Any chance that this Doctor Bishop or someone in his family might have known about the mine?"

"I doubt it," Paul replied. "His kids are teenagers and he told me that they were all fascinated when they found the mining claim deeds. His father, Marvin Sr., had never mentioned ever owning the claims and the deeds were locked away in an old safe that had been in Marvin Sr.'s garage in Pittsburg up until 5 years ago. I don't see any involvement on their part."

Paul went on to tell Buck about the outburst from Marvin Sr. and that it appeared that Marvin Sr. had allowed someone to work the mine. Since Marvin didn't really believe there was anything of value in the mine he gave this person permission with no written contract or anything.

Buck pulled out his cellphone, hooked it up to his laptop and downloaded the pictures of the pin he took in the mine. He then looked over the forensic reports that had been uploaded so far. The forensic team had found some fingerprints. Many were degraded, but they were working through them. They had found a bunch of residue on the old mattress and were separating out the stains to run DNA. They were not hopeful.

He had an email from Dr. Parker saying that she would be doing the autopsy on the young woman this afternoon and asked Buck if he could join her. He checked his watch.

His email notification chimed and he looked to see what had come in. There was a new email from Professor Standish. He opened the email and read the preliminary report. The report covered everything they had discussed earlier in the morning. Buck saved it to the murder book.

"Paul, I am going to drop in on the autopsy of our newest victim. Why don't you follow up on the information you got about her so far?"

Buck stood up and started to close down his laptop when one of the deputies walked in and handed him a piece of paper with eleven names and addresses on it.

"Sheriff asked me to put this together for you. It's everyone we know of who were once in the 10th Mountain Division."

"Thank you, deputy," said Buck. He looked over the list and handed it to Paul.

"Go ahead and start working through this list. I will call you when I am done at the autopsy and we can split up what's left of the list."

Paul grabbed his computer bag and headed out the door. Buck walked down the hall to find Fitz when a voice called his name. Buck turned around to find two people walking towards him.

"Agent Taylor. Detectives Young and Lee, Arapahoe County District Attorney's office. Do you have a few minutes for us?"

Buck checked his watch. He had about an hour before the autopsy, so he followed the detectives into an interview room. They asked him to hand his service weapon and any backup weapons he had to a deputy standing outside the door, which he did and then they closed the door and asked him to take a seat.

Detective Young was about forty years old, Buck figured. He was tall and appeared to be very fit. He had blond hair which was starting to turn grey and bright blue eyes. His partner Detective Lee was a short Asian woman. She looked to be somewhere in her thirties and she had dark hair and dark eyes. She smiled at Buck as he sat down.

Chapter Fifty-Four

Detective Lee read Buck his Miranda rights, which was a standard part of an interview like this and Buck declined counsel and signed the paper indicating such. Buck had nothing to hide. They asked Buck if he minded if they recorded the interview and he told them that was fine. Detective Young asked him to tell them about the events leading to the shooting. Buck knew that they probably already had a copy of his statement and that they would use his words now to corroborate what he had put in his written statement.

Buck spent the next twenty minutes describing the events of the search for the ranger's body and the subsequent search of the area that eventually led to the old cabin and the mine. He explained about the explosions and about returning fire and about finding the kids dead along with the old soldier, who had since been identified.

The detectives listened and took a lot of notes on the pads they had in front of them. Buck finished and sat back in his chair. Detective Young opened up a manila folder that sat on the table in front of him and started looking through the pages.

"Any ill effects from the shootout in Durango? I understand you sought professional help?" asked Young without looking up from the papers. He then looked up and stared at Buck.

Buck was caught a little off guard but he remained calm. He had used the same technique himself many times. He was curious how they got his personal medical records. The psychologist he had seen, once, had been at the request of the Director.

Buck calmed his breathing. "No ill effects," Buck said. "I went to the psychologist once, as is routine in CBI for any agent involved in a shooting."

Lee made a note on her pad. Young continued. "From your report, you and the two deputies came under fire and returned fire. Were you able to identify who was shooting at you?"

"Have you ever been involved in a shootout Detective?" Buck asked.

Detective Young looked a little offended. "My record has nothing to do with your actions Agent. Please confine your answers to the case at hand."

"As I stated in my report and also to you just a minute ago. We came under attack as soon as we entered the field. The explosions occurred followed by the shooting. When the cabin exploded, I was thrown to the ground by our tracker who received a serious injury. The deputies identified where the shooting was coming from and they returned fire. The older man charged out of the woods firing as he ran and we all shot back. When the next explosion occurred, we spotted movement in the trees and fired. We had no idea that kids were involved until we cleared the scene. My view of the scene at the large tree was partially blocked by the remains of the cabin."

The questions continued along that same vein for a few more minutes and Buck was getting annoyed. He answered every question truthfully but he started to sense a bit of hostility on the part of Young. Lee hadn't said much during the interview so far. Buck decided it was time to put an end to the interview. He looked at his watch.

Young kept at it. "Do you have any remorse, Agent, for the two kids that were killed or is it just another day for you?"

"Look," said Buck. "No one likes to see kids get hurt or killed. We were in a shootout with an unknown number of individuals. We didn't have time to ask them their ages. We are all saddened by their deaths but it was them or us. They chose the course of action that resulted in their deaths. Now if you have no further questions, I have an autopsy to get to."

Buck pushed his chair back and stood up. He turned for the door when Young said. "So you're a big deal hero cop and you're too good to answer our questions. You have a trail of dead bodies following you Agent and I mean to find out if you're a hero or a killer!"

Buck stopped at the door and turned to face Young who was now on his feet. He started to step towards the table when Detective Lee grabbed Young's arm.

"Tom you're out of line. I need you to back off."

Young looked at Lee and then at Buck. Buck had misread the dynamic. He now realized that Detective Lee was the lead investigator and Young was the pit-bull. It was his job to get under Buck's skin and try to provoke a response and Buck had almost fallen for it.

Detective Young walked away from the table in the opposite direction from Buck. Detective Lee came over to Buck and held out her hand.

"I apologize, Agent Taylor. You have been truthful with us today and I allowed the line of questioning to drift away from the reason we are here. You are free to go."

Buck shook her hand and she signaled the deputy outside the interview room to unlock the door. Buck walked out, retrieved his weapons and ran into the Sheriff, who indicated for Buck to follow him. Once inside the Sheriff's office he closed the door and sat down behind his desk.

"Shit Buck. I am really sorry about that interview. I watched most of it and if you hadn't stopped it, I was going to. Young was way out of line. The interviews with Manning and Sanchez went just fine. Any idea where the hostility came from towards you?"

"No idea. I've never met either one of them."

Buck and the Sheriff talked for a few minutes about both cases. The Sheriff told him that Professor Standish called and reported that his students were having some luck rehydrating the fingers of some of the mummies and were working with his fingerprint tech to try to get some clear prints. They had also shipped the samples off for quick DNA analysis.

Buck thanked the Sheriff and went in search of Fitz and Steiner.

Chapter Fifty-Five

Buck found Fitz and Steiner in their cubicles. Both were on the phone but Fitz held up a finger and pointed to her visitor chair. Buck lifted a pile of file folders off the chair, set them on the floor and sat down. Fitz spoke for a few more minutes and then hung up.

"Hey, Buck. How's the serial killer case coming?" she asked.

"Good. Heading for the autopsy in a few minutes. Did you talk to Max Clinton at the State Crime Lab?"

Fitz told Buck she had spoken with Max and had gotten the information on Corrine Everheart. She told him she had just gotten off the phone with a very nice detective in Charleston, West Virginia and that he was familiar with her disappearance in that city and would send her everything they have on her. She was no stranger to the police in West Virginia. He was also going to start running down missing children around ten years old and see what turns up. She told him that Moe was in the process of uploading the kid's pictures to the missing and exploited children's database and was going to send out a national alert to see if they could figure out where she grabbed the kids.

"I heard you had a little run-in with the Detective Young. Also heard you kept your cool. Thought you might be interested in knowing that I have the ballistics report. Came in about an hour ago. They only matched one bullet from the rifle you were using and that was a non-fatal wound in the old man's shoulder."

Buck let that sink in a minute. "I wonder what his deal was then? I felt like he was mad at me and I have no idea why."

"Shit, Buck. You've been through more on the job in the last two months than most cops deal with in a whole career. My guess is he was just jealous and wanted to see how far he could push you. Good for you that you didn't respond."

"Thanks, Fitz. Hey, do me a favor and ask the Sheriff if you can send a copy of the report to my Director. I'd really appreciate that. By the way, does it say who had the kill shot on the two kids?"

She clicked open a page on her laptop and turned the screen so he could see. Buck read the report and then stepped back. His expression said it all.

"Thanks, Fitz."

Buck headed down the hall to the Sheriff's office. He stuck his head in the door. "Earl, you got a minute?"

The Sheriff waved him in and he shut the door.

"Looks serious Buck. What's up?"

"Fitz just showed me the ballistic report on the two kids. I just wanted you to know that Sanchez took the death of those two dead kids really hard and was struggling with the possibility that he was the one who killed one or both. I thought you should know his mental state before you show him the report. I also asked her to send a copy of the report over to CBI if it is ok with you."

"Sure thing Buck and thanks for the heads up on Sanchez. This is gonna hurt him bad if that's the case. He's a good deputy. Would hate to lose him over this."

Buck stood up and walked out of the Sheriff's office. He walked out the front door and headed for the hospital and the autopsy on the girl from the mine.

Dr. Parker was already underway when he entered the autopsy suite and apologized for being late. Buck stood in the corner as Dr. Parker and her assistant went through the autopsy step by step recording everything she did on both video and audio. Buck had stood through many an autopsy in his career but he never got used to seeing young people on the table. He noted that the girl seemed very thin for her height. She also had other scarring on her body that looked older than the cut marks. Now that the body was washed, the number of cuts and slices was impressive.

Dr. Parker concluded the autopsy while her assistant closed up the Y incision. She removed her gloves and apron and walked over to Buck.

"Afraid there is nothing unusual here Buck. She died of massive blood loss caused by the cuts. She does have evidence of some superficial bruising but those appear to be several weeks old. I do not think they are related. She is also very malnourished. Probably twenty maybe twenty-five pounds under average weight for her height. We'll have the results of the tox screen in a week to ten days. I hope they find something because the idea that she suffered through this torture while she was awake is going to keep me up nights."

"Thanks, Doc. By the way. How you doing with the mummies?"

"Last time I spoke to the pathologists next door, they had gone through ten of the bodies and were going to stop for the day and pick it up tomorrow. I will email you a preliminary report tonight but it will be almost identical to the report on this young lady."

She turned to leave but Buck stopped her. "Almost identical Doc. What's different?"

She signaled for Buck to follow her and they headed to the room next door that was being used as an additional autopsy suite. One of the mummies was still on the table and she pulled back the sheet to expose the body.

"I will tell you Buck, in all my years of doing this work in LA I never worked on a mummy before. Professor Standish and his team were incredibly helpful. It was quite the learning experience, if you like to learn stuff like this." She pointed to the cuts on the chest of the mummy.

"Professor Standish and Dr. Richland both agreed that the cuts on the mummies appear to be deeper than those on our young lady next door. Their opinion is that the mummies they have looked at so far were mutilated by a man. There was also vaginal tearing evident. In other words, these ladies were raped just prior to their deaths."

She continued. "Our young lady has no sign of being raped or sexually abused in any way. In comparing the cut marks from our victim to the others, they cannot say with one hundred percent certainty that our victim was the work of a man. They feel the cuts were done with a lot less pressure and some even appeared to be tentative. They were not as smooth and clean as on the mummies even though the same knives were used. The end result was the same. She still bled out and died just like the mummies, but my guess is it took longer."

Chapter Fifty-Six

Buck leaned back against the counter and let what Dr. Parker just said sink in. Because all the mummies were women and the latest victim was also a woman he hadn't really thought about the fact that the serial killer could be a woman. He felt a little sexist. Women were just as capable as men at creating evil but his mind automatically went to a man because of the conditions. The brutality of the torture, the work being done in a mine, the bodies just left to mummify and the fact that the crimes were committed during the late fifties or early sixties. It all added up to a man being the perpetrator.

Since the latest crime imitated the original crimes in such great detail, his mind just went to the same place for some of the same reasons. The doer was a man. Could he be that wrong? He was going to have to change the way he looked at the crime.

"You ok Buck? You look perplexed," said Dr. Parker.

"No, not perplexed. Pissed off," replied Buck. "I feel like such an idiot. It never crossed my mind that the killer of our latest victim might be a woman. I made a judgment without having all the facts."

"It's ok Buck, we all do it. Now you have the facts so go look at this case from a different angle."

Buck thanked the Doctor for her time and walked out of the hospital to his car. He opened his phone and called Paul Webber. Paul answered and Buck asked him if he had eaten dinner yet? It was getting late and Buck had realized, too late, that he had already missed lunch. He asked Paul to meet him at "The Ranch." "The Ranch" was a really good steakhouse in town. It was mostly a local joint and didn't have the same kind of prices some of the other restaurants in town had.

Paul Webber found Buck seated at a booth at the back of the restaurant. Buck had his back to the wall. Force of habit. Paul slid into the booth and the waitress came by. He ordered a beer and pulled out his notebook.

Buck filled him in on his conversation with Dr. Parker including the possibility that the latest victim was killed by a woman. Paul looked at Buck with a surprised look in his eyes.

"Wow, Buck. Never even considered that as a possibility. A woman serial killer? There aren't many of them."

He looked pensive for a minute and Buck said. "Paul. What are you thinking?"

"I was just wondering if our current serial killer could be a female relative or someone like that who has or had a close relationship to the old serial killer?"

Buck thought about that but held is thoughts as the waitress came by to take their orders. Once the waitress left Buck took a sip of his soda and looked at Paul.

"Great thought Paul. Let's put that on the back burner for a minute. Fill me in on your conversations with the 10th Mountain veterans."

Paul opened his notebook. "Of the eleven names on the list I was able to meet with nine of them today. I'll tell you Buck; it is really sad. These guys gave everything for their country and half of them can't even remember their names. Six of the ones I met today have serious Alzheimers. Their families let me look through some of the memorabilia they kept but I couldn't find anything related to a Richard Smiley. Two of the vets still had all their faculties. One guy thought he remembered a Richard Smiley but he wasn't sure. The other one didn't recall the name but he had some great stories to tell me. The last poor fella has been bedridden for decades and is in some kind of comatose state. I have two more to see tomorrow."

He read through his notes. "Oh, here it is. One guy suggested I call Sam Brinkman; he operates a small 10th Mountain Division museum in Minturn. He said they used to keep records of the guys who went through training. Might find something on Richard Smiley there."

The waitress delivered their steaks and the conversation lagged while they ate. Paul mentioned that he had talked to Ashley Baxter at the office but she hadn't had any luck looking for Richard Smiley either. She was expanding her search to other states and she was waiting for the army to get back with her. Paul asked if Buck knew how the other case was going and Buck filled him in on the identity of the man and the woman. He told him that they were publishing the kid's pictures to see if they could attract some leads.

Once finished with dinner Buck laid out the plan for the next day. He asked Paul to follow up with the last two vets. He took the phone number for Sam Brinkman and said he would follow up with him and he told Paul to meet him at the Sheriff's office at lunchtime and they would strategize further. The got up, paid their bill and headed for the parking lot.

Paul hopped in his car and headed for his hotel. Buck decided to take a walk. The night was cool and fall crisp and he needed to clear his head. He was mad at himself for almost getting lured in by Detective Young. He was also mad that he had been so focused on the location of the crime and the fact that, old mines and rough men go together, that he ignored the possibility that the new killer could be a woman. He wondered if he was losing his touch.

Buck walked a couple blocks and stood looking out over the Roaring Fork River. This time of year the river was fairly low and it sparkled in the moonlight. He wished he had grabbed his flyrod out of his car. There was nothing like fly fishing to clear one's mind. Once that little fly hit the water, all your focus had to be on the interaction between the fly and the fish. You couldn't think of anything else.

He thought about the times when Lucy use to sit on the bank of a river somewhere and watch him fish.

Even though she never took up the sport, he just loved having her there and she seemed to feel the same way. She would sit on the bank and later, after she got sick, in a lawn chair and read or crochet. He missed her alot and he was also glad she wasn't here right now because she would kick his ass for having doubts about his abilities. She was one tough Latina. Buck stepped away from the river and pulled out the phone number Paul had given him. It was late but this was important.

"Sam Brinkman."

Buck introduced himself and apologized for the lateness of the call. Sam told him not to worry, that since his wife died a few years back, he usually was at the museum late. Buck explained the reason for his call and the information he was looking for. Sam promised to get back to him as soon as he had anything to share.

Chapter Fifty-Seven

Buck had just finished entering the latest information in the murder book on his laptop and was getting ready to look through the latest forensic updates when his phone rang. He looked at his watch and noted the lateness of the hour but he answered the phone.

"Buck Taylor."

"Agent Taylor. Sam Brinkman here. I hope it's not too late?"

"No, Mr. Brinkman. I was just doing some computer work."

Sam interrupted. "I found some information for you and I knew you said this was important, so I wanted to get back to you right away."

Buck smiled. "Mr. Brinkman, I didn't expect you to work on this tonight."

"Not to worry, Agent Taylor. I don't have anything to go home to and I do love a challenge, so I got right on it. Took a bit to find the right timeframe but I do believe I found the information you were looking for."

Sam Brinkman went on to explain that there was indeed a Richard Smiley in the 10th Mountain Division during World War II. He had been in the training class during the winter of 1943 at Camp Hale in Minturn. Sam went on to explain that when he left the training camp, he was a corporal. He also told Buck that Corporal Richard T Smiley was killed in action in Italy in April 1944.

Buck had started to feel upbeat when Sam called. Now his bubble just burst. "Mr. Brinkman. Any doubt about the information?"

"Unfortunately, not. I have a copy of the telegram from the army to his mom and dad. Sad. He was only 22 years old. War is such a waste of young lives. Sorry I don't have better information for you."

"That's ok, Mr. Brinkman. You have been a huge help." Buck stopped short as an idea bounced around his brain. "Sir, if I could ask you one more thing? Does your information list where the soldiers are from or where they enlisted?"

"Yes, sir. It actually lists both, if that information was available at the time. You need to remember that this was during war, so the record keeping might be a little messy. A huge number of young men joined the various services during the war. Many were underaged and used fake ID's and many joined to escape the law or a bad marriage or some other reason. Patriotism was not always the reason for joining the military."

"Can you possibly email me a list of the soldiers who were in the same training class as Corporal Smiley along with their home cities or where they enlisted?"

"No problem. I will get on it right away."

Buck knew there would be no arguing with Sam Brinkman. Sam was on a quest and Buck figured he'd have the list on his computer in the next couple hours. He gave Sam his email address and thanked him for his help. He sat back in the desk chair and thought about the information Sam Brinkman had given him. Someone had given false information to Marvin Davis when that person asked for permission to work one of Marvin Bishop's mining claims. Unless Bishop was mistaken and had the name totally wrong, the person who had used that name didn't just pull it out of thin air. That person had some kind of relationship with Richard Smiley.

Buck started viewing the forensic results when his computer notified him of an incoming email. Buck was wrong. It didn't take a couple hours for Brinkman to pull together the information Buck had asked for. It took less than an hour. He made a mental note to stop in and visit Sam Brinkman the next time he was in the Vail area.

Buck opened the email and clicked on the attachment. He looked at the list that Brinkman had put together. There were one hundred and fifty names on the list and he slowly perused the list. He found Richard Smiley about two-thirds of the way down the list. Richard Smiley had listed his hometown as Monroe, Virginia and he had enlisted in Roanoke, Virginia. He ran his finger down the list. He was able to find six other enlistees with some town in Virginia listed as their home address. He found that seven men enlisted in Roanoke. There were also six more who had nothing listed for the state of their enlistment. He copied down the names on the pad on his desk.

He started to look for the list of the local 10th Mountain vets when he remembered that the list was printed and he had given it to Paul Webber. He hated to stop when he felt he was just starting to get momentum but he didn't want to wake Paul. Besides he needed some sleep himself. He closed his laptop, turned off the lights and laid down on the bed.

The ringing phone snapped Buck awake out of a deep sleep. He grabbed his phone off the table next to the bed and looked at the number.

"Hey, Hank. What's up?"

"Mornin Buck. Did I wake you?" Hank Clancy asked.

"No. I had to wake up to answer the phone," Buck said and he heard Hank laugh on the other end.

"Listen, Buck. Check your email when you are fully awake. One of our clerks worked overtime but she thinks she might have found something for you. She could not find any kind of active multiple victim murder investigation from back in the fifties and sixties in Colorado but she did find old records of six women who went missing around the same time period."

"What makes her think these six women might be connected to our case?"

"According to the reports from local investigators, these six women were traveling across the country for various reasons and the last place anyone ever saw or heard from them was in Colorado."

"Excellent Hank. I will pull up the email and take a look at the files. Any chance there might be fingerprint cards on these women?"

"These six have print cards but remember this was a very transient time in America. After World War II and Korea, a lot of people were on the move. I looked at the files and most of these women were escaping something. Abusive husbands, bad relationships and some just had a whim to travel. Not a lot of people were fingerprinted in those days unless they got caught. A couple of them were picked up as vagrants or prostitutes. Not unusual for a single woman on the road. Take a look. My clerk is continuing to follow up and I will call you if we find anything else."

Buck thanked Hank and climbed out of bed. He opened his laptop, put on his reading glasses and opened the email and the attachment. Hank was right. Most of these women had lived horrible lives but the thing that struck him most is that most of these women probably had tried to disappear. It was just pure luck that someone had actually missed them.

Buck was just about to call Paul Webber when his phone rang. It was Ashley Baxter from the office. "Hey, Buck. I found Richard Smiley. The Army is sending me his file. Should have it in a few minutes."

"Nice work, Ashley," said Buck. "Send it to me as soon as you get it and thanks."

Buck hung up and called Paul Webber. Paul had just arrived at the home of the tenth name on his list. Buck asked him to take a picture of the list and email it to him. Buck hung up and headed for the morgue. On the way, he called the Sheriff.

"Hi, Earl. Can you have your fingerprint tech meet me at the morgue?"

"Hey, Buck. She is already there. The Professor and the pathologists think they have had good luck rehydrating a couple fingers on each mummy and they want to get them into the system."

Buck told the Sheriff about the files that Hank Clancy had sent him and said he would meet the tech there; he was on his way. He hung up his phone jumped in the shower and then found his cleanest shirt and pair of jeans. Buck could feel the momentum building.

Chapter Fifty-Eight

The fingerprint tech was uploading a print scan into her computer when Buck walked into the morgue. He opened his laptop and pulled up the files from the FBI and clicked on the fingerprint cards. He slid his laptop over to the fingerprint tech and stepped back to give her room to work. The two pathologists were at the other end of a long row of morgue tables and were working with Professor Standish and two of his students as they ran the digital fingerprint scanner over the hand of the next body.

"Professor. Looks like you've had some success?"

The Professor turned to look at Buck. "Much more than we dared hope for. We used some different techniques that have been used on mummies by other archeologists over the years and we found two methods that worked really well. We are now in the process of checking with the scanner to see if the prints are legible."

Buck was just about to ask about the process when he heard a shout from the fingerprint tech. "GOT ONE!!"

Buck and the Professor turned and headed over to the tech. She was almost shaking with excitement.

Buck looked at the scan and the old print card side by side, just as she had and he could see it as clear as day. They had their first hit. He slid his laptop back around and clicked on the file for Martha Collins.

Martha Collins was 22 years old in 1963 when she ran away from an abusive marriage. She was originally from Appleton, Wisconsin. Her mother reported her missing two weeks after she left her home. No missing person's report was filed by her husband. Buck just shook his head. She had been arrested in Denver in June of that year for vagrancy. She never made her court appearance and an arrest warrant was issued for her. She was never heard from again. That is until now.

Buck stepped away from the tech and called Hank Clancy. Hank answered and Buck filled him in. Hank sounded almost as excited as the fingerprint tech was. He told Buck that the clerk had found two more possibles and she was emailing them over to him. Buck hung up and congratulated the tech and the Professor and his team. Nothing they had so far would help them find out who the killer was but it would go a long way to giving some of these families closure.

Buck transferred the rest of the fingerprint cards to the techs laptop and closed his computer. He would let them get on with their work. He headed for the door when he ran into Dr. Parker coming down the hall. She too, looked very excited.

She held up a paper as she approached. "We identified your victim." She handed Buck the paper. It was a copy of an AFIS report. "Her name was Margret Mary Trumaine. According to the report she was listed as a runaway. She had just turned twenty-one years old and her prints were on file in New Orleans because she was involved in a bar fight and had been arrested with her boyfriend. A bench warrant was issued a month ago for failure to appear."

Buck looked over the report and pulled out his phone. He dialed the number on the report.

"Stevenson."

"Hi Detective Stevenson, my name is Buck Taylor and I am an agent with the Colorado Bureau of Investigation. I think we found a young woman you have been looking for."

Buck took a few minutes and explained the circumstances surrounding his call. He told the Detective about what they had found in the mine and the hit they just got back from AFIS.

"That's really a shame, Agent Taylor. That young girl never had a chance. She had an abusive father and an extremely abusive boyfriend. By the time I had contact with her she was so far under his thumb I couldn't get her back. She was very meek and mild. Unfortunately, the fact that she is dead doesn't surprise me. I expected her boyfriend would do it but a connection to a decades-old serial killer case. That's fascinating. You get done with this case you should write a book. Can you send me a copy of the autopsy report for my files?"

"Sure can, Detective. Would you be able to email me a copy of whatever you have on her? I'd like to get to know her a little better."

"You bet and thanks for the call." Buck and Detective Stevenson exchanged email addresses and Buck hung up.

Dr. Parker looked at him. "You don't let any grass grow under your feet do you Buck?"

"Can't afford to. The dead can't speak for themselves. That's my job. This young girl didn't ask to die this way and I won't let her death be meaningless."

Dr. Parker could see the intensity in Buck's eyes. She realized that everything she had heard about his dedication and his pit bull attitude was true. Buck thanked the Doctor and headed for his car. He headed for the Sheriff's Department. There was a bug in the back of his brain and he couldn't quite get it to development.

Buck pulled into the parking lot, grabbed his backpack out of the hatch and headed inside. The desk officer buzzed him in without checking his ID. He walked into the empty conference room and pulled out his laptop and his notepad. He grabbed a bottle of Coke from the small refrigerator in the corner and sat down.

The first thing he pulled up was the forensic reports. He searched through until he found the evidence summary. The techs had found several fingerprints and it always amazed him that they could pull prints that were decades old but under the right conditions there was no telling how long prints could last.

It was obvious from the report that the killer hadn't used gloves or he had and just got careless. They found partial prints on some of the knives in the leather bundle. They pulled a decent print off a ceramic coffee mug that was also in the cabinet with the leather bundle and they pulled a couple usable prints off the kerosene can and off the fuel cap on the kerosene stove.

The forensic techs had run the prints through AFIS and also through the military but so far hadn't gotten any hits. This didn't surprise him. Fingerprinting was only used in dealing with criminals so if the perp had never had any contact with the law the chances of his prints being in the system were slim to none. He didn't know if the military printed enlistees but he doubted it. During the war, he imagined they just ran as many men as possible through the enlistment process with very few questions asked.

Chapter Fifty-Nine

Buck was going through the report looking for the evidence that could relate to the newer killing when Paul Webber entered the conference room. Paul looked exhausted.

"What's going on Paul?" asked Buck. "You look beat."

Paul explained that he had just spent four hours with two 10th Mountain Division vets in a retirement home just north of town. "These guys love to talk about their time in the 10th. Their stories are incredible. I wish I had the time to write their stories down. Someone should. What incredible men."

"So, besides the stories, were they any help with Richard Smiley?"

Paul opened his notebook. "Both men remember a Richard Smiley but they couldn't agree if he was killed in Italy. One thought he was and one thought he wasn't. They had a lot of arguments like that as they were telling me their stories. They did both remember that Smiley was one of the hillbilly boys. They said that several hillbillies from back east somewhere, had all come into the unit together. Said they were thick as thieves and pretty much stuck together. Said the other guys in the unit used to call them squirrel eaters and most of the unit stayed away from them."

Buck asked Paul to pull out the list of the vet's names he gave him and he opened his laptop and clicked on the attachment from Sam Brinkman the 10th Mountain Division museum curator. Paul slid him the list. Buck opened his notepad to the list he had created from Sam Brinkman's list of the men who enlisted in Roanoke Virginia. It was a long shot but then, so far, everything was. He checked the names on Paul's list and then on his list. No matches. Paul could see the frustration on Buck's face.

Buck pulled his laptop closer and started working his way down the list from Sam Brinkman. Buck had listed only the men who indicated they were from Virginia and had enlisted in Roanoke. He remembered that Sam had told him that some names on the list didn't have that information. Buck had planned to go back to them after he checked out the ones on his list. Now was the time.

Buck found six names on the list that did not contain either their hometown or their place of enlistment. Buck pulled out his phone and dialed Sam Brinkman. Sam answered his phone and listened as Buck told him what he was looking for. Sam Brinkman told him he would get back to him as soon as he had what he needed. Buck hung up.

Buck now took the time to update Paul on the morning's activities in the morgue. Paul was fascinated with the whole idea of fingerprinting the mummies. He was also thrilled that they had identified their victim. The conversation reminded Buck of something he meant to do and he opened his email and sure enough, there was the email from Detective Stevenson. The file from New Orleans was attached. The note in the email from the Detective said, "Thanks for the autopsy report and the photo. Definitely our girl. Heading over to her mom to make the notification. Let me know if you need anything else and good luck."

Buck opened the file. The first thing he noticed was how much the young girl had changed. The girl on the morgue table was much thinner than the girl in the booking photo. Her hair was also shorter now and had a tint of blue color in a streak down one side. Her booking photo showed a girl with bright eyes and blond hair. She looked ten years younger in the booking photo. She had gone downhill fast.

Buck read the booking information and read through the arrest report. Detective Stevenson was very thorough and Buck appreciated how well organized the reports were. He stopped reading and turned his computer around so Paul could see it. Paul read the report and commented about a tragic life. Buck couldn't agree more.

Buck had just stood up from his chair when Fitz walked into the room. She looked as tired as Paul did. She filled Buck in on her case. The pictures they had posted on the Missing and Exploited Children's website had been paying off, at least in the quantity of information they were getting, if not the quality. They had a few decent leads on several of the children and had already arranged with the police in Kansas City and Omaha to take DNA swabs of possible extended family members for two of the kids. DNA had already linked the momma, Corrine, with one of the kids. The oldest boy that had been killed, was her biological child.

Fitz excused herself so she could get back to answering calls. They had brought in several of the volunteer reserve deputies to help out with the calls, many from the news media around the country. Their case had gone viral. Fitz wasn't sure that was necessarily a good thing. She picked her coffee mug up off the table and headed out the door. Buck started to pace when his phone rang.

"Agent Taylor, I have the information you were looking for," said Sam Brinkman.

Buck had no doubt that Sam Brinkman would come through. "Thanks, Mr. Brinkman. Go ahead." Buck grabbed his pen and his notepad.

"Only one of the six names you gave me came from Virginia. Thomas Hawkins listed his hometown as Lynchburg, Virginia and he enlisted in Roanoke. Can't tell you why it wasn't in the report. Like I said last night. This was war and a lot of things slipped through the cracks. I also called one of my contributors in Vail. He wasn't in this unit but was in the unit that completed training just before this group but he remembers the hillbilly boys. Said they were an odd group and they stuck to each other like glue. Didn't have any contact with them after he shipped out. I hope that helps?"

"Thanks much Mr. Brinkman. Helps a lot." Buck hung up his phone and filled Paul in on the conversation. Paul read through his notes. "I spoke with Mr. Hawkins's son yesterday. This is the guy I mentioned who was bedridden and comatose. His son said his father was injured in an accident and had been bedridden ever since. He has been comatose the last two weeks. The doctor doesn't hold out much hope."

Buck sat back in his chair. Something was really nagging at him but he just couldn't put his finger on it. He was just about to say something when his phone rang.

"Buck Taylor."

"Agent Taylor, Frederick Standish here. Do you have a minute?"

Buck said he did and the Professor filled him in on their progress. They had identified five of the women so far and had just opened up the fingerprint cards for the two most recent reports that Buck had sent the fingerprint tech. The Professor was ecstatic about their success and Buck was impressed with what they had been able to do so far. The Professor hung up and promised to report back. Buck filled in Paul.

Buck's phone rang again and this time he recognized the number and answered the call.

"Yes, Sir?" he said

"Buck, I just heard from Max that Professor Standish and his team are having some pretty good luck with getting prints from the old victims. Anything on the newest victim?"

Buck told the Director that, so far, they didn't have anything on the killer. He filled him in on the information they received from Sam Brinkman and also from the detective in New Orleans on the latest victim.

The Director seemed very interested in the 10th Mountain connection to the original crime. They talked strategy for a few minutes then Buck hung up.

Buck pulled up the forensic report on his computer and looked through the evidence collected section. He found what he was looking for on the second page. The techs had pulled a relatively fresh DNA sample from the old straw mattress. There was a small stain on the old horsehair blanket that covered the mattress. The note indicated that they had not found a DNA match in the database.

Chapter Sixty

Buck asked Paul if he could run down the street and pick up a couple deli sandwiches. Paul headed out the door and Buck spent the time going back through the murder book on his laptop. That little nagging bug was still in the back of his mind and he couldn't shake it. He knew that solving crimes as complex as this were in the details, so Buck went back to the details.

Buck was still reviewing the photos and the evidence notes when Paul returned with a couple Italian subs. They took a break and ate their sandwiches. Buck got up to throw away the sandwich wrapper when his phone rang. It was Max Clinton, the head of the State Crime Lab. Max was excited. She told Buck that they had gotten a DNA hit off one of the mummies. It wasn't a solid match but it was definitely familial. She said it was possibly a cousin or an aunt or uncle. She forwarded the information to the Galveston, Texas police department since the DNA report had been filed by them. She was waiting to hear back.

Buck and Max talked a while about the progress and how much success they had been having with this case and how nothing related back to the killer but the fact that they could identify these victims was pretty amazing. Buck was just about to say something else when the nagging little bug hit him right in the forehead. He told Max he would call her later and hung up.

Buck sat down and looked at the list from Sam Brinkman and looked at the notation he had made next to Thomas Hawkins's name. He looked at Paul.

"You said Thomas Hawkins was bedridden and comatose right?" he asked.

Paul checked his notes. "Yeah. Bedridden for several decades, comatose in the last two weeks. What are you thinking?"

"Was Hawkins injured in the war?" asked Buck.

Paul looked at his notes. "His son just said he was injured in a car crash. Didn't say when or if he did I didn't write it down. What are you thinking?"

"What would cause an active serial killer, who had already killed fifteen women, to suddenly stop killing?"

Paul thought about it for a minute. "Typically, it would be death or imprisonment." Then Paul's face lit up. "Or an accident that left him a quadriplegic. Shit!"

"Exactly," Buck replied. "Head downstairs to the archives and see if the clerk can find a report on an accident from some time in the sixties that left the victim a quadriplegic."

The Sheriff stuck his head in the door. "You guys are getting pretty loud. You got something?"

While Paul grabbed his notepad and headed out the door, Buck filled the Sheriff in on what they had discovered today. The Sheriff sat back and listened. He was aware of all the activity at the morgue. The thought about the accident he felt was on the right track. He told Buck to let him know if he needed more help and he headed for his office.

Buck picked up his phone and dialed Virginia Gonzales, the Pitkin County Attorney. Virginia picked up her phone. "Hi, Buck. Figured you'd be calling sooner or later. What do you need?"

Buck spent the next twenty minutes walking her through the evidence they had developed so far. She too, was impressed with the work the Professor and his team had been able to do. Science was amazing. Buck asked her about the possibility of getting a warrant for fingerprints and a DNA sample from Thomas Hawkins. Virginia thought for a minute.

"Buck, I agree with your theory. We are a little light on physical evidence linking Thomas Hawkins to the mummies but I think I can get Judge Donnelly to issue a warrant for the samples. Give me a little bit and I will call you back."

Buck hung up. The momentum was definitely building. He pulled his laptop closer and started inputting what they had learned in the past couple hours. He also shot a quick email to the Director to let him know what the latest theory was.

Buck hated waiting but he had no choice. They had a lot of irons in the fire and Buck just needed to wait to bring it all together. The samples from Thomas

Hawkins could seal the deal. He pulled up the evidence report from the murder book and went back to the second page. As he had read before, the techs had found what they felt was a fresh stain on the old mattress blanket but they had not been able to find a match in the national DNA database.

Was it possible that someone related to Thomas Hawkins had decided to start down the same road? The mine shaft was not easy to find. He doubted that someone who just happened upon it, would suddenly decide to become a serial killer or that someone who had the makings of being a serial killer, would go looking for a great place to kill people and would think the shaft was perfect. Those were just too far in the extreme to be plausible. But someone who knew the original killer and had been able to discuss it. That was more of a reality. Especially the methodology of the crimes.

It was not easy to discern from the mummies, how they were killed. As the bodies shrunk, a lot of the slices and cuts had closed up. The only way someone would find out how they died was to discuss it with the killer. Buck thought for a minute. Paul had mentioned that he had spoken with Thomas Hawkins's son. Buck figured that this son would be Buck's age or older. Buck couldn't recall ever reading about a serial killer who started his career that late in life. Of course, it was possible that the son was a killer for a long time and had just not been caught but Buck recalled the conversation with Dr. Parker and about the uncertainty about the killer being a man.

Buck picked up his phone and called Max Clinton at the crime lab. "Hey, Buck. How's my favorite cop?" Typical Max. Always answered his calls the same way.

"Hey, Max. Got a question. The stain the techs found on the old mattress blanket that they have listed as sample 17. Do we know if it came from a man or a woman?"

Buck could hear Max clicking the keys on her computer. "According to the report the sample came from a woman. What are you looking for Buck?"

"Just a wild hair. Did the lab do a DNA comparison between the victim and the sample?" More keys clicking

"The lab did do a comparison," said Max. "The sample did not come from the victim. That should be in the notes in your murder book."

Buck looked at the note section of the forensic report. "I don't see that in the report. When was the report you are looking at uploaded?"

Max put Buck on hold for two minutes. She came back on the line apologetic. "Sorry Buck, the tech just uploaded the latest report twenty minutes ago. If you have had the report open it probably didn't refresh, so you don't have the latest version."

Buck said, "no worries Max." He hit the refresh button on the report and sure enough, there was the note. He thanked Max and hung up.

Buck called over to the Clerk and Recorders Office and asked the Clerk if she could check a few birth records for him. He had no idea how long Thomas Hawkins had lived in the valley but it was worth a shot. He gave her the information and she promised to call back as soon as she had something. Buck sat back and closed his eyes.

Chapter Sixty-One

The Clerk from the Clerk and Recorder's Office called back and gave Buck the information he had been waiting for. There were four birth records related to Thomas and Judith Hawkins. Thomas and Judith had two sons, Thomas Jr. born in 1950 and Mathew born in 1952. She also found a death certificate for Mathew in 1953. Cause of death was listed as undetermined. Buck assumed it was probably SIDS related. Back in those days, many children's deaths, if spontaneous, were listed as SIDS. Sudden Infant Death Syndrome. It was a catch-all phrase for "we don't know what caused the death."

She also found two birth certificates under Thomas Hawkins Jr. and Sarah Jane Westover. They had two children. Thomas the third, born in 1985 and Alicia born in 1995. Buck thought, "a change of life baby." He thanked the Clerk and hung up.

Paul came rushing back into the conference room carrying in a very old dusty file folder. "It took some time to go through the boxes but we think we found it."

He laid the file on the desk and caught his breath. Buck waited.

"Thomas Hawkins was involved in a single-vehicle rollover accident in July of 1964. It happened between Carbondale and Aspen. According to the report the car slid on the rain-soaked highway and crashed through a barricade and rolled down the embankment. It wasn't discovered for three days, until a highway road crew stopped to check out the damaged guardrail and spotted the car in the ravine. Thomas Hawkins was the lone occupant in the car and had been crushed when the car slammed into a tree at the bottom of the ravine. Hawkins suffered serious internal injuries and a broken neck. The investigating deputy made a note in the accident report that the doctors did not think that Hawkins would survive." Paul stopped to catch his breath and Buck pulled the report across the table and started going through it himself.

Paul came around the table and Buck slid the report over to him. There was obviously something else he wanted Buck to see. He flipped a couple pages and slid the report back to Buck. He pointed to a faded note written by the deputy along the edge of the page. Buck pulled out his reading glasses and looked at the note.

Paul saw that Buck was having trouble reading the note, so he filled him in. "The deputy made a note to check on the condition of the female victim. Identity unknown."

Buck looked at Paul. "You just said that Hawkins was the lone victim. What does this mean?"

Paul smiled. "I think someone doctored the final report. The official accident report makes no mention of a female victim. I think someone missed this note from the deputy when they typed up the final report. Someone hid the fact that Thomas Hawkins was not alone in his car at the time of the accident."

Buck removed his glasses. "Shit Paul. Do you think this could have been victim number sixteen and the accident happened before he had a chance to finish the job?"

Paul responded, "it's possible but why would someone cover it up? Do you think someone in the Sheriff's office, at the time, knew about the killings and was trying to protect Hawkins?"

Buck looked at the signature on the report. Deputy Ernest Rivers. Buck grabbed the report and headed out the door to find the Sheriff. He found him sitting in his office reading a report. The Sheriff looked up.

"Do you remember a Deputy Ernest Rivers?" Buck asked.

The Sheriff thought for a minute. "Ernie was a deputy back in the sixties. Why? What up?"

Buck set the accident reports on his desk and explained the anomaly. The Sheriff looked at the reports, reread the accident report from the deputy and the final accident report and set the reports back down on his desk.

"Got me, Buck. Old Tom Glover was Sheriff back in those days. He was a tough old bastard and he ran a tight ship. Nothing happened in this county that Tom

Glover didn't know about. I can't believe one of his deputies would fake a report. To what end?"

Buck replied. "Maybe to hide a serial killer?"

The Sheriff sat back and scratched his head. "Fuck, Buck. How confident are you that Hawkins is the guy? Maybe it was just a simple clerical error."

"Is this Ernie still around? Can we talk to him?" asked Buck.

"No, Ernie died about ten years back," responded the Sheriff.

Buck gave the Sheriff the rundown on what they had. When Buck finished, the Sheriff just sat there. "Ok. What's the next step, the DNA and fingerprint samples?"

"Yeah. Soon as I hear back from Virginia. Do you know the family?"

"No," replied the Sheriff. "Let me know when you are ready to head over and I will come along."

Buck left the Sheriff's office and headed back to the conference room where he filled Paul in on the conversation he just had with the Sheriff.

"Do you really think a cop would cover up multiple murders?" asked Paul.

"I don't think so. I mean it's possible Earl is right and it's just a clerical error. What bothers me is that there is no follow up from the deputy. That I can't explain."

Buck had just sat down at the conference table when Paul grabbed his notebook and started furiously flipping pages. He stopped and read his notes.

"Fuck," Paul said. "Excuse me. I thought so. Maggie Stevens."

"Maggie Stevens what?" replied Buck.

"Maggie Stevens is the owner of the Jackpot Bar and Grill. I spoke with her early on when we were trying to get a line on our victim. She mentioned that she had lived in Aspen since her accident. She said she was involved in an accident in the sixties and had no memories of the event before waking up in the hospital."

Buck looked at him. "Go talk to her and see if you can jog some of her memories. We might have a living breathing victim of our serial killer?"

Paul grabbed his notebook and his backpack and headed out the door.

Chapter Sixty-Two

Buck was starting to get a little antsy, so he decided to take a walk down to the river. He hated waiting for things to happen and it seemed that that was all he was doing today. They had made a great deal of progress in a short amount of time and he felt they were right there. As he stood at the river's edge and watched the water flow by, he felt that they were close to wrapping this one up.

He was about to head back to the Sheriff's office when his phone rang. He checked the number and answered the call.

"Hey, Virginia. Are we good?"

Virginia Gonzales responded, "got your warrant. What are you waiting for?" She laughed.

"Awesome. Can you fax it over to the Sheriff's office? Oh, I hate to do this but do you think you can get warrants for the rest of the family as well?"

Buck explained why he needed the rest of the family's DNA. He waited for a response.

"You think someone else in the family is our new killer. Seriously. A family of killers living here in Aspen and no one knew. You have got to be kidding.   Ok, I will try but see if you can get them to give the samples voluntarily."

Virginia hung up and Buck walked back the three blocks to the Sheriff's department. As he entered the building, the desk officer handed him the fax copy of the warrant. He buzzed Buck through the door and Buck headed for the Sheriff's office.

The Sheriff was talking on the phone, so Buck waved the fax and pointed to the conference room. He nodded and Buck headed for the conference room. Buck was closing up his laptop when the Sheriff entered the room. He slid the warrant over to him and put his laptop in his backpack.

"Can you have your fingerprint tech meet us there?"

The Sheriff pulled out his phone, called the tech and gave her the address. He told her to stay in her van until he called her to come in.

Buck called Paul who, said that he was just wrapping up with Maggie Stevens and he would meet them at Thomas Hawkins's house. Buck and the Sheriff walked out of the building and climbed into the Sheriff's car. He pulled out of the parking lot and headed for the address on West Hallam Street. He pulled to the curb behind the county's forensic van and signaled the tech to wait. He and Buck crossed the street and walked up to the cute little Victorian house.

The Sheriff knocked on the door. The door was opened by a middle-aged, heavy set women with grey hair and glasses. He introduced himself and Buck and asked if they could come in. Once inside Buck closed the door.

"How can I help you gentlemen?" asked Sarah Jane Hawkins.

They had agreed on the way over to let the Sheriff do most of the talking since these were his people. Buck was never offended at being considered the outsider. Many times it proved valuable to have the locals handle the locals.

"Ma'am, we have a warrant to get a fingerprint scan and DNA swab from your father-in-law." The Sheriff handed her the warrant.

She looked at the warrant, confused and unsure what to do. She stepped to the door to the living room and called out. "Tom, can you come here a minute? The police are here."

Tom Hawkins came walking in wiping his hands on a rag. He was medium height, slightly overweight and he had a short haircut and a neatly trimmed beard.

"What do you mean the police are here. What do they…" He stopped short and looked at the Sheriff and Buck. His wife handed him the warrant. He pulled a pair of reading glasses out of his pocket and read the warrant. He looked up at Buck and the Sheriff.

"What the hell is this all about? You want fingerprints and DNA from a man who is on death's door and has been bedridden since 1964. Are you kidding?"

The Sheriff looked at Buck. Buck responded. "We have reason to believe that your father was involved in several murders during the late fifties early sixties."

Sarah Jane Hawkins put her hand in front of her mouth. Tom Hawkins looked at Buck as his anger seethed. "What the fuck are you talking about? You think my dad is a serial killer? How dare you come into my house and make that kind of accusation! Get the fuck out!"

Buck stepped forward. "Mr. Hawkins, I know this may be a shock but we wouldn't be here if we didn't have proof. The warrant gives us permission to be here and to take the samples. You are welcome to call your attorney but he will tell you the same thing."

Buck watched as Tom Hawkins slowly balled his fists and he stared daggers at Buck. Buck looked him in the eye. "Mr. Hawkins," Buck said softly. "Please think very carefully about what you are about to do. We understand your anger but the samples are important and you do not want to make the situation any worse."

"Thomas step back." The voice came from a short elderly woman with a walker who entered the room. Her words to Tom seem to diffuse the situation instantly. He turned and was about to say something when she held up her hand and silenced him. "He may be your father," she said. "But he is still my husband and I will deal with this."

Tom Hawkins started to protest but once again his mother raised her hand for silence. Tom backed off and sat down at the kitchen table.

"Gentlemen, I am Judith Hawkins. If you would follow me, please."

The Sheriff pulled out his phone and called the fingerprint tech to come in. He was just putting it away when Paul Webber arrived at the door. Paul looked around at those assembled and wondered what he had missed. The Sheriff, Buck, the fingerprint tech and Paul followed Mrs. Hawkins through the house to what was obviously an addition that had been built onto the original house.

Chapter Sixty-Three

She pushed open the door and they all entered a very cozy if not very large room. The oxygen tank in the corner hissed as Thomas Hawkins breathed. He was lying in a hospital bed with the blanket pulled up to his chest. He had on striped pajamas and was clean shaven. It was obvious to everyone that Thomas Hawkins was well taken care of.

Mrs. Hawkins sat down on the chair that was next to the bed and held her husband's hand. She nodded to the fingerprint tech who pulled the portable digital fingerprint scanner out of her backpack and ever so gently slid it across his fingers. She then pulled a DNA swab out of her pack, broke the packaging and gently lifted the old man's lip and swabbed the inside of his mouth. Mrs. Hawkins sat silently and watched, holding her husband's hand the entire time.

The fingerprint tech opened her laptop and pulled up the prints that had been recovered at the mine. She spent a few minutes comparing the prints from the mine to the scans and then she looked up at Buck. She nodded her head. Mrs. Hawkins lowered her eyes and a tear fell on her hand.

Buck turned his head and noticed Tom Jr. and Sarah Jane standing in the doorway. They both looked stunned. Tom finally broke the silence. "Mom, did you know about this?"

She looked at her son. "I would like to talk to these gentlemen alone for a minute. Will you please excuse us?"

Tom Jr. looked hurt and like he wanted to fight but instead he just turned around and walked out. Sarah Jane followed closely at his heels. Buck asked the fingerprint tech to go back to the kitchen, finish her analysis and log the report. She nodded and left the room.

Buck, the Sheriff and Paul Webber stood and watched Mrs. Hawkins. She was looking at her husband and no one wanted to disturb her. She finally reached over and took a tissue from the box on the table and wiped her eyes. She looked up at Buck and the others. She asked Buck to close the door.

Mrs. Hawkins kissed her husband on the forehead and then began. "My husband was a good man. Up until his accident he took very good care of the boys and me." She wiped her eyes and Buck could see the sadness in that statement. "He was a loving husband and father but I always sensed that there was something beneath the surface. He worked a lot of late hours in those days but his paychecks never revealed any extra money. Up until you walked in I always believed that he was having an affair or many for that matter. He would always shower before coming to bed, after a long night but I could always smell the sex on him. It never occurred to me that he might be a killer. He never seemed the type but I know he was troubled. I was young and naïve and despite what I have just told you I always loved him. I still do. When our little Mathew passed away, he was the rock I depended on."

She sat for a minute and looked down at her husband. She wiped more tears away from her eyes. No one spoke.

"I can only assume that from the young lady's reaction, that his fingerprints match fingerprints that were found at a crime scene. What will happen now? He doesn't have many days left and I assume you can't arrest him. What's next?"

Buck looked down at Mrs. Hawkins. "I am not sure Ma'am. That will be up to the county attorney. May we ask you a couple questions?" She nodded yes and asked Buck to please open the door. Buck turned and opened the door and saw a new person in the room. He was the spitting image of Tom Jr. This would be Thomas the third. They all rose from the couch.

Paul pulled out his laptop and turned on the voice recorder app. He nodded to Buck. As the others all listened, Buck walked Mrs. Hawkins through the evidence they had gathered over the last couple days. She had no idea that her husband had been in contact with the owner of the mining claim. She told them he had worked as a mechanic for the Aspen Skiing Company almost from its inception. They talked about his skills as a metal worker and welder. Periodically there would be a gasp from one of the family members especially when Buck described the scene in the mine.

Mrs. Hawkins held her husband's hand through all of Buck's questions. For a frail little old lady, she was amazingly strong. He hoped the crash wouldn't come later but he knew it would. It always did.

Buck asked Mrs. Hawkins if she would allow them to search the house and property. She said she would and then he asked if the rest of the members of the family would allow them to take DNA and fingerprint samples. They still needed to eliminate them as suspects in the recent murder. They all agreed.   Buck asked Tom Jr. if his daughter was around. Tom told Buck that she had left the week before to go back to college in Florida.

Mrs. Hawkins looked up at Buck. "I assume you will want to see his jewelry collection? He thought I didn't know about it but I did. I just assumed it was to help him relive his conquests. I had no idea they were what you would call trophies."

Buck looked stunned, "yes Ma'am."

"Tommy, would you please show these gentlemen your grandfather's toolbox? The trophy box is in a space in the wall behind the toolbox."

Paul stepped through the door and followed Thomas the third. The Sheriff stepped out of the room and called dispatch to send out his forensics team and he asked that they dispatch a couple deputies and to notify the Aspen Police and let them know what was going on.

Buck sat with Mrs. Hawkins. He needed to clear up the anomaly with the accident report. He waited until the Sheriff returned. "Mrs. Hawkins, have you ever read the report about the night your husband was injured in the accident. We found a discrepancy and unfortunately there is no one left alive, except you, who might be able to explain it."

Mrs. Hawkins sat there for a minute and looked at her husband. She finally smiled through the tears and looked at Buck. "I had asked Tom not to change the report but he wanted to do it for me."

"I'm sorry Ma'am. Who is this Tom that you are talking about?" At this point, Tom Jr. and Sarah Jane stepped into the doorway. Mrs. Hawkins looked at them and then back at Buck.

Chapter Sixty-Four

The affair with Pitkin County Sheriff Tom Glover had started innocently enough. Tom was a deacon in her church and they had met at several of the church's social events. Her own Thomas never wanted to attend church with her. She never understood why until today.

It had started out as just coffee but she was feeling that her husband was growing more distant from her every day. A few months before the accident it had turned into something more than just coffee. She had been feeling seriously underappreciated and she needed someone to talk to. She called the Sheriff to see if he would like to stop by for coffee. Her Thomas was at work and her son was in school.

The coffee visit had turned into two hours of intense lovemaking. It was funny. Judith didn't feel any regret after it happened. She still loved her husband but the time she spent with Tom Glover was something else entirely.

Tom was the one who came by the house that day to tell her they had found Thomas's car in the ravine and that he was on his way to the hospital. It was touch and go whether he would live or die. Tom Glover now became her rock.

"Tom told me about the woman they had found in the ravine. She had been thrown from the car and was seriously injured. He wanted to protect me from public ridicule, so he told me he would take care of it." Mrs. Hawkins said.

She had begged him not to do anything that would jeopardize his career and he had laughed at her. He was the Sheriff of the county and he could do anything he wanted to. "He asked Ernie to remove any mention of the girl from his notes. Tom wrote the accident report up himself and Ernie signed it without question."

A tear formed in her eye. "Tom helped me get through all the hard days that would follow, as I had to deal with Thomas's injuries, get a job and keep my son fed and clothed. Tom was always there for me."

Buck asked her how long the affair lasted. She looked down at her hand holding Thomas's hand. Softly she said, "it lasted until the day Tom died, almost ten years ago. That was the saddest day of my life."

Her family just stood in the doorway in shocked silence. Their whole world had been torn apart today. It was horrible to watch. Tom Jr. and Sarah Jean excused themselves and walked out the front door. The forensic team arrived just as they were leaving. The Sheriff stepped away to give the team instructions and asked the fingerprint tech to get the swabs from the rest of the family.

Paul returned with Thomas the third and walked into the room. In his hands was an old cardboard cigar box. He handed it to Buck. Buck opened the box and just as Mrs. Hawkins had said, the box was filled with jewelry. Buck was no jewelry expert but nothing in the box looked expensive. Some of it looked like it might have sentimental value.

Mrs. Hawkins held out her hand and asked to see the box. Although it was evidence, Buck wanted to gauge her reaction now that she knew the truth about where the pieces came from. He handed her the box and she slowly opened it. She sat for a minute and just looked inside the box. Finally, she reached in and started moving pieces around. She got a funny look in her eyes. Buck watched her as she seemed to count the pieces one by one. She did this several times. She looked up and Buck thought he could see fear in her eyes.

"Ma'am, is something wrong?" Buck asked.

Mrs. Hawkins sat quietly for a few minutes just looking in the box. She closed the box. "There is a piece missing," she said.

"Are you certain?" Buck asked. He took the box from her hand and opened the lid.

"There were sixteen pieces in the box. I checked it every now and then to be reminded of how many women he had cheated with. The piece that's missing was a little jade horse on a silver necklace."

The house was now full of forensics people and Mrs. Hawkins asked Buck if he would close the door. Paul reached behind him and pushed the door shut. Buck was trying to understand what was happening. There were fifteen pieces of jewelry in the box and they had fifteen bodies in the morgue. The numbers worked unless one of the pieces belonged to the sixteenth victim. The woman who almost died in the accident that night. Paul was thinking the same thing as he looked through his notes.

"Agent Taylor. What I am about to say is very hard for me and it will destroy my son and his wife." She paused for a minute and let go of her husband's hand.

"My granddaughter Alicia found the jewelry box. I saw her with it one day when she thought I was asleep on the couch. She was coming out of this room and headed back to the garage. She had spent several days in here talking with her grandfather, over the summer, when he had a lucid moment." She started to cry.

She looked at Buck with pleading eyes. "Please don't say anything to my son."

Buck looked at Paul. "Would you have one of the techs look through Alicia's room and quietly see if they can find anything that might contain DNA? Toothbrush, hairbrush, anything."

Paul left the room and Buck reached over and rested his hand on Mrs. Hawkins's hand. "I hope I have done the right thing?" she said.

Buck stood up. He left Mrs. Hawkins sitting there with her husband. The poor woman's entire life had just unraveled. He felt bad for her. He walked through the house and stepped out onto the front porch. The Sheriff walked up beside him. Together they just stood there in silence.

The Sheriff finally broke the silence. "Hard day my friend. Wouldn't want to be these folks."

Buck looked at him and shook his head. He told the Sheriff about the conversation they had had about her granddaughter. "What are we going to do?" he asked.

Buck knew exactly what they were going to do. "As soon as the DNA results are back and we confirm what Mrs. Hawkins told me, we are going to issue an arrest warrant for Alicia Hawkins and have the Jacksonville, Florida police arrest her. I will let Hank Clancy at the FBI know. He might want his guys to track her down since she could be considered to have fled the state to avoid prosecution."

The Sheriff pulled out his phone. "I'd better call Virginia Gonzales and see how she wants to handle this. We certainly can't arrest the old guy but I'm not sure what to do." He stepped away and walked across the lawn.

Paul stepped out on the front porch. "I just spoke with Maggie Stevens at the Jackpot Bar and Grill. She confirmed that she had a little jade horse pendant on a silver chain but that it had disappeared from the hospital after the accident. She never saw it again until a young girl showed up at the bar a week or two back and was wearing a little jade horse pendant. Something in her mind triggered a memory and she asked the girl where she got the necklace. The girl told her she found it in a pawn shop in Florida. Maggie didn't think anything of it once the bar got busy but she swore that the girl was watching her the rest of the night."

Chapter Sixty-Five

Buck asked Paul to head back to the Sheriff's department and upload his notes to the murder book. Paul headed for his car. Buck took another pass through the house. Mrs. Hawkins was still sitting quietly next to her husband. As Buck looked in the door, she smiled at him and lowered her head. Buck checked in with the forensic team. He found the Sheriff and told him to call if they needed him. He would be back in the Sheriff's office in the morning to file his reports and put the finishing touches on the murder book.

As he walked towards his car, he pulled out his phone and dialed Max Clinton. He told her what had happened in the last couple hours and asked her to rush through the DNA samples she would be receiving for Alicia Hawkins. She promised to get her team on them as soon as they arrived. She ended the call the way she always did.

"God will watch over you, Buck Taylor. You are a good man. Stay safe."

Buck hung up his phone and walked to his car. He sat in his car and pulled out his phone again. He called the Director, who answered on the first ring.

"Hey, Buck. What's up?"

Buck filled him in on the day's events. The Director listened carefully. He asked a few questions and then said, "you guys did a great job, Buck. You solved fifteen decades-old serial killings and are about to close out a serial killer who is just getting started. Congratulations."

Buck thanked him, hung up and sat for a few minutes. He started his car and pulled out. He had intended to go back to his hotel and work on the murder book but the car seemed to have a mind of its own and he found himself parked along the river. He stepped out of the car and walked to the edge. The moon was full and the water sparkled. He stood there just watching the current when he sensed a presence behind him. His hand went instinctively for his gun.

"Sorry to have spooked you, Agent Taylor." Buck relaxed and turned around. PIS stood behind him and smiled.

"I heard it was rather a rough day."

Buck smiled and filled PIS in on the events of the past couple days. PIS listened quietly. Buck asked PIS how his shoulder was doing and PIS told him that he had been hurt worse and not to worry. When Buck was finished, he sat down in the cool grass and looked out over the river. PIS sat down next to him and that is where they stayed until the sun came over the mountains. Buck finally stood, shook PIS's hand and walked to his car. When he turned and looked back at the river, PIS was gone. Buck laughed and started the car.

The next few days were a blur as Buck and Paul continued to pull together forensic reports and log incoming information into the murder book. Virginia Gonzales had decided to indict Thomas Hawkins for the murders in the mine. She did not issue an arrest warrant because she knew he wasn't going to be alive that much longer. Professor Standish and his team had continued making progress and had identified nine of the fifteen women. He wanted to keep going but he had serious doubts that they would ever identify all of them. Hank Clancy agreed and by the end of the week he had pulled his clerk off the case and assigned her other work. Buck found out later that the clerk received a commendation for her excellent work in piecing together the victims.

Fitz and Moe Steiner continued to follow leads on the kids from the other mine. They had solid DNA matches on two of the kids and were waiting for the families to arrange flights to Colorado. The Missing and Exploited Children's Network had led to the possible identification of two of the other children and those leads were being followed up by police departments in St. Louis and Fort Collins, Colorado. The phones were still ringing but not as often. Corinne Everheart's uncle in West Virginia had arranged to have her remains and the remains of her identified son shipped to him for burial.

Major Richard Cranston, the Army CID investigator, arranged to have James Michael Forester's remains shipped to an Army base outside of Washington, DC. Buck had no idea how the Army was going to handle his burial and he decided he really didn't care. As far as Buck and the Sheriff were concerned, it was now an Army matter.

Buck had stopped by the Hawkins home a few days after that fateful day. To say the family was morose would be an understatement. The family moved around like zombies. All but Mrs. Hawkins. Buck found her sitting, in the cool afternoon air, on a love seat on the front porch. She was wrapped in a blanket and was just staring into space when Buck walked up the sidewalk.

Buck sat next to her and she put her hand on top of his. Softly she said. "Thomas will be at rest soon. He will face the lord and have to answer for his deeds. My solace is in the fact that you might give closure to those who have lost loved ones. Thank you for all you have done."

Buck started to stand up when she said, "please find my granddaughter."

She pulled her blanket around her a little tighter and looked across the yard.

The DNA from a toothbrush, that the forensic team found in Alicia's room, was a solid match for the stain on the old mattress blanket from the mine. Virginia Gonzales issued an arrest warrant for the murder of Margret Mary Trumaine. The FBI had also issued a federal arrest warrant for murder and interstate flight to avoid prosecution. The FBI, along with the Jacksonville Police, raided her dormitory but there was no sign of Alicia. All her belongings were still in her dorm room but Alicia was nowhere to be found. The FBI reported back that there was no sign of a little jade horse pendant on a silver chain.

Buck and Paul finished compiling the murder book and Buck emailed a copy to the Sheriff and to

Virginia Gonzales. They boxed up all the physical evidence that had been returned from the state lab along with samples from the morgue. The Sheriff had his evidence clerk label and seal the boxes and take them to storage.

Paul headed back to Grand Junction the next morning. Buck found himself standing knee deep in the cool waters of the Roaring Fork River. After several hours, he had only landed one fish but it didn't matter. He could feel his mind clearing more and more as he focused on the fish

Epilogue

Alicia Hawkins was hardly recognizable. She had a dark tan and she had cut her hair short and died it purple. The phone call from her older brother had come just in time. He didn't want to believe the things they were saying about her and he wanted her to come home to clear her name. She promised she would. She had made a promise to her grandfather. She would finish his legacy. One day soon, she would return to Aspen and finish his job.

Alicia hated the fact that she couldn't go home for her grandfather's funeral. She now, more than ever, understood him. She understood the force that drove him to do what he had done. She could feel that force growing stronger in her every day.

She had managed to get out of her dorm room and across the street to the park just before all the cops showed up. She was surprised to see the men and women with their FBI emblazoned jackets. It made her feel important. She sat in the park and watched for several hours as they carried out her stuff and talked to the other students in the dorm.

She waited until dark and then hitched south until she got to Tampa. She bought some purple dye at a local drug store and rented a cheap hotel room. When she was finished, she looked in the mirror and was pleased with the transformation. Over the following couple weeks she made her way farther south until she couldn't go any further.

Alicia walked out of the bar and stepped into the warm Key West sun. She put on her sunglasses and looked from side to side. She spotted the young girl a block down the street. The girl had arrived on the bus two days ago and looked lost. Alicia had been watching her since she arrived. She looked like a runaway and she was perfect.

The sun was setting and all the tourists were heading to the beach to wait for the green flash. People swore that the flash was visible, for just a second, just before the sun went down but Alicia had never seen it. She really didn't care. She watched the girl walk along the beach looking in the trash cans as she passed. Occasionally she would pull something out of the trash look at it, sniff it and eat it.

Alicia watched the young girl walk along the rocks towards the small tropical forest. She reached her hand into the back pocket of her shorts and felt the thin knife. She reached up to her neck and wrapped her hand around the little jade horse pendant on the silver chain. She smiled a wicked smile and headed off after the girl.

ACKNOWLEDGEMENTS

A special thank you to my daughter Christina J Morgan, my unofficial editor-in-chief. She devoted a significant amount of time making sure the book was presented as perfectly as possible. Any mistakes the reader may find are solely the responsibility of the author.

Also, I would like to thank my family for all their encouragement. I have been telling them stories since they were little and I always told them that someone should be writing this stuff down. I finally decided to write it down myself.

I want to thank my closest friend, Trish Moakler-Herud. She has been encouraging me for years to write my stories down. I hope this will make her proud.

Finally, a very special thanks to my late wife, Jane. She pushed me for years to become a writer and my biggest regret is that she didn't live long enough to see it happen. I love her with all my heart and miss her every day. I think she would be pleased.

ABOUT THE AUTHOR

Chuck Morgan attended Seton Hall University and Regis College and spent thirty-five years as a construction project manager. He is an avid outdoorsman, an Eagle Scout, and a licensed private pilot with a passion for camping, hiking, mountain biking, and fly-fishing.

He is the author of his first crime novel called *Crime Interrupted.*

He is also the author of *Her Name Was Jane*, a memoir about his late wife's nine-year battle with breast cancer. Morgan has three children, two grandchildren, and two dogs. He resides in Lone Tree, Colorado.

Buck Taylor will be back for another investigation in

Crime Unsolved.

Coming Summer 2018

Made in the USA
Lexington, KY
10 January 2019

When a local wildlife ranger goes missing in the rugged mountains south of Aspen, Colorado, the local sheriff launches a massive manhunt. Buck Taylor volunteers to help in the search and what the searchers uncover will shake this small mountain town to its core.

With years of hard-earned experience, Senior Agent Buck Taylor from the Colorado Bureau of Investigation will need to use all his talents to help solve a murder, unravel a series of years old kidnappings and solve several, decades old serial murders with a current twist. As talented a sleuth as there ever was, Buck is known for his dogged determination. Buck's last case—a Mexican drug cartel attempting to set up shop in a small mountain town- had served as a productive distraction from the grief etched into his heart by the death of his wife of thirty-five years.

Now, as he turns his attention to the trouble in Aspen, Buck finds himself drawn into one strange situation after another. But as Buck focuses on the two different cases, his intrepid group of helpers including one of Aspen's most "colorful characters" will face danger on several fronts. With serial killers, kidnappers and kids in the mix, it is going to be a crazy ride.

Crime Delayed is a thriller that will have readers burning through the pages.

ISBN 9780998873039

90000

9 780998 873039